Skinned bodies and garages, but w: the 'victims' are fou..... .. .. there a mistake at the morgue? Is the murderer a serial killer with a gruesome fixation on taxidermy?

Human killers aren't the responsibility of the Templars, even non-knight ones, but when a vampire is found dead and skinned north of the city, Aria suspects the killers aren't human. She'll need all of her friends – both alive and dead – to help catch these killers before they strike again.

Bare Bones

By

Debra Dunbar

Formatting by Anessa Books

CHAPTER 1

So it's a love charm?" Janice tilted the amulet, regarding it with a skeptical eye. The reporter was sprawled on my couch, her long legs propped up on my coffee table. She was wearing her usual trim slacks and well-tailored, button-down shirt, but the new copper highlights in her hair and mascara on her lashes heralded the significance of today's activities.

We were going to find Janice a boyfriend.

Not that I was anybody's idea of a matchmaker. Nor was I a posterchild for success in love. My last significant relationship had been over two years ago. Right now I was alternating between lusting over a vampire that I couldn't have and sending mixed signals to one of my gaming friends.

I should be full steam ahead with Zac, really I should, but it was hard to be enthusiastic about someone when I was meeting that other, completely unsuitable, person every night for a few hours of food, wine, and occasional discussions of matters that concerned the supernatural community in Baltimore. But today wasn't about *my* love life or lack thereof, it was about Janice, who had been on a steep downward slope ever since her divorce.

Maybe today was also a *little* bit about me. I'd never get over grieving for Raven if I didn't make the effort to crawl out of my hermit cave.

"No, it's not really a love charm. It's an illusion charm."

I didn't want to tell her that the charm would make her more appealing than usual. That sounded horribly insulting and Janice didn't need any more blows to her ego. The idea behind the spell was that she would stand out from the crowd, draw the notice of any men within a twenty foot radius. The rest was up to her. She had four hours to convince the man of her choice that she was worth knowing the next day, worthy of a phone call. It was a four hour window of attraction.

That was a lot of pressure on a woman, especially one who had been avoiding the dating game since the ink dried on the divorce papers three years ago. Which was why I was going with her. And why we were not going to a pub either.

"I can't believe I'm trolling for guys at the Walters Art Museum," she grumbled.

This again. "You need to go where there will be men who share your interests. You like historical items and art. It's the perfect place."

She squinted at the amulet. "No one asks women out at the Walters Art Museum. Maybe we should go to a bar where the lighting is dim and guys have their beer goggles on."

Janice was no great beauty with her long face, sharp nose, and thin build, but she wasn't homely by any definition of the word. The woman had amazingly long, shapely legs and pretty brown eyes. Guys didn't find her unattractive, they just didn't *notice* her. And they'd be less likely to notice her in a bar full of scantily clad barely-legal girls.

I sighed. "Plenty of guys go to the Walters. They

have swords and armor on display. There's more than just the usual art gallery crowd there. Trust me. If it doesn't work, I'll craft another amulet and we'll try somewhere else."

Janice clenched her jaw and draped the amulet over her head with a determined glare. "Let's go."

I held up a finger. "One more thing."

She watched in interest as I pulled a bracelet out of a bag and handed it to her. It was a complicated design of interlocking silver rings, reminiscent of chain mail. It was the reason I had some seriously dark circles under my eyes today. The amulet would help her stand out in the crowd, but this bracelet was the magical item I was more proud of. It recharged through kinetic energy as she walked, kind of like some watches did. The amulet would draw men in, this bracelet would make sure those she attracted were kind and loyal—and that they stayed that way. The last thing Janice needed was some player or a guy who only wanted to drain her bank account and head to Bermuda. This bracelet should protect her from hurt.

If it worked, that is. I wasn't exactly a Grand Magus. There was only so much a self-taught Templar could do when it came to the magical arts.

"Pretty." Janice put it on and shook her wrist, admiring the silver links. It *was* pretty, glowing a faint shade of blue as it moved on her arm. "Hey, I've been meaning to ask you, what do you know about demon possession?"

I blinked at the abrupt segue, feeling a chill at the very topic of demon possession. "A lot actually, but it's mostly academic. Priests deal with exorcism, not Templars."

We could do it, but given our inclination to

forcibly banish demons at the point of a sword, priests were a better choice. The possessed human was less likely to die if a man of the cloth cast out the demon. Now, once it was cast out, all bets were off and we were happy to step in with a sword and take care of any demon foolish enough to hang around post exorcism.

Janice picked up her purse, pulling out her phone. "I've had two people in the last few days claim that family members were possessed. I know it's a full moon and all that, but it seemed like a trend. One woman is having an exorcism done on her brother tomorrow and I was thinking of taking her up on the invitation to watch and report on it." She scrolled through her calendar. "It's in Canton. You can go with me, or I can text you the address if you want to drive separately."

I hated to disappoint her but most demonic possessions were nothing more than a psychotic break or other type of mental illness. Now that epilepsy was recognized for the medical condition it was, reports of possession had gone down significantly. Plus most priests were well trained in guiding their flock toward mental health services when someone claimed demonic possession. This was probably just a feel-good visit by a priest prior to recommending a good psychiatrist.

"You should go ahead and go," I told her. "But it will probably end up being a human interest piece on the need for additional funding for the treatment of mental illness rather than any kind of supernatural phenomenon."

She nodded. "Yeah. That's what I was thinking, too. Either way it will be a good story. Come along with me."

"No thanks." The idea of intruding on a woman

and her mentally ill brother as they received spiritual counseling seemed wrong. I didn't want to be that gawking stranger at their family crisis.

"Seriously, I want you to come. You're a Templar. I'd like your take on it, your expert opinion."

Ugh. Although it's not like I had a ton to do lately other than my part-time coffee shop job, Wednesday night Anderon game, and the occasional dinner and a movie with Zac. "I'm not an expert on psychiatric issues. I'm going to feel like an idiot standing there watching a priest tell a woman her brother needs therapy and pharmacology."

Janice grinned. "Come just in case it's a real demon. I've seen vampires, a necromancer, corpses that have been killed by an angel and demons. I've interviewed mages who have been involved in human sacrifice. This might be nothing more than a human interest piece, but just in case it really *is* a demonic possession, I want you by my side."

It made me feel good that I was the one she wanted by her side. Me. Things might have been a little boring the last four weeks, but after seven months in Baltimore I finally had friends, a hobby of sorts, and a guy that I might think about calling my boyfriend. Someday. Maybe.

Or not. Yeah, those mixed signals.

I put an arm around Janice's shoulders and gave her a quick hug. "Okay. I'm in. Now let's get going before the Crab Rangoon and decent wine are gone and all we're stuck with is tortillas and tap water.

We parked a few blocks out from the museum. I breathed deeply once inside the building, feeling the pull of history surround me. The Walters Art Museum was like a sanctuary to me. Whenever I felt stressed or lonely, I'd come here and browse the exhibits, admiring the paintings, the sculpture, and of course the arms and armor. Helms, hilts, daggers, shields and spears. I'd press my hand against the glass, trying to be as close as possible to such treasures. I envisioned my ancestors with such swords and armor as these, dressing for battle against an evil foe, confident that God would guide their hand and make their aim true.

I had no such faith. I constantly doubted whether my sword swung on the side of righteous justice or not. It was so difficult to judge when there were no definitive lines between good and evil. No wonder Templars had refused to judge at all for the last eight hundred years.

Except for me that is. I'd made that judgement last month and taken a life. It still hovered over me like a cloud. He'd been a murderer, a skilled magician that no prison would have been able to hold, but I still wished there had been an alternative to sticking my sword through him.

There wasn't. It was done, and it was my burden to bear. I'd face judgement on that when I died, but until then I tried to put it behind me. I wasn't going to dwell on that today. No, today Janice and I were heading to a special exhibit of twelfth century illuminated manuscripts where Janice would scope out the eligible men while I pressed my nose against the glass and admired the calligraphy and artwork. There was an unveiling of some additional pieces to the exhibit, and in keeping with the posh tone of the museum, a special sponsor's reception. The Ainsworth family were significant donors, although we'd always declined the invitations for these events given our distance from Baltimore.

I lived here. I was an Ainsworth. I might as well

go and enjoy some food and drink, rub elbows with the sort of people who donated large sums of money to museums, and set my friend up with one of them.

And Janice was indeed attracting attention. It wasn't the crazy, celebrity rock-star kind of attention, but men were definitely noticing her. They struck up conversations with her at the drink table, and edged up to speak to her as she admired the manuscripts. Before long I noticed her in conversation with a man so tall he nearly dwarfed her. He bent his blond head to listen to something she was saying, extending a glass of wine to her with a long-fingered hand.

"So, what do you think?"

I smiled, leaning back against the man behind me. "I think she's gonna get laid."

Zac snorted. "*Someone* should."

It was a gentle dig at our lack of mattress-action. Not that I blamed him. A guy was bound to get frustrated going out with a woman for over a month, making out a few times only to be pushed away with excuses about work and exhaustion.

I had good reasons to hold back on this relationship. I'd been numb after Raven's death and the events of last month. I saw Zac at the Anderon game and usually was talked into a once-a-week date. He'd gotten the clue after the first week and backed off, taking the slow and easy approach—one that I knew wasn't what he'd hoped for.

Zac was cute with his floppy, over-long brown hair and glasses. Really cute. Sex with him would be fun. It was the afterward that worried me. Crossing that bridge meant we couldn't easily return to the friend-zone, and I liked Zac—liked him as a friend. I felt as though I'd be using him by having sex with him. And that just seemed wrong.

Although both Sean and Petie at the coffee shop assured me that men were perfectly happy to be used if it meant they got to get horizontal with an attractive woman. In spite of their assurances, I still felt like I'd be a total jerk sleeping with Zac and keeping our relationship on the back burner.

He smiled and I wavered in my resolve. "I meant what do you think about the manuscripts? You went on and on about them Friday. I expected to hear a twenty minute lecture on their...something or another."

Sheesh, poor guy. I probably owed him sex after boring him to death Friday night. Yes, I probably did owe him sex. Or at least second base.

I took a step closer to Zac, giving him my sexiest smile. "In a day of e-mail and text messages, such calligraphy is truly a work of art. And I really like the leopard. Yeah. I think I like the drawing of the leopard best."

Zac took the glass of wine from my hand and placed it on a nearby table. "Me, I'm partial to the dude playing the harp. It really adds to my comprehension of the Latin, or whatever that is."

I turned my attention back to the manuscript, placing a finger on the glass. "It's Latin. Don't ask me to read it though. I'm barely proficient. I ran away from the tutor every day and hid behind the tapestries in the dragon room. And I cheated, copying Athena's old tests and essays."

I felt an arm around my waist, the press of a masculine body against my back, a warm breath against my hair. "You had a dragon room?"

"When you've got a house with nine bedrooms you've got to have some way of differentiating them.

Mom and Dad's. Athena's. Roman's. Mine. The five others were named by their decorating theme. The dragon room has tapestries with a dramatic graphic rendering of St. George and the dragon."

"Sounds Gothic. And sexy." His breath stirred my hair.

Okay, this was getting rather intimate for a posh museum gala. "Gothic, yes. Sexy, no."

The image of me on the bed, Dario's weight on top of me, his eyes black with blood lust flashed into my mind, and suddenly I felt breathless. Blood lust scared the heck out of me, but Dario on top of me... Mmm.

But Dario was a vampire, and sex with him would involve a donation of blood, along with an addiction and obsession that would lead to my early death.

Zac pressed against me, oblivious to my thoughts. "I hear they have a spiral staircase here, made of stone like in the castles of Europe."

They did. I loved the stone steps. The turn of the staircase was so narrow it was difficult to walk down.

Zac's arm tightened around me. "We can be alone there. Just you and I."

That was a cold splash of water on my libido. Oh, Lord. He wanted to make out on the museum staircase. "Are you kidding me? There are no doors and it's a major attraction. We wouldn't be alone for long."

"Spoilsport. Come on. Live a little."

I looked over at Janice, happily in conversation with the tall, lanky blond man. Zac was right. I *was* a spoilsport, and I'd strung him along for a month. I needed to live a little, have some fun, take some risks, especially after everything that had happened in the last month. Although it wasn't exactly mature for a twenty-six-year-old woman, a Templar, a representative of the Ainsworth family who had donated to this museum, to be making out with a guy on the spiral staircase.

It wasn't exactly mature, but I needed to be immature just for a moment. I'd mended fences with my best friend only to have her die horribly. I sat across from a vampire I longed for every evening, knowing he was leaving our "business" meeting and going to spend the rest of his night with his blood slave, Giselle.

Giselle. Even her name was beautiful. *Her* parents hadn't saddled her with something like Solaria Angelique Ainsworth.

I leaned back against Zac. "Okay. But not the staircase. I know somewhere a bit more private."

Zac seemed onboard with that idea. Certain portions of his body seemed *very* onboard with that idea. I felt giddy, like a naughty schoolgirl sneaking off between classes with a hot boy. Shooting one last glance at Janice, I took Zac's hand and twirled out of his embrace. "Come on, babe. All these manuscripts have got me hot and bothered."

Yeah, that was about the extent of my skills in sexy-talk. I'm not sure Zac even heard me. He followed behind as I led, holding my hand in a tight grip. We edged our way out of the reception, through an empty room with Egyptian pottery, then past cabinets with filigree jewelry.

"Here."

"Here" was a broom closet at the back of the museum. I giggled as Zac spun me around, pushing me against the door and kissing me. The heat soaring through me had just as much to do with the fact that someone could walk in on us at any moment as the skillful way his mouth moved on mine. I gasped, breathless as Zac's lips traced their way across my jaw and down my neck.

"Come on. Let's get into the closet." Not something I thought I'd ever be saying to a guy. Then again, I never thought I'd be getting frisky in a museum broom closet with Zac either. He was fun. He was nice, and cute. He made me laugh. And this whole thing was like champagne in my veins, taking my mind off everything that had happened in the last thirty days.

I pushed him away, laughing as I turned around and flung open the broom closet door. Something toppled out on top of me the second I opened it, knocking me to the ground. My first thought was that whatever had been leaning against the door was far heavier than a broom. It smelled a lot worse, too. It smelled like blood.

I held back a scream as I tried to shove what appeared to be a freshly butchered side of beef off of me. Zac didn't have my restraint, and I was oddly amused to hear his high-pitched shriek. Amused until I got a good look at what I'd just pushed off to the side. It wasn't a huge chunk of beef at all, but something just as unlikely to be found in a museum broom closet.

It was a human body—a freshly skinned human body.

CHAPTER 2

D ETECTIVE TREMELAY WALKED into the room and did a double take, his eyes widening as he saw me. "Ainsworth. Why am I not surprised?"

Zac's naughty intentions had vanished with the presence of the grotesquely skinned body. Honestly, mine had, too. It wasn't just the shock or the ick factor, but the blood now decorating my shirt and little black skirt. It didn't do a lot for my sex appeal.

The one good thing in all of this was that Janice had texted me to say she was leaving to have coffee with her tall blond guy before all this went down. It was a relief she hadn't been here. I didn't want to ruin what had most likely been the best, or only, dating experience she'd had in years.

"Tremelay. Glad you could join the party." I grinned at the detective, noticing Zac shoot me a narrow eyed look as I did. "I opened the closet door here, and this body fell out on top of me."

Tremelay looked down at the aforementioned dead body. "And what exactly *were* you doing in a broom closet? Did you break some priceless Ming Dynasty pottery and hoped to do a quick clean up?"

"We were going into the closet for a bit of private time." Zac's tone bordered on the hostile side. "Just Aria and me, you know?"

Tremelay's head shot up and so did his

eyebrows. "A closet? Ainsworth, you were getting it on with this boy in a closet?"

Crap. The detective was twenty years older than me, and now I felt like I was all of twelve years old. And Zac wasn't exactly a *boy*. He was my age. Give or take a year.

Although everyone did seem to think I was older than I truly was. Probably not after admitting to almost making out in a broom closet, though. And from the sudden amount of tension in the room I got the feeling that Zac was thinking about opening up a whole can of whoop-ass on the detective. I'm sure the only thing holding him back was the pistol at Tremelay's hip and the fact that a police record wouldn't do Zac's career any good.

Still, his surge of caveman testosterone was making me rethink this whole dating thing. If he was this way now, was I going to need a restraining order in a few months? I might have just been saved from an obsessive boyfriend by a dead guy in a broom closet. I might need to have the "let's be friends" talk with Zac sooner rather than later.

"Any idea who the dead man is?"

Now it was my turn to do the raised eyebrow thing. "Seriously? He's been skinned. The only way I know it's a 'he' and not a 'she' is the lack of boobs and the lap sausage."

Which also had no skin on it. The body was like an anatomy class dummy, only oozing blood. "I think he was killed fairly recently. Maybe he's one of the museum attendees? Or employees?"

Tremelay turned to the Man-In-A-Suit, who I presumed was in charge of the museum. "Well?"

The guy knotted his hands together, carefully avoiding any position where he might actually catch a glimpse of the dead body. "All the employees working today are accounted for. We're going through the sign-in and checking it against the people still in the museum, but we don't keep track of when people leave. Out of one hundred sixty some visitors today, there are probably only forty left in the museum."

I looked again at the body. We might have to wait for a missing person's report and the M.E.'s findings before we could discover the identity of this man. There were no clothes, no wallet, nothing but a naked guy without the slightest bit of skin on him. Not even any fingerprints to check. Hopefully the guy had something about him that allowed us to get a positive ID sometime this century.

Us. I doubted that normally I'd be included in this investigation, and there was still a chance I wouldn't be, even though I'd been the one who found the body. A murderer who skinned their victim could be a psycho with a thing for taxidermy, or it could be something else. I'd only be involved if it were "something else."

Two guys wheeled in a stretcher. Another with them began to snap pictures. Tremelay took out his little notepad and began to write. I got the feeling that my presence was no longer needed, and I was sure that Zac was itching to get out of here.

"We good?"

Tremelay looked over. "Yep. I'll call you if I need you, Ainsworth."

I knew he would. And as much as I wished my life would return to normal, part of me wished I would get that phone call.

CHAPTER 3

I T WAS THE sort of gorgeous fall day where everyone, residents and tourists alike, were flooding the Inner Harbor. After the excitement at the museum, my coffee shop shift and solo night watching television seemed mind-numbingly dull. Dario had cancelled our scheduled meeting due to some vampire business, and I was restless and bored. By ten at night I'd called Janice to let her know I wanted to join her for the demon exorcism.

Which might not be a demon exorcism, but was better than sitting in my apartment all day.

I'd arrived at our meeting spot early just so I could soak up the sun, relax in the hard metal chair and enjoy a cold beer and some oysters. Two teenagers were eating ice cream as they sat on the brick sidewalk just outside the roped off area for outside dining. A couple with three rambunctious children in tow consulted a map and looked around, pointing at various landmarks. The guy at the table next to me hammered his crab claws violently, digging in the shattered shells for meat with the point of a steak knife.

I loved people watching almost as much as I loved the oysters, topped with a spray of lemon juice and a heaping teaspoon of fresh horseradish. The guy next to me gave up hammering and I heard the teenage girl on the other side of the rope say something that grabbed my attention.

"I want a vampire."

So did I, but I didn't think the girl with her jean shorts and sky-blue T-shirt wanted an actual, real life vampire. Maybe she meant like in the movies. I hadn't hung out with teenagers since I'd been one myself, but I remember mooning over romantic leads and wishing my very human boyfriends were more like the perfect guys on the silver screen.

"Get over it, Becca," the boy responded. "Like, you're seriously going to hunt down a vampire and jump her? You're such a baby sometimes. Grow the fuck up."

Brother and sister and not boyfriend and girlfriend? I remembered similar arguments with my own siblings, without the cursing and vampire reference though.

"That was the deal," the girl shot back, her voice crackling with anger. "I help us sneak out and get away from Grandmother, then you help me find a vampire."

Oh sheesh. Kids sneaking out. Been there, done that. I looked quickly over at the two, judging them to be about sixteen or so. The boy had black hair in an overgrown buzz cut. The color made him look Goth in contrast to his pale skin. The girl was equally pale, her long, golden-brown hair with streaks of blue and pink pulled back into a ponytail. The profile of her face showed a cute upturned nose and an excess of eyeliner, as well as neon-pink lip gloss.

"Whatever." I could practically hear the eye roll in the boy's voice. "You wanna kill yourself messing with vampires, have at it. I'm sticking with humans."

Smart boy.

"Where's Lawton?" The girl asked, abruptly changing the subject like teens seemed to do. "He was supposed to meet us here. Think he's okay?"

The boy made a frustrated sound deep in his throat. "We should have ditched him days ago. He's home with his family. Something about his dad needing help and his kid's baseball game. I can't wait around for him. I've gotta change and stop by the bitch's house for my backpack and some cash."

I blinked, disturbed by the boy's callous language. And what friend of theirs could have a kid old enough to be playing in baseball games? But before I could eavesdrop further, Janice showed up. She was all aflutter with sparkling eyes and a very carefully put together skirt and sweater-set combo. I was dying to pump her for details on yesterday, to see if the charm worked or not, but waited for her to settle in with a beer and a few oysters first.

"So...how did things go with the tall blond guy?" Finally. I was squirming with excitement. Judging from her happy expression, things had gone very well indeed.

Janice blushed. I don't think I'd ever seen the reporter blush. "We have a date tomorrow night. He's already texted me."

We both squealed and stomped our feet, which caused our waiter and several other patrons to turn and stare. Even the two teens looked our way before moving off the step and heading down the pathway toward the aquarium. I didn't care. It's not like the little outdoor raw bar was particularly upscale, and I was thrilled for my friend.

At least *something* had gone right yesterday.

"So..." Janice squirmed, giving me a sly smile. "His name is Sean Merrill. He's a real estate developer in Harford County. Divorced two years with no kids. He was already hinting at taking me to an upcoming campaign fundraiser for one of the mayoral candidates. If things go well tomorrow night, I might be shopping for a black-tie dress."

Wow, she really *had* hit the jackpot. "That's awesome!"

She grinned. "I know! We'll have to double-date with Zac one night."

A double date with Janice and her new beau wouldn't exactly send the "just friends" message I needed send to Zac. Darn it. It sounded like such a fun, mature, adult couple thing to do. It sucked that the one guy in the last two years that I really wanted to be with was dead. Or undead, actually.

"Sean really wants to meet you." Janice nodded enthusiastically. "In fact, at first I thought maybe he was interested in you, not me. He saw your tattoo and commented on it. He was fascinated to hear that you were a Templar. Couldn't stop asking me questions about you. I was starting to get a bit jealous." She laughed. "After you went off with Zac we got to talking and suddenly he was asking me to have coffee with him."

Maybe I was overly suspicious, but that whole speech worried me. The guy *could* be a history buff who did lots of reading about the Crusades. Or maybe he was less interested in Janice until he realized I was already taken. Still…

"You wearing your bracelet?"

Janice hid her wrist, shooting me a guilty look. "I love it, Aria, really I do. It just bangs on my keyboard when I'm typing and I forget to put it back on."

"You really should wear it. Just in case." How

the heck could I say it might protect her against sharks in the water? Might. If I'd done the spellwork correctly, that is. It sucked that I had no one to call about these things, to double check my magical work.

Janice scowled. "Just in case what? I'm okay with the attraction charm, but if Sean needs the equivalent of a magical roofie to want to date me, then I'm not interested."

I raised my hands. "Okay, okay. It's not another attraction charm or anything though. It's meant to shield you. I'm sure Sean seems nice and everything, but the bracelet will let you know if he doesn't have your best interests at heart. It will protect you in case he's just some player."

"Oh." Janice looked only slightly mollified. "I can protect myself. It is pretty, though, and I know you worked hard on it, Aria. I don't want to seem unappreciative. I'll try to remember to put it back on after I'm done typing."

Janice was never done typing. I'd just have to rely on women's intuition—both Janice's and mine— to clue us in if Sean was a scumbag or not. It's not like I was one hundred percent sure the bracelet charm would work anyway.

"So, how are things with you and Zac?"

Janice had the sly look on her face. No doubt she'd seen him with his arm around me at the reception. She'd been privy to my angsty discussions about my love life, or lack thereof. She'd also met Dario and Tremelay. And she'd admitted to being Team Tremelay, despite my repeated assurances that we were just friends as well as sort of investigative partners.

What to say? I didn't want to ruin Janice's fresh

bloom of possible love with my decision to dump Zac. That girlfriend convo would have to wait for a few days at least.

"Well, we went off for some adolescent nookie in a back closet, but I was cock-blocked by a dead body."

"What?" Janice shrieked.

Oh yeah. I'd forgotten that she hadn't been there for my tussle with a corpse. The police weren't particularly forthcoming when it came to releasing such gruesome details to the press. It had probably come across the police blotter as a medical emergency on Charles Street. It's not like they made a habit of pronouncing anyone dead on the scene either. Even though the guy was without a doubt deceased, they would have claimed he was dead-on-arrival at the hospital.

"Yep. Dead man in the broom closet. Actually he was skinned, and I don't think he'd been in the closet for long. Or dead for long, actually. There was no way to ID him, so I'm waiting for Tremelay to call me with the M.E. results."

Although he might not call. If this was just some whack-job murderer, he'd have his hands full and no reason to waste time bringing his supernatural expert into the loop on a case that was not in her realm of expertise. I'd need to read about it in the paper eventually, along with all the other curious folk in Baltimore.

"Skinned? As in the dead body did not have any skin on it? Holy shit. I'm so pissed that I missed that. Of course the police are going to put the lid on all the details. Damn it."

Yep. Sometimes you were in the wrong place at the wrong time. And by that I meant me, not Janice.

"Hey, everyone needs a day off. You were having coffee, entrancing the oh-so-eligible Sean Merrill with your considerable charm." I patted her hand at her disgruntled noise. "You'll be first in line when they find the Psychotic Skinner. In the meantime, you've got that great human interest piece about demonic possession and the lack of funding for mental health services."

She smiled. "Yeah. There's that. Are they seriously, calling him the Psychotic Skinner? Can I quote that?"

"*I'm* calling him the Psychotic Skinner. As far as I know, the police have not yet given the killer a catchy tweet-worthy name."

"Figures." Janice shoved the tray of oysters over to me. "Slurp down the last one and let's get going. I'm thinking it would be really bad form for us to be late to an exorcism."

I wasn't one to let shellfish go to waste, so I did as Janice said and we hustled to her car.

The event was taking place at a lovely single-family home in the Canton neighborhood. It was a short drive from the harbor and there was plenty of parking was available both street side and in the wide driveway leading to a two car garage. Janice chose to park on the street. We walked up to the door past beautifully manicured hedge and rang the doorbell. A distraught woman answered. She wore yoga pants and a fitted T-shirt, her hair a messy bun on the top of her head.

"I'm Janice Oswald. The reporter from *The Sun*."

The woman grabbed Janice's hands, practically dragging her into the house. I followed, looking around with curiosity. The inside was just as neat and clean as the outside. The oak furniture had clearly been bought from the same high-end collection. Accent pieces were color coordinated in burgundy with splashes of light green that gave the décor a modern flare. The carpet was white plush and I grimaced, checking my shoes for dirt. Clearly this woman didn't have kids. Or pets.

"He's upstairs. He just got home a few moments ago. Father Bernard is already here."

I hadn't been introduced yet, and the sister of the possessed man didn't seem to care, so I followed them up the carpeted stairs and down a hallway to a large bedroom. Inside was a man who looked to be in his early twenties. He wore jeans, a T-shirt promoting a band called Rabid Rabbit, and had a backpack slung over one shoulder. In the other corner was a priest, looking like he'd rather be anywhere but here on a Saturday afternoon.

"That's Bradley. At least, it used to be Bradley. Now it's a demon in Bradley's body."

"Would you knock it off Amanda? I've gotta go. I just stopped in to grab my backpack and some cash. I don't have time for your crazy demon-talk." Bradley looked hunted as his eyes darted from his sister to the priest, then to the doorway that I was blocking. His head wasn't spinning around. He wasn't frothing at the mouth and spouting curses in arcane languages. He wasn't levitating and convulsing. This didn't look like a demon possession to me. Maybe the sister was the one who needed therapy and good pharmaceuticals, not her brother.

And how the heck were they living in this sweet home in Canton, anyway? The sister wasn't any older than I was, and her brother looked maybe twenty-one or two. I didn't get the feeling this was their parents' home. Had the sister married well and her brother was sponging off of her, taking up residence in one of the guest bedrooms, sleeping all day and getting drunk at Rabid Rabbit concerts at night? Not that I wanted the white plush carpeting, but I was having a serious case of house envy here.

The priest sighed. "Bradley, I'm going to ask you a few questions—both you and your sister. She's very concerned about you."

Frustration flashed across Bradley's face. "Will this take long? I've got a job interview in an hour."

"That's *not* Bradley." The woman pointed dramatically at her brother. "He hasn't been himself since yesterday. A job interview? Oh, please. Bradley hasn't looked for a job after he got fired from the Crab Shack last year. He doesn't eat meat, but I caught him eating a twelve ounce filet last night. I saw him doing the laundry this morning."

Poor Bradley. What a control freak he had for a sister. I folded my arms across my chest, continuing to think some very uncharitable thoughts about this woman.

Janice was busy taking notes. I looked over her shoulder and saw something about dietary changes and personality disorders.

"Bradley? What do you have to say to this?" The priest wiped a hand across his sweaty brow.

Bradley slid the backpack off of his shoulder and dropped it onto the crimson and black bedspread. "Seriously? After all the complaining she's done since I quit college, I finally get my act together and she calls in the church?"

He had a point. The situation was looking less like an exorcism and more like a reality show episode. Crazy Housewives of Canton: Sisters Who Nag Their Younger Brothers.

"He's a demon," the sister shouted.

"You're crazy," he shouted back.

This was getting tedious. It was time for the priest to do his thing so Janice could get her story and I could get back to...whatever it was I needed to do on a Saturday afternoon.

"Why do you think he's been possessed by a demon?" I asked the sister. "Has he been involved with the occult in the past? Has he been ordering books on summoning and black magic off the internet? Is he drawing sigils in a binding circle in your basement?"

Now everyone was looking at *me* instead of Bradley.

"Nooooo," the sister said, eyeing me as if *I* was the one needing exorcism. "But there was the blood. And I overheard him talking to some friends in the driveway about killing people."

"Blood?" All of us asked at once. Well, except for Bradley, who looked rather irritated at this point.

"There was blood all over his clothes and on his body. It was last night, right when he started eating meat and doing this whole job-search thing. He came home covered in blood, tried to sneak into the house. When I saw him, I felt afraid. It wasn't just the blood. He looked... I don't know, he looked swollen and was moving funny."

"Oh for fuck sake, Amanda!" Bradley threw up his hands and paced a few steps. "I was in a fight. Some guy jumped me in an alley, stole my wallet and beat me up. Of course I was swollen and bloody. And I was sore. And I was limping. And yes, I probably said I wanted to kill him. Do you blame me? Shit woman, get off my back."

Amanda winced. I narrowed my eyes,

wondering if this was the talk of a young man who'd just had enough of his meddling sister, or something else. I could see having this kind of argument with Roman. Well, without the profanity, anyway. Obsessive sister. Fed up brother. Poor Janice. I wasn't even sure she could get a story on mental health services out of this family drama.

Except Bradley didn't look all that worse for wear today. If he'd been beaten up enough last night to be bloody and swollen, then he'd sure healed up quick. I would have at least expected colorful bruises and a few bandages. The guy looked fresh as a daisy.

"I'm going to suggest some family counselling," Father Bernard interjected, stepping between the two siblings. "I'd be happy to provide weekly sessions, or I can refer you to a few secular therapists who specialize in group sessions."

Amanda and Bradley glared at each other around the priest. Neither seemed particularly happy with the idea of weekly therapy.

Father Bernard turned to face the sister. "In the meantime, I'd like Amanda to work on holding back a bit, giving Bradley the room to grow and change. Unless he's doing something that endangers himself or others, he should feel free to try new foods and explore different career options."

Amanda gave a short, grudging nod.

"And you." The priest turned to point at Bradley who took a wary step backward. "Your sister has given you opportunities most young men never have. She deserves to be spoken to with respect, her concerns heard. Can you do that?"

Bradley's nod mirrored his sister's.

And there we were. Another episode of Drama in Canton.

Janice tapped her pen against her lip. "Father, can you do the exorcism anyway? Just in case?"

I choked back a laugh. Always the reporter, Janice was determined to salvage something from this story. There might not be demons or psychiatric issues, but even if nothing came of it, Exorcism in Canton would make a better story than Family Drama in Canton.

Father Bernard raised his eyebrows. "But there's no indication that demonic possession is in play here. I honestly believe with a month or two of weekly counselling sessions, Amanda and Bradley can resolve their differences."

"I think Amanda might be able to accept that and be more receptive to group counselling if she could put these ideas of demonic possession to rest."

Janice was good. Really good. Next time I had to go before the Elders, I was taking her. The woman could negotiate like a boss when there was something she wanted.

The priest thought for a second and nodded. "I guess it wouldn't hurt. Amanda, would that satisfy you? Will you agree to let your brother have space to grow and change if I can show you he's not possessed by a demon?"

The sister hesitated then nodded. "Yes. I'll even start buying burgers if you can guarantee that he's truly my brother and not some monster that's taken over his body."

"Then let's proceed." Father Bernard walked over to his bag and began removing supplies.

Bradley exploded in anger. "No. There's no way I'm standing here while this guy throws holy water at me. This whole thing is stupid."

"But it will get you to your job interview in

time," I interjected. "And it will get your sister off of your back. Ten minutes, tops. Splash some holy water, say a few words in Latin, and you'll be on your way."

Janice turned to Amanda. "This is going to satisfy you, right? If Father Bernard does the exorcism and no demon comes flying out of your brother, will you admit that this is Bradley and not some doppelganger?"

Amanda swallowed hard a few times and nodded. "Yes, I'll admit I was wrong."

"Fine." Bradley threw his hands outward in exasperation. "What do I do? Let's get this over with so I can get out of here."

The priest asked him to lay down on the bed, shifting the backpack to the floor. Then Bradley closed his eyes and placed his hands on his chest as Father Bernard began chanting, and flicking him with water. I looked at my phone and moved out of the doorway, my foot hitting the backpack. It squished slightly like it was crammed full of sopping wet clothing or Jell-O or something. Yuck. What the heck did he have in there? I grimaced, wondering briefly if there was more bloody clothing in the bag. Was it really a job interview that Bradley was so desperate to get to, or was he involved in a little extracurricular illegal activities? If he'd pissed off his supplier, then that would have explained the beating and the blood, although not the remarkable healing abilities he seemingly possessed.

The holy water was flying thick and fast by this point, making me think it was a good thing the white plush carpeting had ended in the hallway, and that Bradley had hardwood floors in his bedroom that matched the oak furniture.

"I'm going to need to change my clothing," Bradley complained. "Probably throw the bedding in the dryer, too. Can't you use less of that stuff?"

The priest ignored him and continued. I'd never been to an exorcism before, but this certainly didn't seem to bear any resemblance to the ones I'd read about. There was no screaming. Bradley's body remained on the bed instead of levitating above it. I'd hoped for at least a few vehement phrases in arcane languages, but no. Bradley just lay on the bed, complaining. Janice, and Amanda, were going to be disappointed, because I got the feeling that Bradley had most definitely *not* been taken over by a demon.

The priest evidently had reached the same conclusion. He stepped back, shaking his head as he put the leafy sprig and water back in his bag. "He's not possessed. Will you now believe, as he said, he's just become motivated to get a job and do his own laundry, and decided to eat meat?"

Bradley snorted, flicking holy water from his hair and face as he rose. Without a care for those of us in the room who were complete strangers, he began to strip off his shirt and shimmy out of his pants. Before I had a chance to turn my head, he'd re-dressed himself and draped the wet clothes over the edge of a laundry basket.

I felt a bit sorry for the guy. How embarrassing to have your sister call in a priest just because you ate a steak and had a job interview. Reaching down, I picked up the backpack and handed it to him, noticing that it was really too heavy for my bloody clothes theory. What *did* the guy have in here, bricks? Squishy bricks?

"Thanks." His eyes darted to my tattoo and narrowed. "You're the Templar."

I was *a* Templar. I wasn't *the* Templar. His choice of words was really odd. Suddenly my sympathy was gone, replaced by suspicion. Yes, some people did recognize the mark. Rob at the records office had. Some of the LARP people had. Occasionally I'd served a latte to a history buff who had. But this was a twenty-one-year-old guy who, up until last week, hadn't done more than lay around the house, eat tofu, and listen to Rabid Rabbit.

"Yes, I'm a Templar." I might be the only one living in Baltimore, but I wasn't presumptuous enough to call myself *the* Templar.

"Cool." He reached out to touch the tattoo on my wrist and I jerked my arm back. There was a limit to my politeness, and letting a strange guy feel up my tattoo was way past that limit.

"A Templar." Father Bernard seemed impressed, nodding and smiling at me as he put the rest of his gear away. "God be with you."

"And with you, also," I replied.

Bradley stepped closer, well into my area of personal space. "Can I buy you dinner tonight? Or drinks? Or a cup of coffee?"

What? Seriously? The guy had just been through an exorcism that had left him drenched with holy water and now he was asking me out—a stranger who'd witnessed the humiliating event. Bradley seemed to have forgotten all about his job interview and was giving me what was clearly his best attempt at a sexy come-hither, smoldering look.

"No. I have a boyfriend." Zac wasn't a boyfriend, but he made a good excuse not to go on a date with this creep.

"You sure? I know a great brewpub downtown. They've got a good menu. Farm to table with local, grass-fed beef."

That did sound yummy, but not with Bradley. "No, thanks." I looked pointedly at my watch, then over at Janice. "We really need to get going. I've got a million things to do."

I didn't, but I did want to get out of here before Bradley made me even more uncomfortable than I already was. Janice grimaced in sympathy, exchanged information with Amanda and we hotfooted it out the door to her car.

"What a bunch of weirdos," she said once she had the car in gear and was backing out of the driveway. "How about that sister? And what was it with the white carpeting?"

"I know. In my house that would have been stained with wine or mud in about five seconds. And Bradley? Just as I was starting to feel sorry for him, he turns into a creeper. Think he has a white van in the garage?"

Janice snorted. "I think he's probably got bodies in the garage."

CHAPTER 4

I KICKED OFF my sneakers, threw my keys on the table, and placed my sword gently on the kitchen counter before plopping down on my sofa. It was still early. I had hours before I needed to meet Dario.

Never did I think I'd feel bored again. The first six months here in Baltimore had been lonely. I'd spent my time at work or harassing Dario in downtown pubs, trying to find something to entertain myself that didn't cost money.

August had been a whirlwind of activity and sleepless nights. The job with the vampires. The necromancer. The demons, and angel, and death mages. I'd found friends. I'd lost one of the best friends I'd ever had. I kinda started dating a guy. But right now, I had nothing to do and it was driving me nuts.

Actually I had research to do. Gah. I never thought I'd be tired of paging through manuscripts and magical texts, but I really wanted to *do* something today. A month of scouring every reference I owned on demon marks had left me with nothing beyond the notes Raven had made before she died. I needed to find a way to get this mark removed, but I'd run out of ideas.

Dark Iron had a ritual that he'd given to Raven, but he was dead and I wasn't sure what my friend had done with the information before she'd died. Had Dark Iron taken it from her? Had she left it in the car or her purse? Who knows where those had ended up after she'd died. And honestly, I wasn't sure that Dark Iron hadn't given her a bogus ritual as a red herring.

Although Raven would have known. She was skilled enough to have scented out a fraud. That ritual was the only hope I had right now of getting rid of this demon mark, and I had no way to find it either among Raven's effects or Dark Iron's. I couldn't exactly call Haul Du and ask to see their grimoires without arousing suspicion. Besides, none of those mages would speak to me, let alone hand over a former member's magical diary.

So, as futile as it might be, I was going to take yet another look through my reference books and hope that some miracle jumped out at me from the pages. I flicked on the television, reached down to the coffee table to pick up the Lemegeton that Raven had given me, and knocked something over. It was the fox figurine. Again. I felt the hair stand up on the back of my neck as I picked up the resin object and turned it over in my hands. It was warm, and I wasn't sure if the ruby eyes were reflecting sunlight from the window or if they were glowing.

Glowing or not, this figurine had been on the shelf when I'd left. And now it was sitting on top of my copy of Peterson's *Monsters of the New World*. Was someone messing with me? I'd warded my doorway. Dario was the only one who could get past the deadbolt and the magical locks, but it was daylight, and even he should have triggered the spell that would alert me someone had been inside my apartment.

All the other figurines that my great-grandmother Essie has sent were still on their respective shelves, gathering dust. What was it with the fox? There was only one way I could set my mind at ease, and I was looking for an excuse to procrastinate on my magical research anyway, so I picked up the phone and dialed my great-grandmother.

Essie had a cell phone. And she made very good use of the internet for a woman over a century in age. No one was really sure how old she was, and it would be terribly rude of us to ask. I'd never known my famous grandfather, Tarquin Ailpean Ainsworth, who'd died when my father was only seven, but *his* birthdate, marriage date, and date of death were all recorded in the family bible. If I were to conjecture, I'd put Essie's age at between one hundred and twenty and one hundred and thirty.

And the woman didn't look, or act, a day over eighty. Of course, Tarquin hadn't just brought home a raven-haired beauty from Hungary when he'd married Essie, he'd brought home a talented witch. I fingered the Lemegeton by my side, hoping that I'd inherited more from Essie than my dark hair.

"Hello?" Essie shouted into the phone. "Aria? You okay girl? Any more demons or angels you need to get rid of? How's that hot vampire of yours?"

Essie was obsessed with Dario, more so than even I was. "We're just friends, Gran. I've gone on a few dates with a human named Zac. He sells medical equipment."

I heard a grumble from the other end of the line and knew Essie thought a human sales person was quite a step down from the sexy vampire. Of course at her age, dying from blood loss after a wild three to six months of amazing sex wasn't really a deterrent.

"Gran, I gotta ask. What's up with the figurines? I mean, they're cute and I love that you send me stuff like that, but is there something else about them I should know?"

"They're vessels. *Lelek raktarban.*"

Vessels I understood, but vessels for what? And *Lelek raktarban* sounded like something really tasty for dinner.

"*Lelek.* For the holding of souls."

I felt a wave of cold at her words. Last month I'd helped take down a group of death magic practitioners who had crossed the line from icky animal sacrifice to using humans *and* using their souls. It had involved a very expensive soul trap that had been stolen from a mage in Argentina—a soul trap that I still had, hidden away in the back of a kitchen shelf. I still shuddered to think of the thing, buried behind fifty packets of ramen noodles. I didn't want it, but wasn't sure how to get rid of it without implicating myself in Dark Iron's death. Plus the idea of it falling into the hands of someone who might wind up using it made me feel sick. I didn't want the soul trap. And I wasn't sure I wanted these *Lelek* either.

"Umm, what am I supposed to do with them? I don't do that sort of magic, Gran. And one of them, the fox, keeps moving."

She laughed. It sounded eerily like a cackle. "Oh excellent! A wayward spirit has found a home in one. And the fox too? This soul is there to help you, to share his knowledge with you. That's why he's chosen to live inside the fox."

I was getting the idea that these soul vessels weren't like the soul trap hidden behind the ramen, or like the ones used in necromancy. "Chosen? So this is like a familiar only not furry and not likely to violate the no-pet clause in my lease?"

"No." Essie made an impatient noise. "Familiars are non-human spirits who choose to inhabit an animal body and attach themselves to a human who had proven worthy in magic. They serve to store energy and to act as a catalyst for spells. These *lelek raktarban* are vessels. They are objects that have been magically enhanced so they are attractive to wandering souls."

I still didn't fully understand this, but the fact that my great-grandmother had gone to the trouble of buying all these different figurines, then painstakingly spelling each of them meant the world to me. Essie was cagy with her magic. None of us had ever seen her spell books or knew where she did her work. Most of the time she just seemed like an eccentric, elderly lady, until she flicked her wrist and sent a tennis ball plowing into someone's stomach.

"So I could end up with..." I counted the figurines, "...a dozen of these souls, moving all over my apartment with their glowing eyes?"

"It is rare to even be host to *one*, dear. They are mostly empty hotels, but if a soul is drawn to you and wants to help, he will pick the vessel best suited to his purpose."

So the fox. Wisdom and knowledge, Gran had said. I did want to clear up one major concern, though. "Human souls only, right? I'm not going to get demons or malignant spirits taking up residence in these things?"

That would be totally creepy. I imagined waking up to find the figurines lined up at the edge of my bed, staring at me with glowing eyes as I slept.

"They house only human souls."

I shook my head, looking down at the sitting fox, its bushy tail curled around its legs. "Why me? Why would a spirit be drawn to help me?"

"Only you can answer that, Aria. And you may never know why or even who this spirit was when alive. Some souls do not rest. Some spirits wander. A few of these choose to make use of their time by assisting someone they deem worthy."

"Assisting how? Because it doesn't speak. It just relocates the little fox figure around the apartment. And I think maybe its eyes glow."

"Eh. Sometimes the soul can't figure out its way around the *lelek raktarban*. You'll just have to pay attention and be patient."

I picked up the figurine. It felt so warm in my hands, as if there really was something living inside the resin. The fox appeared to grin saucily at me, his eye's twinkling. Pay attention. It seemed to like my coffee table a whole lot. That wasn't much to go on. The table was filled with books, an old coffee mug, a box of tissues, and a dirty bowl that once had held cereal.

Ugh. I was a total slob. Maybe that's what my spirit-helper was trying to tell me. Clean up, girl.

"Thanks, Gran. Love you."

"Love you too, Aria. Give that vampire a big old kiss for me. One with lots of tongue."

I rolled my eyes and disconnected the call, setting the fox figurine down on the table once more. There were just too many variables going on here. Yes I'd clean, especially the dirty dishes, but I also needed to make it easier for whoever this was inside the fox to communicate with me.

Foxy went back on the shelf and I went to work, tidying up and separating the books that were on the coffee table. One went on the floor by the television, one on the kitchen counter, one on the edge of the couch and so on, until they were a good distance apart. If the fox was back on the coffee table, then I'd figure my message had something to do with either the table itself or the box of tissues. Hopefully the fox would instead move toward one of the books.

As a precaution, I went and picked up the other animal figures. They all felt cool, with none of the glowing eyes of the fox figure. Good. One spirit taking up residence in my apartment was enough. Hopefully soon this one would start to do more than just creep me out with random movements, otherwise foxy might find himself in a box on his way back to my great-grandmother in Middleburg, Virginia.

CHAPTER 5

THE VAMPIRE REFILLED my wine glass, nudging the plate of calamari over toward me. "So the exorcism sounds like it was a complete waste of time."

I shoved a few of the fried squid pieces in my mouth. "Yeah, I don't even think Janice can get a good human interest story out of it. Maybe if she wants to do something Geraldo-style. I was disappointed. I've never seen an actual exorcism and I was looking forward to it. The priest said he'd call me if another one came up, but that he hasn't had a true exorcism in over a decade."

Dario made a sympathetic noise and sipped his wine. "Speaking of Janice, how did the attraction charm go?"

Oh sheesh, I'd been so busy telling him about the exorcism that I'd forgotten the museum. "She did meet someone she liked and is going out on a date with him tonight. But get this, I opened up the door to a broom closet and had a dead guy fall out on top of me."

The vampire blinked, his mouth open in astonishment. "You *what*?"

"I was at the museum, and a corpse fell out of a closet. Knocked me down. I thought it was a side of beef at first because the body was completely skinned."

Dario shut his mouth with a snap. "Skinned? As in no skin at all? Like at a slaughterhouse?"

"Yeah. What kind of crazy freak skins his victims?"

The vampire raised his shoulders and shook his head. "That's revolting. So what did you do when this corpse fell on you? And why were you going into a broom closet at a museum?"

Oops. "Umm, I was getting a broom? Anyway, I called the police. Tremelay came down. I guess he spent the rest of the day interviewing museum attendees and employees. Someone had to have seen the killer sneaking a skinned body into a broom closet."

"I'd assume so." Dario took a sip of his wine, a faint smile twitching at the corner of his mouth. "A skinned corpse falling out of a broom closet on top of you. I wish I wasn't dead during the day. I would have paid good money to see that."

It was like we were an old married couple, out each night to drink wine and discuss our day's events. Weird as it was, I liked our few hours every evening together. I just had to not think about where he was probably going afterwards. Did he sit like this with Giselle discussing her day? Did he tell her what was going on with the *Balaj*? A truly horrible part of me hoped not. I wanted these sort of things to be just between us. She could have the ecstasy, the sex and the blood. Just let me have this bond, unshared with another.

Okay, I was lying. I didn't want her to have the ecstasy, the sex and the blood, but since I wasn't supplying it, I really didn't have any room to complain. Life wasn't fair. I needed to put on my big girl panties and deal. Plus, it's not like I hadn't been two seconds away from getting busy with Zac in a museum closet. I was such a hypocrite.

"I haven't heard any updates from Tremelay," I told Dario. "Although I'm not sure I'll find anything out if it's just some whacked-out serial killer. I hear those bath salts users turn cannibalistic, maybe they also develop a weird taxidermy thing?"

He shrugged. "All I know is I'm a vampire, and *I'm* weirded out by this whole thing. I wonder what he did with the skin."

Hopefully the police could figure that out. "Well, it wasn't in the broom closet. But enough about me, what's going on with you guys?"

I finished off the last two bites of calamari and cradled my wine. I was probably a little tipsy at this point. Dario always ordered the good stuff and he was pretty heavy-handed when it came to filling up my glass.

"There have been a batch of killings north of the city that have us worried." Dario's tone was casual, his eyes fixed on the swirl of red in his wine glass. "In case they come to your attention I want you to know that they are not sanctioned in any way by our *Balaj*. We suspect a group of renegades has banded together and is testing our ability to hold the outer edges of our territory. We'll take care of it ourselves."

My fuzzy wine-brain cleared right up at his words. "What kind of killings?"

"Humans. We found a disposal site with the bodies. They'd died of blood loss. Some of them showed signs that they'd been aggressively fed from over the course of a week."

All I could do was wonder how this was any different from the blood slaves that Dario's *Balaj* took. Yes, *they* seemed to make it several months. No doubt the taking of other prey each night and the support of their family allowed the vampires to keep the relationship going for an extended period of time. But still—how could they blame other vampires for not having such restraint, especially if they were starving and outcasts?"

"How many humans died?"

"Six." Dario frowned, glaring at the glass as if it were the wine's fault. "At first we thought it was a starving rogue who was gorging himself, but each vampire leaves their scent, their mark, on the victim. We sensed at least four different vampires. A common dump site means they are working together. One renegade is troublesome. Four is cause for worry."

At least I had some solace that blood slaves such as Giselle and Sarge came into these relationships willingly. I doubted these renegades got consent from their victims. "Is Leonora sending a group out to track them?"

Dario nodded. "We're leaving tomorrow right at first dark. I'm not sure how long it will take. I'll text you, but our meetings may need to be on hold for a while."

I opened my mouth only to snap it shut. I desperately wanted to ask him to check in with me each evening, so I knew he was okay. That wasn't my place, though. "Let me know if you need my help," I said instead. "It's not like I'm doing anything right now beyond research, the occasional LARP and RPG, and my shifts at the coffee shop."

He tilted his head and gave me that smile of his that made me want to throw my panties at him. "Bored?"

"Yes," I grumbled.

"So I need to scare up a hydra or open a portal to hell? Can't have my Templar getting bored," he teased.

I didn't need that kind of fun. "Just let me know if you need a woman with a good sword arm, okay?"

He nodded and saluted me with his wine.

"And...be careful." My face felt on fire just saying that. It got even hotter at the intent look on Dario's face in response.

"You're concerned about me?"

Oh sheesh. "Of course. I mean, we're friends. And we're kind of diplomatic liaisons, business partners. Yes, I'm concerned about you."

Thankfully my embarrassing speech was interrupted by my phone. I'd had it on do-not-disturb, so this was probably one of my family.

It was Tremelay. I shot Dario an apologetic grimace and he waved for me to take it. I'll admit my pulse raced a bit at the thought that there might be something going on that would require my help.

"The dead guy at the museum?" the detective announced without any sort of greeting or preamble. "His name is Brian Huang."

"Huh." Did I know this guy? Was his name supposed to mean something to me?

"Do you know how hard it is to identify a skinned body? There are no fingerprints. No easily identifiable facial features. No tattoos or moles or scars. It's impossible. Guess how we ID'd him. Guess."

Heck if I knew. "Dentures?" It was a long shot, but I remember reading a crime fiction where a victim was identified through distinctive dental work.

"Close. Dude had a knee replacement. They're numbered and registered. The M.E. pulled the number and bingo—Brian Huang."

Again I grimaced apologetically at Dario. This was interesting and all that, but I didn't see why the detective had called me. Unless he just wanted to chat and we'd become the sort of friends who talked about this stuff. Maybe. I had these scheduled debriefings with Dario. I met with Janice regularly to exchange info. Why not Tremelay? If this kept up, I'd need to have them all in one room to do it all at once, like a press conference. It would save me repeating everything three times and playing a torturous game of telephone.

"Ready for the weird part? Well, weirder than a skinned guy in a museum broom closet?"

Yes. Yes, I was.

"No missing person's report. His family claims they've seen him since the murder. In fact, we accounted for him at the museum. He was at the reception area and my records show we spoke to him when we were clearing the crime scene."

Dario looked intrigued and I realized that he could probably hear every word Tremelay said. Vampires. I'd need to be careful what calls I took when he was around. It would be horribly embarrassing if someone let slip a personal bit of information.

"Identical twins? Or maybe Brian Huang is a common name and there's another guy with the same name and knee replacement?"

"Not twins according to hospital birth records." Tremelay snorted. "Maybe he's a clone. After what I've seen in the last month I'm not ruling out alien body snatchers."

Body snatchers. Right. "Maybe the hospital screwed up the knee replacement ID. Typed a seven instead of a one or something?"

"Come on, Ainsworth. I thought you'd be the first to be on board with my alien theory."

Normally I would, but I'd just spent a disappointing afternoon at a non-exorcism. "So, what's the next step?"

"Well, we also considered the possibility of a screw up in registering the knee replacement, so we're checking similar numbers to see if any of them line up with a missing person's report. It's gonna take forever, though. In the meantime I'm going to ask Brian Huang to meet me and answer a few questions. It's a long shot that he'll have any information, but I've got a skinned body and not a lot else to do until the researchers run through the device registration possibilities."

"Soooo...what can I do to help?"

I heard Tremelay sigh. "I don't know. Cookies. A batch of cookies would really help."

My eyes met Dario's. We both shook our heads, eyebrows raised. "What are cookies going to do?"

"Keep me in a good mood. Show up tomorrow at ten with cookies, chocolate chip or peanut butter, and I'll let you listen in while I talk with Huang."

"Am I allowed to do that?" I knew he'd been skirting the line of police procedure with my involvement in the death mage case. Having me hang out on the other side of a two-way mirror while he interviewed a potential...witness? Suspect? I was pretty sure that wasn't permitted.

"Heck, he's not even a person of interest. It's just

an informal chat that we're doing at the station as opposed to me going to his house or on a street corner. No biggie."

"Umm, okay." It's not like I really had anything else to do besides scour my research texts for the umpteenth time for info on demon marks.

"Cookies. Don't forget the cookies."

Cookies? Like *I* knew how to make cookies. We had servants growing up, a cook. I was lucky I could microwave a frozen dinner. The only chocolate chip cookies this guy was getting were ones baked by a bunch of Keebler elves. And the more I thought about it, the more annoyed I got. So the only help I could provide was baking cookies? What was I, some kinda Betty Crocker? Should I show up tomorrow in a poofy 50's era dress with hot-rollered hair and false eyelashes?

But I *did* want to listen in on the interview because I was bored and this skinner serial killer was the most interesting thing that had crossed my path in weeks. If I had to run by a bakery on the way, so be it. Although I was tempted to burn a batch of cookies into a rock-hard, blackened crisp, just to teach the detective a lesson.

"I'll be there." I hung up the phone and plastered a smile on my face as I looked up at Dario. He had a wary expression on *his* face—one part amusement, one part terror.

"Are you going to poison him with your baking?"

Now my smile was real. Dario didn't care that our dinner had been interrupted by a call from another man. He wasn't getting all puffy-chested and demanding to know who Tremelay was. Heck, he'd met Tremelay and hadn't reacted that way either. This was so nice, not having to worry about misplaced jealousy.

But I wasn't going to think of that now. Not when I was enjoying the company of a charming vampire. And not tomorrow when I was listening to the police interview someone who could be a murder victim—or suspect.

CHAPTER 6

I WAS UP early for once, breakfasting on the box of cannoli that Dario had insisted I bring home with me. Things were looking up. I was going to watch the cops work their magic. I had no one trying to kill me or my friends. There was nothing supernatural going on that required my attention.

Of course, a glass half full was still half empty. I had a demon mark on my waist. And sometimes at night, right when I was about to drift off to sleep, I saw the emptiness of death in Dark Iron's eyes, saw the blood flowing around my sword blade, coating it crimson.

Did soldiers feel this way? Did cops feel this way? If it hadn't been for Dario helping me clean up the mess, hiding what I'd done from the police who would have a very different opinion of my taking justice into my own hands, I might have fallen to pieces right then and there. It was justified. It was the right thing to do...wasn't it? I was a Templar, and I needed to protect pilgrims on the path. If that involved spilling the blood of murderers, then that was a cross I'd need to bear.

But I'd stabbed him in the back. I'd made my decision to deliver justice a split second too late and stabbed him in the back. That was just as hard to live with as the fact that I'd taken a human life.

I pushed those memories into the dark corners of my mind, pulled my drapes open as far as they'd go, and danced around my apartment in my pajamas while eating pastry, trying to start the day off without the nightmares that came in the dark. The radio station had a classic rock thing going on and I was digging it—digging it so much that I almost missed the little resin fox figurine perched on top of a book by the bathroom door.

Ah. My resident spirit was pointing me in a direction, and that direction was Peterson's *Monsters of the New World*. I patted the fox's pert little nose and put it back on the shelf, grabbing my coffee before curling up on the couch with the Peterson book.

An hour later and I still didn't know what I was looking for. After getting sucked into Wendigo lore, I'd fallen into the abyss of Mothman legends. It was after nine o'clock when I reluctantly set the book aside, wishing I had more time to delve into the section on Lupe Garou. Almost as an afterthought I left the book on the sofa, opening it randomly to a page and wincing as I thought what my father would say if he saw what I was doing to the binding of the book.

Librarians, even Templar ones, took the preservation of the written word very seriously. Cracked spine aside, I was hoping that the spirit in the little fox could somehow manage to flip to the page I needed to read. If he could move the figurine around, I assumed turning pages wouldn't be too much of a stretch.

Throwing on some clothes and yanking my hair back into a pony tail, I went to put on my sneakers and hesitated. What the heck had I stepped in? Or rather, what the heck had I kicked? I didn't always look closely at my footwear, and these were a retired pair of running shoes, neon-bright in pink, blue, and yellow. Whatever I'd kicked had stained the blue toe to dark purple.

Yuck. I slid on another pair, but took this shoe over to the sink. It could have been anything—pizza, car oil, barf.

It was blood. I could tell from the red of the water, from the faint smell it gave off. My mind slid back into memories of a month ago, of me standing in the shower fully clothed as the water ran red down the drain.

Get a grip. I hadn't killed anything. I'd probably stubbed my shoe against some roadkill while walking. Yeah, because I wouldn't notice almost stepping on a dead possum in a gutter. Whatever it was didn't matter. The stain was coming off my shoe. The water was now running clean. No harm, no foul.

I left the soggy shoe in the sink to dry and skipped out, grabbing one more cannoli for the road.

It was a beautiful day, the sun beating down with a fierce intensity that belied the September date on the calendar. I headed west from my Fells Point apartment, swooping through the harbor area to swing by the bakery. I could have picked up cookies at Holy Grounds, the coffee shop where I worked, and taken a few moments to socialize and chat with co-workers unlucky enough to be working on this gorgeous day, but instead I kept going up the narrowing streets to the huge brick building that looked more like a turn of the century clothing factory than a bakery.

Normally showing up at a bakery after nine o'clock in the morning meant you were left with whatever the morning crowd didn't want. That usually included things like black olive bagels, anise flavored cookies, and those donuts with the jelly in them. That was not the situation at Dill's. Even at this late hour of the morning the cases overflowed with a huge assortment of cookies, donuts, and pastries. Pies and cakes in their glass displays took up an entire wall of the shop. Three people were ahead of me to place their orders and two staff were on the phone, filling orders for delivery.

In record time I was out of there and on my way to the station, a huge box of assorted cookies in the passenger seat. Tremelay had given me directions that led me through western Baltimore to a large industrial-looking brick building with rows of small, squinty windows and a huge white-columned entrance that looked like it should have been attached to a southern estate instead of this soulless edifice.

No wonder the guy needed cookies. I'd need more than pastry coming here to work each day. Hard liquor, perhaps.

I parked and trotted up the absurd white steps, sending my cookie box through the metal detector along with the contents of my pockets.

The sword was in my car. Even the best crafted look-away spell wouldn't keep the metal detector from going crazy at my weapon. I hated to leave it behind, but couldn't exactly bring it into a police station. Besides, I was here to watch them conduct an informal interview with a museum employee, a mistaken victim of a serial killer. No need for a bastard sword when I was in a station full of armed officers better equipped to take down a human threat than I was.

"Whoa! Dill's!" Instead of greeting me, Tremelay snatched the box of cookies and caressed the lid. If only a man would show *me* that much affection.

Before I could reply there was a crowd around the cookie box. "Any chocolate chip?" "Ones with pecans?" "How about cinnamon spice?"

Tremelay wrapped his arms protectively around the box and glared at his co-workers.

"I brought three dozen," I told him. He might want to consider sharing. I heard things at the station could get pretty frosty when someone refused to share baked goods.

"Afterward." He shooed at the other cops, who tried to take advantage of his one armed hold on the box with attempts to grab it from his hands. "You guys make me drop these and I'm gonna have to discharge my service weapon."

We elbowed our way past the hungry cops and into a little room with a huge picture window. I'd seen these two-way mirror things in hundreds of movies. I'm pretty sure by this point none of the folks being interviewed were fooled by the mirror.

At this moment, the room on the other side of the window was empty. Tremelay put the box of cookies down on the table and opened them, offering one to a guy who'd come into the room with us. He was less slovenly than Tremelay with a neat crease in his dark pants and starch in his white shirt. The two cops were about the same age, but this one had lost a good bit of his blond hair, the remaining amount trimmed short. In spite of the stereotypical affection toward donuts—and the verified fondness for cookies—this guy had managed to keep his midsection in the range of what I'd expect to see on a somewhat active middle-aged man.

"Norwicki," he announced, crumbs decorating

his bottom lip.

"Ainsworth," I replied. No one had offered me a cookie yet, but since I'd bought the darned things, I went ahead and reached for one. I half expected Tremelay to slap my hand out of the way, but he generously allowed me to take a peanut butter.

"You the Templar?" I nodded and he continued. "Where's your sword?"

"In the car." Duh. Like they'd let me carry it around here.

"Can I see it?"

What was it about cops and my sword? I swear if there was a choice between seeing my boobs and my sword, they'd pick the sword.

"Where is Huang?" Tremelay interrupted, looking at his watch. "If he's a no show, we need to send someone around to his house to pick him up."

"Riiight," Norwicki drawled, sneaking a hand into the cookie box. "The Lieutenant is never going to go for that. He's obviously not our victim since he's walking around alive with his skin still on. We can't strong-arm a citizen just because there was a mistake coding his medical implant."

"Little too much of a coincidence in my opinion," Tremelay replied, ignoring the cookie theft. "Guy works at a museum, is there on the day a body winds up in the museum broom closet, *and* happens to have a medical device registry number that shows up in the corpse."

Norwicki stuffed the whole cookie in his mouth, managing somehow to speak while chewing. "People do win the lottery. People do sometimes get hit by lightning. And people do sometimes work in a place where a dead guy is found with an implant that traces back to them. What are you saying, Tremelay?

You think Huang switched knee implants with the victim, then skinned him and stuffed him in a back room at work? There's nothing that points to him as the killer. Nothing. It was a freak chance thing that the dead man's implant matched Huang's."

He had a point. "Aren't those devices shipped in batches?" I chimed in. "Hopkins probably does a ton of knee replacements. Heck, there are hundreds of joint replacement specialists in the Baltimore/D.C. area. It's not that far of a stretch to think that Huang may have gotten his replacement from the same batch as the victim and the numbers were only one digit off. Someone does a typo and bingo—two guys in Baltimore with the same implant registration number."

Tremelay glared at me as if I were Judas. I felt suddenly guilty and pushed the box over toward him. Maybe another chocolate chip cookie would ease the pain of my betrayal.

"Let it go, Tremelay," the other detective said. "This is Baltimore. We've got enough to deal with without harassing some museum employee with a bad knee. The M.E. John Doe'd the vic. They'll hold it longer than usual because of the circumstances of the murder. We'll keep checking missing person's reports and eventually we'll get a hit."

The detective had a point. If my theory about the artificial joint batches was correct, then the guy lived in the area at the time of the surgery. He was either visiting or he still lived here. Eventually someone would report his disappearance, and most likely sooner rather than later. I couldn't see vagrants with expensive knee replacements, and nothing about the guy's teeth—which were all frighteningly visible on his corpse—seemed to indicate long-term drug use or lack of annual dental care. *Someone* had to be missing this guy.

At that moment the door opened to the interview room and we all snapped to attention. A uniformed officer escorted an Asian man in and motioned to the chair, asking him if he'd like water or coffee.

"Coke? Orange if you have it."

The officer tilted his head, his expression confused. "Orange soda? We don't have any of that but we do have the regular Coke."

Huang thanked him and the officer left. No one made a move to go into the room. Norwicki and Tremelay watched through the mirror, as did I. The man slumped in his chair, legs wide and hands shoved in his pockets in a stance that was at odds with what I'd expect from a forty-year-old museum employee.

He looked like a nervous teenager, bouncing his knee and glancing around the room.

"Rock, paper, scissors?" Norwicki asked.

"Nah. I got it." Tremelay closed the lid on the cookies and gave his partner a warning glare before leaving to enter the room with Huang. The man straightened up as the detective walked in, clasping his hands on top of the table, still bouncing his leg at a frantic pace.

"Mr. Huang. Thank you so much for coming in today." Tremelay put a folder on the table and sat across from the man. "I know we spoke to you about the body found at the Walters the other day, but some interesting facts have come to light."

Brian Huang fidgeted, picking at his nails. "Yeah?"

Yeah? This was a man who had a Master's

degree and five years of employment at the museum as a curator.

"The dead body has a knee replacement, and the serial number is registered to you."

Huang's leg abruptly halted its frantic movement. "Well, I'm obviously still alive."

"I see that," Tremelay smiled. "It's quite the coincidence, though. A dead man at your place of employment has a medical device that links to you."

"What are you getting at?" Huang's voice was squeaky, panicked. "Are you accusing me of something? You think I ripped out my knee and surgically implanted it in someone else before killing them?"

"Of course not. I just need to follow up. I'm sure you understand." The detective opened the folder and pulled out a picture, sliding it toward Huang. "Do you recognize him?"

"No," the man shrieked. "How the hell am I supposed to recognize him? He's got no face."

Tremelay slid the photo back into the folder. "Where were you the evening before?"

Huang took several deep breaths, his leg starting its bounce again. "I was at the museum from five to midnight. We had the exhibit to prep, plus there were some loaned artifacts coming in from a museum in South Carolina. Elsa Cartwright, the curator of the weapons exhibit, was there with me. We catalogued the loaned items and readied the displays. I went home at midnight and was back at the museum at eight to get things ready for the donor reception."

Thorough, and he had witnesses to his alibi. But there still was time after he'd left the museum to have killed and skinned the victim. I was assuming he had keys to the building, and that his wife might not notice that he'd arrived home closer to two than twelve thirty or one.

Wait. He wasn't a suspect. He was supposedly the victim by his knee replacement ID. The guy probably had nothing to do with this. Tremelay had him here just to gather information, not accuse the man. As Huang had said, he could hardly have removed his own implant and put it in the victim. This was just a bizarre coincidence.

Tremelay obviously felt the same. He noted the man's comments, then stood, thanking him for coming in. The detective was escorting him to the door just as the officer arrived with the man's soda.

Huang took it and nervously fiddled with the pull tab, then followed Tremelay out of the interview room.

"What do you think?" Norwicki asked.

I shrugged. "Someone screwed up coding the guy's medical device. Probably someone getting a knee replacement the same week as our victim."

Norwicki nodded in agreement. "Try convincing Tremelay that. He's gonna be a dog with a bone on this case, and the man doesn't believe in coincidences."

The detective might not, but I couldn't see how this was anything else. No other explanation made sense. We were looking for a psychotic killer who skinned his victim, and I truly doubted Brian Huang had anything to do with the murder, in spite of his eccentricities.

CHAPTER 7

NORWICKI AND I had reopened the cookie box and helped ourselves by the time Tremelay made it back in.

"Hey," he protested, shutting the lid after grabbing another chocolate chip for himself. "Well, Huang was a bust, and we're back to square one. I still think something is fishy with that guy, though."

Norwicki gave me a knowing look reached for another cookie, jerking his hand back as two beeps went off. Like a synchronized water ballet, both detectives checked their cell phones and exchanged tired glances.

"Got a murder, this one with her skin still on," Norwicki announced as he stowed his cell phone in his pants pocket.

"Yeah," Tremelay grumbled, looking through the big glass window into the now-empty interview room. "Guess our John Doe has to step aside until we get another lead." He looked over at me and smiled. "Wanna ride along, Ainsworth? I feel bad that this wasn't more exciting."

I had nothing else to do today. "Sure. I think a dead woman is a fair trade for a couple dozen cookies."

At the mention of the baked goods, both detectives eyed the box. "We won't be back for hours," Tremelay announced. "I leave these at the station and there won't be any left."

Oh for Pete's sake. You'd think the guy never had a cookie before in his life. "Share, you selfish pig. You're gonna get fat if you eat all those cookies yourself."

Tremelay and Norwicki both instinctively sucked in their stomachs and looked down. Vanity knew no age limit.

"Oh all right." Tremelay finally capitulated. They each took a few more cookies and deposited the nearly-empty box on a desk just outside the door to the interview room. Within seconds, other cops had descended on it like a pack of piranhas.

We walked out to the unmarked car, Tremelay still chewing over the not-Huang case. "You know if it's a serial killer, he's going to kill again. It's not like this guy wakes up one day and decides to peel the skin off someone then never do it again."

"Yeah." Norwicki chimed in. "Even if it's out of state, it'll link in. It's too weird of a murder not to. We'll get him."

Tremelay sighed. "Yeah. I guess. I just hate having this one on the board as a John Doe with no leads at all."

We made our way through the parking lot and I saw Huang next to a car in the visitor space, talking to a young woman. Suddenly he reached out and grabbed her, the pair hugging each other like they had no one else in the world. Their shoulders shook and I realized they were both crying.

His daughter? No, he wasn't *that* old. The girl looked to be about sixteen, too young to be his wife. My stomach twisted at the thought that Huang could be involved with an underage girl, but their embrace, although emotional, didn't seem passionate.

"Coming Ainsworth?" Tremelay called, unlocking the door to the unmarked car.

I turned but not before the couple broke apart from their embrace and I saw the girl's face—the golden-brown hair with pink and blue streaks, the upturned nose, thick black eyeliner, and neon pink lipstick. It was the teenage girl from the Inner Harbor who'd been arguing with her brother outside the oyster shack.

Brian Huang was about as far from a vampire as could be. Either she'd changed her mind, and her gender preference, or they were an odd pair of friends. Suspicious, I grabbed my cell phone and snapped a quick picture of the two, jogging to catch up with Tremelay and Norwicki.

The three of us were settled in the car, me in the backseat, before I remembered I'd left my sword in the trunk of my car. Not that I'd need it. We were heading off to see a routine murder. No need for Trusty there.

"So what's up with this case?" I asked, breaking the silence and putting the thought of a forty-year-old man and a sixteen-year-old girl out of my mind.

"Amanda Lewis," Tremelay said. "Twenty-eight. Made a bunch of money in short-sales when she was barely old enough to buy a beer. She's a financial analyst, but does pretty well day trading, evidently."

Norwicki snorted. "I should be so lucky. My 401k looks like a kid's lunch money."

Dead at twenty-eight didn't sound so lucky to me. "So...? Jealous boyfriend goes homicidal? Robbery gone bad? She spend all that money on coke and tried to stiff her dealer?"

Both detectives shrugged. "Boyfriend is the one

that found her," Tremelay said. "Judging from the hysteria on the 911 call, I'd say he's not a suspect. He thinks it has something to do with her brother. Says he saw a man running from the scene, and is pretty sure it was him."

I looked out the window at the tightly spaced rows of narrow, tall houses, the shadows of the harbor in the distance. The container ships looked so small from here, the rows of gantry cranes at the port like bowlegged stick figures. We made a left, heading north and still east. This neighborhood looked vaguely familiar, but I hadn't been paying attention early on and still wasn't familiar enough with the city to know where I was.

"Who knows," Norwicki said. "Brother could have been in a gang. Maybe the sister saw something she shouldn't have. Or maybe he had racked up debts and was robbing his sister when she came home early from work."

She was killed in her house. It seemed an odd place for a gang to do a hit. We were heading to the more affluent eastern neighborhoods. I couldn't see a bunch of boyz-in-the-hood driving here and storming into a charming Cape Cod with guns blazing. Unless it was vampires. I shivered, hoping with all my might that vampires weren't involved with this murder. *Please Lord do not let me be on the opposite side of a murder from Dario.* We'd just gotten back on good terms after the necromancer thing last month. I didn't want our friendship—or whatever the heck we had—threatened by a dead day trader in Canton.

Canton. I blinked as I realized where we were and why I was recognizing the scenery. In fact, I was *really* recognizing the scenery. Then I went into a state of astonishment as we pulled into a very familiar driveway.

Good Lord. "I know this house. Tremelay, I was here yesterday. I met this Amanda woman as well as her brother, Bradley."

Tremelay put the car in park, and the two detectives swiveled their heads to stare at me in the backseat. I applauded their synchronicity of movement, the similarity of expression. It was almost as if Tremelay and Norwicki had been practicing the move for weeks. I guess that's what happened when you spent more time with your partner than you did with your spouse.

"You *know* Amanda Lewis?"

Wow, they even spoke in harmony. Amazing.

"Yes. My friend is a reporter and she was here doing a piece on an exorcism. Amanda was convinced that a demon had possessed her brother because he'd started eating meat, doing his own laundry and was looking for a job. She even called a priest in."

Norwicki blinked, his mouth open. "Hell, I'd be jumping for joy if my brother started looking for a job, not calling in a priest."

"She sounds like a nutjob," Tremelay growled. "Maybe her brother *did* kill her for nagging him all the time. Can't say I hadn't thought about it a few times with some of my sisters."

I didn't know any of Tremelay's sisters, but judging from his selfishness with the cookies *I* bought, I was thinking they might have had a good reason to nag him.

"Anyway…" I glared at the two detectives. "The priest threw a bunch of holy water on the brother. Nothing happened. Then the brother left to go to a job interview."

It all came back to me in Technicolor—us leaving abruptly because the brother had suddenly turned into smarmy player-boy the moment he saw my tattoo, the stupid white carpeting everywhere. I wondered if Amanda was killed in a room with the white carpeting. I hoped for her sake it had been somewhere with easier clean-up. I could completely see the woman haunting her killer if he caused her to bleed all over the thick, white plush floor covering.

Bradley. Sympathetic at first then a complete creeper. I thought of the Rabid Rabbit shirt he'd had to change after it became wet with holy water. I remembered the oak floors of his bedroom that matched his furniture to a "T". I remembered my foot hitting his backpack, the feel of it squish as if he'd filled it with soggy clothing or Jell-O.

Slow-motion, like a film replay, I again saw my foot hit the backpack. It was the same foot, the same shoe that was drying in kitchen sink because it had been stained with blood.

"Guys? I think maybe the boyfriend is right. I think Bradley *is* involved in his sister's death." I relayed the details of the squishy backpack and my blood-stained shoe.

"Are you sure?" Norwicki asked. "Maybe you accidently kicked a dead possum crossing Pratt Street. It happens."

Ew. No, it didn't happen. "I think I would have noticed that. I'm not positive one hundred percent that the blood was from the backpack, but I'm pretty sure."

"Okay." Tremelay unbuckled his belt and shifted in his seat as he opened the door. "We'll make sure we look for the brother's backpack in the house and have the techs run it through for trace. Ready?"

We slid out of the car. The neighbors were conspicuously outside, trying to look like they weren't gawking while they pruned manicured hedges or nearly wiped the paint off their car in endless circles over the same spot. A few had given up pretending and just stood with their arms across their chest, lips tight as they watched. Tremelay's car was parked half-in the drive, flanked on either side by marked cruisers. Two officers stood outside, ensuring the neighbors kept their gawking to their own side of the property line.

Neither of the detectives had to flash badges. The uniformed officers gave them a nod of recognition, narrowing their eyes at me as I followed Tremelay and Norwicki inside. Not having a badge or my sword, I instead flashed the Templar tattoo on my wrist, which earned me a nod of acknowledgement. It seems Tremelay had been talking and had spread news of me around the station. I wasn't sure if that was a good thing or not.

The white carpet in the foyer and living room was pristine, but as we made our way up the stairs and to the master bedroom, I saw my hopes for Amanda's eternal rest were dashed. Her body lay twisted on the ground, white carpet stained bright red in a lopsided circle around her torso. The padding underneath must have been thick, because I knew how much blood the human body held (thank you vampires) and it all seemed to have been soaked up pretty much directly under her body.

I'd thought she was a crazy pain in the butt when I'd met her yesterday, but now I felt a pang of remorse as well as guilt for my uncharitable thoughts. No matter how unlikeable I found their personality, no one deserved to die like this. Amanda was naked, her legs twisted unnaturally as if they'd been dislocated at the hip. Her arms and hands were covered with slash-marks. Defensive wounds? I couldn't really tell. They weren't the only knife marks. There were also ones along her neck and shoulders, as if someone has slashed in a parallel fashion to her body rather than stab at her.

"How'd she die?" My voice was husky. I'd seen dead bodies before. A month ago I'd seen so many dead bodies I'd become rather numb to the experience, but something about this woman's death seemed so wrong.

"Neck snapped," a tall woman by the bed announced. Others around her were taking pictures or bagging items with tweezers. She stood like Pharaoh commanding the slaves, latex covering her hands and feet as she made notes on a clipboard. "Cuts were perimortum by my initial impression."

"And her hips?" I'd seen my share of knife wounds and blood, but the angle of her legs kept drawing my eyes like a horrible magnet.

"Before death."

I choked back bile. The idea of a woman—a financial analyst, day-trader, brother-nagging woman—having her legs dislocated at the hip, then fighting off an attacker with a knife for God-knows how long until having her neck snapped? In a way it seemed just as horrific as the death magic sacrifices last month. Worse, actually. *Both* legs dislocated at the hip? I knew how strong those muscles were, how big those joints and ligaments were. It must have been excruciating. It must have been damned near impossible.

"How the heck did someone dislocate both her legs?" I had to ask. And I had to look around the bedroom for any sign of a medieval rack or a couple of truck winches.

"I'll know more when I get her back to the morgue," the woman said, tapping her pen against the clipboard. "The boyfriend's story was one guy running from the scene, so this would have been difficult to do. The killer might have brought along some kind of device, but then how could he hold a struggling woman down and hook her up to equipment meant to pull her legs out of joint? Either he was inhumanly strong, or there two assailants."

She was right. I envisioned the strength it would take for one man to dislocate a woman's hips by hand and shook my head. Maybe if he were a vampire, or some other supernatural creature. If not, there had to be some sort of pulley that he used. Otherwise...no way.

"A lot of blood for those superficial cuts," Tremelay mentioned.

Shit, he was right. I hadn't even thought about that, so preoccupied with Amanda's leg dislocation. Where the heck had all the blood come from? Yes, there were a lot of cuts on her arms, hands, and neck, but not enough for the amount of liquid needed to turn the white carpet that glistening shade of ruby red.

The woman walked forward, stepping carefully, and placed one hand under Amanda's shoulder. She cautiously turned the body over and we all leaned in. There, on the back of Amanda's neck, was a large puncture wound.

"But I thought you said she died from having her neck broken?" I stared at the puncture wound, knowing that it would have killed someone within seconds.

"I did. This was postmortem. Very soon

postmortem. Soon enough that a few heartbeats pushed out a good bit of blood. Gravity did the rest."

I didn't get it. "They must have happened almost simultaneously. Maybe the killer intended to stab her and broke her neck in the process?"

She shrugged. "Maybe. I get the odd feeling that he was trying to drain as much blood out of her as possible after her death."

"Like a deer?" Norwicki choked out. His face was full of horror. "Like draining a deer to prep for butchering?"

"Well, he didn't eviscerate her or hang her upside down. Unless he was interrupted before he could get to that, I doubt he was treating her as a trophy kill or potential dinner."

How these detectives went about their jobs every day, I had no idea. Actually I had no idea how this M.E. woman managed. I'd seen a man who had been skinned, and now this? There really were some sickos out there in the world.

There was something nagging at the back of my mind about this whole thing, but I just couldn't grasp it. "Do you think the killers were interrupted?" I asked the woman. "I'm assuming she died this morning and was found pretty soon after she died?"

She nodded. "She couldn't have been dead long. The boyfriend had spent the night and gone to work, but had to come back before he was more than a few miles away to grab some papers he'd forgotten. When he found her, she was still warm. He says he heard a door slam, then looked out to see a man running through the backyard and over the fence."

I couldn't imagine running home to retrieve papers and finding my lover dead on the floor. For a brief second I envisioned Dario's reaction to me naked and murdered in my bedroom. He wouldn't have called 911. No, the vampire would have taken it upon himself to find my killer and deliver a very slow and painful death. Of course, he wouldn't have found my body until nightfall. And he wasn't my boyfriend.

What a weird fantasy to be having at a crime scene. I shook my head and tried to rid my mind of all thoughts of Dario. "And the boyfriend thinks the brother did it?"

Tremelay cleared his throat. I jumped, giving him an apologetic glance. Crap. When did I take over the investigation? I was along for the ride. This was a human-on-human crime. Not my thing.

"We're searching for the backpack," he told me. "The boyfriend says that the brother had been living here for the last two years ever since their parents died in a car accident. Seems the stereotypical parasite of a younger sibling, sponging off his business-savvy and successful older sister. They had a lot of arguments. Amanda asked him to move out last night. Boyfriend says he was relieved because the brother was a constant source of tension in the house."

I could imagine. I headed for the bedroom door. "Mind if I check his bedroom?"

Tremelay put out a hand. "No, the techs are in there now. If you want to nose around, it needs to wait until we're done."

"Detective!" A voice shouted up from downstairs. "In the garage. We've found something."

Tremelay ran, me right after him. Norwicki had done a moment of indecisive back and forth, then stayed with the body. As we tore through the kitchen and into the garage we saw two officers. One held a backpack, what appeared to be bloody untanned leather spilling from the top. The other stood by a giant white cooler. I craned my neck and saw what appeared to be a side of beef inside the cooler, packed with ice and water.

What the heck? I was seriously having a déjà vu moment here.

"Is that...is that a human skin?" Tremelay looked rather green as he stared at the bloody leather protruding from the backpack.

"Yes, sir," the tech said. "I'm gonna bag it in the backpack, but we'll get photos of it laid out once I get it to the morgue."

I know I had the same slack-jaw, deer-in-headlights look as Tremelay did. Skinned body at the Walters Art Museum. Skin stuffed into a backpack at a house in Canton. And what was in the cooler. "I'm assuming that's a body in there? That's not lamb or a gigantic pork loin, is it?"

The tech shook his head. "No, it's a body. But not the same body. I mean, the body in the cooler is male, and it's skinned. This skin is male, but it's younger, like that of a teenager. I didn't pull it all the way out because I wanted to preserve any trace evidence, but I could tell."

I felt the weight of Tremelay's stare on me, and I looked up to meet his eyes. "What do you think, Ainsworth?"

I shrugged, because none of this had anything to do with me. "I think you've got a crazy serial killer on your hands, Detective. That's what I think."

CHAPTER 8

THE FOX WAS back on top of the Peterson's book when I got home, but none of the pages had been moved. Hoping for the best, I started to read about chupacabras. As interesting as it was, I kept thinking of what we'd found at the house in Canton and texting little notes to Tremelay. He hadn't responded, so either he was out of pocket or ignoring me. Probably the latter.

Did the John Doe from the museum have a broken neck too?

Puncture wound to the back of the neck?

Hips dislocated?

Was skinning cleanly done, or evidence of defensive wound/knife cuts?

I figured it would take a while for the medical examiner's office to get around to the bodies, and skin, from the Canton house, but hopefully they'd performed the autopsy on the John Doe. If we could just figure out what was similar and what was different between them, maybe we'd have a direction to go in. Right now other than cross comparing medical implant records and missing person's reports, and searching for Bradley Lewis as a "person of interest" we had nothing to go on.

We. When would I get it through my thick head that this was a human serial killer? As intriguing as it all was, I was a Templar and a part-time barista. Tremelay was kind enough to loop me in as a friend. That was it.

And he was busy. I needed to stop texting him and continue to read about chupacabras.

I was just starting to get to the intriguing part, where Peterson discussed the times chupacabra had been mistaken for werewolves, when there was a knock on my door. The book had amazing full-color, detailed photography of the corpses of each, pointing out the differences in physiology as well as hair patterns, so I was reluctant to answer it. Janice always texted before she came over. Dario wouldn't be here during daylight hours and he just opened the door and let himself in anyway. Whoever it was could just go away.

Another knock. "Solaria, I know you're in there. Answer the door."

The last person I ever expected was at my door—my mother. I practically dropped the book on the floor in my haste to let her in, all sorts of horrible scenarios running through my mind. We Templars were pretty good about keeping in touch via modern communication methods, but certain things required a personal visit—things like sharing the news of a family death.

Oh, God. My Dad? He always seemed so healthy, but things happened. It couldn't be Essie. My great-grandmother was probably one-thirty if she was a day, but I honestly expected her to outlive us all. Besides, I'd just spoken to her yesterday. Jet? Oh, not Athena's new daughter. We'd had a huge family party two weeks ago when she and Pietrus got home from Korea with her. I thought of the little girl's thick black hair that stood out from her head like one of those troll dolls, her round, pinchable cheeks, her sweet, rosy bow of a mouth. Not Jet.

I threw open the door and stared mute with panic at my mother.

She didn't look sad, she looked stern. And that sent a wave of relief through me that nearly brought me to my knees. I was used to stern Mom. Heck, that's about all I'd gotten from her since I'd refused to take my Oath. She wasn't here to tell me of a loved one's death, she was here to pester me about something, and when Mom had *that* look on her face, she was hard to resist.

I was one of the few who ever successfully resisted, stubborn intractable child that I was.

Moving aside to let Mom in, I suddenly realized how absolutely unprepared I was for visitors. Trusty took up the majority of my kitchen counter. The sink was full of dirty dishes—most of them coffee cups. Clothing lay across the back of my sofa, hooked on chairs, puddled on the floor. It looked like I had a habit of disrobing as I walked about my apartment and just leaving my clothing where they dropped— which actually was the truth. I lived alone, and modesty wasn't my thing. I twisted my T-shirt in my hands, suddenly regretting I'd chosen to wear the one with giant red lips emblazoned across the front.

Mom looked down at my T-shirt and I swear I saw a smirk before she carefully schooled her face into one of cool determination. "This is a nice little apartment, Solaria. You've made it quite homey."

By which she meant it was just like the mess I'd kept of my room back home. Oh well. One of the advantages of being an adult was being able to have a week's worth of dirty coffee cups in the sink and throwing your clothes all over the place.

"I'd have cleaned a bit if I knew you were

coming." I moved a few piles of books off the sofa. "Sit. Can I get you something to drink? I can make a pot of coffee. Or wine?"

I didn't normally have wine, but knowing Dario was going to be out of town for a while had driven me to an impulsive purchase of Chianti. I envisioned myself pouring a glass each night, an hour after sunset, as a sort of nod to whatever the heck we had going on. And they say I'm not romantic.

My mother sat on the sofa, looking over the research books I had on the coffee table. "I'll have some wine."

Ugh. That Chianti had cost me a fortune, way more than I'd usually spend for wine. Outside of Emergency Beer, I didn't buy the pricey stuff. My wine usually came in boxes—the cheaper the better.

I went into the kitchen, trying to turn my reluctance to share my wine into a proper sense of hostesslike graciousness. I'd scolded Tremelay for not sharing the cookies. I should be willing to let my own mother have a glass of Chianti.

In all honesty I was broke. I needed to face the fact that I couldn't make it here in Baltimore on a part-time barista's salary. The vampire money was down to a few hundred and I needed that for next month's rent, not expensive wine. Sadly being Baltimore's Templar didn't come with donations from the city, and Tremelay had never offered any kind of payment for my supernatural advisory experience. Not that he could probably get that sort of thing past the city accounting office anyway.

I should just take the stipend money my parents deposited into a checking account for me. Heck, there had to be over ten grand in there by now since I hadn't touched it in seven months. I hated sponging off my parents like that but I *was* doing Templar stuff here—just not stuff that any other Templar had done for hundreds of years.

Which is why I hadn't taken my Oath. Oath equated to Knighthood which equated to a generous allowance commiserate with level. Sounded great until I read the fine print and realized that I'd be at the beck and call of the Elders, researching what they wanted me to research, guarding the Temple when they said so, going to retrieve artifacts with only a moment's notice. I'd be owned, and I wasn't about to be owned.

"Here you go." I handed Mom a glass of wine and sat down beside her, curling my fingers around the fine crystal of my own glass. Silently I looked over to the window, across the rooftops to the north of the city. *This one's for us.*

It might not be an hour after sunset, but it was the thought that counted, right?

"I see you're looking into chupacabra," Mom commented, looking down at the Peterson book. "I took one out in Puerto Rico a few years back. Nasty thing. Much taller and bulkier than the werewolves up in the Appalachian Mountains. They usually have a set of spikes that run from their shoulders to mid-back. Not always, though. There are a group in southern California that look more like overgrown coyotes with a bad case of mange."

"That was a chupacabra in Puerto Rico?" I asked. "You never said."

Mom was a Guardian and most of her responsibilities lay with the Temple and the Holy Lands, but every now and then a Guardian was sent off to dispatch a troublesome supernatural creature. Templars had become rather live-and-let-live about the monsters we would have killed centuries ago, but when one threatened a religious institution we stepped in.

Who was I kidding? It was all about the money. If a city or a Cardinal waved a bunch of "donations" in our face, we were happy to go kill chupacabra in Puerto Rico. Things hadn't really changed all that much since the Crusades.

"Yeah. Nasty thing. Hope I don't ever have to face a nest of them again. There was a moment in that fight when I wasn't sure I was going to make it." She sighed and took a sip of her wine. "Wow, this is really nice, Solaria. Excellent choice."

And that was my mother, casually discussing her near-death experience at the claws of a violent goat-sucker, then praising my selection of wine in the next breath.

I loved her. I admired her and growing up I'd wanted to be just like her. I guess I kind of was, in my own not-a-Knight way. Same sword, different path.

"But I'm not here to discuss my adventures in Puerto Rico." Mom set her wine down on the table.

No, of course she wasn't. She was here to lecture me about taking my Oath. She was here to tell me my little juvenile tantrum needed to come to an end. She was here to inform me I needed to be a responsible adult and become a Knight as all my family had, as all my ancestors before me had. I took a big gulp of my Chianti, sending a silent apology to Dario who would have scowled to see me slugging down a quality wine like this.

Then I stiffened my spine. I might be a child having a rebellious tantrum in my mother's eyes, but plenty of people saw me as an adult, as someone they could trust, as someone they could rely upon to protect them from the monsters of the world— human or otherwise. Tremelay didn't see me as a child, neither did Dario. And Raven hadn't either. I'd be polite. I'd be welcoming. But ultimately my mother was going to leave here disappointed.

"Well. Let me see it," my mother demanded.

That hadn't been what I expected at all. I gaped at her. "Huh?"

Mom actually looked hurt. "Solaria. Something this serious and you didn't think to come to me? I'm your mother. Show me the demon mark."

I was speechless that she knew. And speechless with anger that Athena had betrayed my confidence and told my secret. If she hadn't been adjusting to motherhood, I would have been tempted to drive down to Virginia and punch her.

"Come on. Let's see it."

Things might have been strained between us, but she was still my mother. My Dad was brilliant. He was the best researcher, the best Librarian I'd ever known, but Mom...she was fierce. If anything had threatened Dad or us children, she would have moved the stars above to defend us. And she would die before seeing a demon take our soul.

I lifted the edge of my shirt, scooting over on the couch so she could see the round mark on my waist.

Her fingers brushed the mark and I told her everything—the innocent Goetic summoning gone wrong, the banishment with Athena, the summoning with Raven, and my suspicions that Balsur had sent one of his minions to masquerade as an angel to lead me to sin.

Not that I had needed his help. I thought of my sword slicing so easily through Dark Iron's back and told my Mother about that, too. Then I cried, throwing my arms around her like a child looking for comfort.

She didn't hesitate to put her arms around me and hold me close, murmuring soft words into my hair as she rocked me. It was then I realized that whatever I'd done, or not done, my mom would never forsake me. Never.

When I pulled back I saw the tears in her eyes, the grim determination in the set of her jaw. If Balsur had shown up in my apartment right now, I had no doubt that he'd meet his match. This was my mother, the woman who battled chupacabra, the woman who rammed her sword down an ahuizotl's throat, the woman who wore the scars of garuda bites like a badge of honor.

My mom was badass. And if I became half the woman she was, I'd be so proud.

"I don't know much about demons, Aria, but I'll be damned before I let one of my children lose their soul to one."

Crap, I was going to cry again. I sniffed, taking a second to get my emotions under control. No one since Raven had been so determined to help me. As much as I admired my Mom, Raven had probably been in a better position to assist. She at least had been a mage knowledgeable about demons. Mom was just good at killing things.

But then again, we had all the knowledge of the Templars at our disposal. Dad's research ability combined with Mom's warrior skills might just save my soul. But Dad... Oh he'd be so disappointed in me. I took the shortcuts he had always been so vocal in criticizing. I'd summoned Goetic demons. And this was what happened when you went to the underworld for knowledge instead of doing the proper legwork.

"Don't tell Dad," I pleaded.

Mom's eyebrows arched upward. "I absolutely *will* tell your father. There are no secrets between partners. Someday you'll understand that. There is nothing I can keep from him. Nothing. It would violate every bit of trust we share."

Even though I hated the thought of Dad knowing I'd been demon-marked, it warmed my heart that my parents had such a bond. Polar opposites, they'd always had a passion between them that had been rather embarrassing as a child. Roman had found his match with Hilda. Athena had absolutely found her match with Pietras. I wished I could find the same kind of love.

My thoughts veered straight to Dario. There was something there—something beyond simple lust. There was respect. There was friendship. There was a connection, caring. At first it was all hormones, but somehow in the past month what we shared had deepened. Was it when he'd faced down his own *Balaj* to buy me time to negotiate with the necromancer? Was it when he'd chased me down outside a pub, leaving his date behind to ask me what I needed? Was it when he'd come, no questions asked, after I'd killed Dark Iron and was having a morality meltdown?

Or was it the last month of casual conversation each and every night over wine and Italian food? I got the feeling that I'd already found the kind of love my parents had, only with a vampire. Why couldn't he have been a Templar? Why couldn't he have at least been not undead?

"Your father and I will do everything within our

power to help you, Solaria." Mom's hand stroked my hair. "In the meantime, do *not* summon any demons. Keep the channels between you and the underworld closed."

"Six weeks until Halloween." She knew, but I had to say it. Halloween meant three days when the veil between the worlds was thin. No summoning would be necessary for demons and other beings to cross over. I'd been surprised that there had been no visits from Balsur in the last month, but higher demons were known for their patience, and his minion had been banished hard by an experienced mage. Still, I'm sure the temptation to cross at Samhain would be more than any demon could bear. We already had a link. This would be the perfect opportunity to show up and push me right to the edge.

All he had to do was threated my family or those I loved. If Balsur got his claws on little Jet, on my nephews, on Dario or any of my family, I would bargain my soul away in an instant. I'm sure he knew that. And I was sure my mother knew it, too.

Again she brushed my hair with her hand, pulling her fingers gently through the dark snarls. We were so different in our physical appearance— her with wheat-colored, curly hair and dark-gray eyes, me with my sable-almost-black, straight-as-a-stick hair and bright blue eyes. My great-grandmother's hair. My great-grandfather's eyes. Could I ever live up to their legacy?

"I don't care if he's Satan himself, this demon will not take your soul," my mother vowed.

And I believed her. Because nothing, nothing in the whole world, could prevail when my mother demanded otherwise.

CHAPTER 9

"Yes on the puncture. Yes on the broken neck. No on the defensive wounds. No on the dislocated hips." Tremelay relayed the information as if he were checking things off a list. "The doc thinks the puncture is to drain as much blood as possible so the skinning process is cleaner. Of course that means there's a whole bunch of blood somewhere near the museum. I can't imagine that someone would haul a skinned corpse away from the kill and skinning site so that they could stuff the body in a broom closet, though. Makes me wonder if they didn't *want* it to be discovered at the Walters. Like it's part of his ritual or something."

"Sicko." I commented, thankful that at least the victims were dead before they'd been skinned. Although those dislocated hips of Amanda Lewis made me sick.

"Amanda Lewis wasn't skinned, but the puncture and broken neck are a connection between the two murders. And get this. Ready? Ready?"

I smiled at his excitement. "Ready."

"The boyfriend came in to give a description. He's pretty sure the guy fleeing the scene was the brother, although he only saw him from the back. He also described a few friends of Bradley Lewis that had made him nervous—a man and a girl. The description he gave of the man sounded an awful lot like Brian Huang, so we showed him a group of pictures and he picked Huang out."

Wait. Girl? I immediately thought of the scene in the police station parking lot, with Brian Huang hugging the girl from the Inner Harbor. "Was the girl like a little girl, or a teenager?"

"Teen. High school. Said she had brown hair with pink and blue streaks, and wore a ton of makeup."

What would a forty-year-old museum employee, a high school girl with a heavy hand at the eyeliner, and a deadbeat college-age guy who liked a local band have in common? I could see Bradley maybe dating the high school girl, but what was up with Brian Huang?

Bradley was fleeing the murder scene. Was he the psychotic skinner, or had he just come upon his sister's body and feared he'd be blamed? There was that skin in his backpack—that was damning. Either way, there was no denying the connection between the three, or Huang's doppelganger victim in the museum closet.

I tapped my chin in thought. "So Brian Huang's knee replacement and his working at the Walters that day wasn't the coincidence we thought it was. I don't know if he's the killer or both he and Lewis are. Or the teenager, although somehow I doubt she has the strength to overpower either victim let alone dislocate Amanda Lewis's legs."

"Yeah, I'm thinking either Lewis or Huang or both. I've already got a warrant out on Lewis. And now have probable cause to go bring Huang in for additional questioning. I've got a car heading over there now." Tremelay sounded smug. It *was* progress.

"How did Huang know Amanda and Bradley Lewis? Stock investments? Something with her work? Was she a frequent visitor to the Walters or a donor? Was Huang a Rabid Rabbit fan?"

"We're trying to figure that out. Wait—who is Rabid Rabbit?"

I waved a hand even though Tremelay wasn't there to see it. "A band. Bradley had one of their T-shirts on. I'm just throwing it out there."

The detective made a grunting noise. "Serial killers usually work alone, so I'm thinking it's probably Lewis with Huang as an accomplice. Although this could be drug or gang related and they're doing the skinning thing to throw us off."

I remembered how revolted Dario was about the whole skinning thing. It just didn't seem like something a killer would do unless they really liked that sort of thing.

"That's a whole lot of work when a drug gang could just toss the bodies over the bridge into the Patapsco River, or ditch them in an abandoned house in Southwest. And it's a pretty gruesome thing to do to a body if you only want to throw off an investigation."

"Yeah. I've prosecuted my share of murderers and as hard-core as some of them are, this kind of thing would probably have them vomiting in the trash can. A couple of bullets, a tire iron beating, or stabbing was about as horrific as they'd get. I can't see any of them sitting down to meticulously take the skin off a body."

So we were back to serial killer, only perhaps one with a buddy. I couldn't imagine Bradley and a museum employee teaming up, but what did I know?

"Speaking of skin, any news yet on the corpse and skin you guys found in the garage?"

"Yeah. No ID on the body in the cooler yet, but the skin is a sixteen-year-old boy that went missing ten years ago in South Carolina. A Lawton King."

"Ten *years* ago?" What had happened in the ten years between a child vanishing and his recent murder?

"I know. Kid vanished one night out of his bed. They never found him or his body, and now his skin turns up, ten years older, in a presumed murderer's backpack.

"The killer preserved the skin somehow," Tremelay continued. "The doc isn't sure exactly how. No dried edges. No trace chemicals to suggest it's been tanned. He's got no idea how the guy did it, but somehow this killer managed to preserve the skin beautifully."

Bleck. This was beginning to sound eerily like a horror movie I'd once watched. I wondered if the killer was intending to sew all these skins together to make a ghastly outfit.

Of course, that was assuming the killers were psychotic killer tailors. Who knows what they were doing with the skin from the guy in the museum closet? Whatever it was, the murderer had to be angry over the loss of the one in the backpack as well as not being able to take Amanda's. Hopefully he'd be angry enough to slip up and get caught before any more people died.

"You get the most fascinating cases, Tremelay," I told him. "I swear you need to write a book or something. Occult gang warfare and now this?"

He snorted. "Right. I'd be happy for a simple drive-by right about now. I'll call you when we bring

Huang in and let you know what happens."

I hung up, kind of bummed that he hadn't invited me down for the second interview. Not that I had anything to do with this case. It *was* interesting, though. And I really appreciated Tremelay keeping me in the loop.

Which reminded me that I should also keep Janice in the loop. I looked at my phone and I was filled with indecision. Tremelay would have a fit that I was telling the reporter this stuff, but I felt like she had a right to know. Her mental health human interest story had taken a deadly turn, and now she'd need to write about a brother who possibly teamed up with a museum employee to kill his sister and at least two other men.

If that's what happened. Yeah, Brandley was positively ID'd as fleeing the scene of Amanda's murder, and there *was* that skin in his backpack, but there could still be a reasonable, innocent explanation for that. Well, for fleeing the scene, probably not for the skin. Maybe Amanda was having a side relationship with Huang that she didn't want her boyfriend to know about. And maybe he was the killer who murdered and tried to skin her, then planted a skin in the brother's backpack?

Innocent until proven guilty. As I put down the phone, I was the one feeling somewhat guilty over leaving Janice out of the loop. She had another date tonight with her new man—actually *we* had a date tonight. I'd managed to wiggle out of the double date thing, but did promise to meet them for coffee after their dinner. I'd wait to hear what came of Huang's interview and if the police managed to catch up with Bradley or not, *then* I'd fill Janice in on what was going on.

After her date, that is. Because the poor woman

deserved a little romance without dead bodies ruining the mood.

CHAPTER 10

"WE NEED TO go retrieve the scroll for this mage," Brandi argued.

Actually she was arguing with *me*. The rest of the group was all on-board with this "quick" little side trip. Finishing up my shift at the coffee shop, I'd headed over to Zac's for my eagerly anticipated Wednesday night Anderon game. We were supposed to be on our Grand Quest, heading out for a four-day hike through the mountains where we would most likely encounter orcs and ogres before making it to the other side, battered but alive. Instead we were debating heading off in a completely different direction. Out of the blue, some mage waved supplies and money at us and we were actually considering this fools' journey.

I swear this expedition was going to take us five years at the rate we were going. Either that or two months from now we'd be informed that our rivals, the Evil Shadow Guys or something or other, had arrived before we had and were waving the Heaven's Shard in the air and dancing around in triumph. Meanwhile we would still be slogging through the marshes looking for this pointy-hat dude's stupid scroll.

"We don't have time for this," I told the group. "The mage can hire some other adventurers, we've got a quest to finish and a tight timeline here."

"He's got an amulet he'll give us to help in retrieving the Heaven's Shard," Truman chimed in. "And he'll outfit us and provide us with a group teleportation spell when we return. That means we don't have to deal with the mountain passes, the orcs or the ogres. Win-win. And we won't lose any time at all."

If the mage came through, that is. I had a bad feeling we'd return to find him dead, or suddenly impoverished and unable to provide us with all he promised. After all, an amulet, a group teleportation spell, and food and supplies for a group of six seemed far more than this stolen scroll was worth.

I lifted my hands in frustration. "Did *nobody* learn from the fourth Crusade?"

They all stared at me. "Don't hire Flemish mercenaries?" Truman guessed.

The fourth Crusade had been doomed from the start. Venice had promised to provide transport ships with the understanding that the participating rulers would provide a certain recompense. When faced with a papal invoice, suddenly the enthusiasm for the mission dried up and scads of highborn found they had to wash their hair that particular year and couldn't attend. Or send money.

That left Venice high and dry with a ton of ships and a buyer with empty pockets. The Doge bargained and the Crusaders found themselves with a side quest in lieu of immediate and full payment— reconquer the city of Zara for Venice from the King of Hungary. I didn't really blame them for that detour since their empty pockets left them with few options. It was the following second side quest that had historians pulling their hair out.

Flush with victory at Zara, the crusaders jumped at the chance to overthrow the Emperor of Constantinople and place the rightful heir back on the throne. Said rightful heir did have a sad tale of cruel uncles, blinding, and imprisonment right out of a fairy tale, but a good chunk of the crusaders were reluctant to march against a Christian foe—even if they were Eastern Orthodox and technically fair game. The party split in two, with half heading to Jerusalem via Syria, and the other half taking over a year to beat their way into Constantinople and restore Alexius to the throne.

The new emperor promptly stiffed them and locked them out of the city. The crusaders found themselves having to winter in a hostile Mediterranean port with dwindling supplies.

The other half of the crusading party had arrived in a timely fashion at Syria. They were soundly beaten on the way to Jerusalem, wondering the whole time where there backup had gotten to. The whole thing fell apart. Both groups splintered, some taking cities here and there, others returning home.

It was an abysmal failure, and one I wasn't about to repeat in this Anderon game.

"Basically half the Crusaders went on a side quest, which turned into several side quests. Fast forward several years and they're all broke. Nobody made it to Jerusalem. Don't be the forth Crusade. Don't be distracted by side quests."

Everyone stared at me as if I had walked in off the street and stole their puppy. Zac smothered a grin. "The mage is waiting for your response. Are you going to take him up on his offer, or head to the mountains?"

"We're not going to be able to retrieve the Heaven's Shard without that amulet," Truman comment. "I'm voting for the side quest."

"Me too," Brandi chimed in. "With the teleportation spell we don't have to deal with the orcs and ogres in the mountain pass."

I put my head in my hands in disbelief. "When it sounds too good to be true, it probably is. We can take any orcs or ogres we encounter. And we don't need the amulet."

"That's two for and one against," Zac commented. "The mage is getting impatient. He's looking at his time piece, tapping his foot."

"I'm in," Chris chimed in.

"Me too," Leon added.

Michelle shot me a guilty look. She was always my staunchest supporter, but it seemed peer pressure had gotten to my only ally in this game. "I'm for the side quest."

"Five for and one against." Zac rolled the dice. "The mage claps his hands together and says 'splendid.' He hands each of you a small bag of coin and gives Bartholomew a map."

"I check the map," Leon, better known as Bartholomew the Druid, said.

"I count the coin." Brandi's Halfling thief always counted the coin. Or appraised any object we encountered. We could be right in the middle of a deadly battle and our thief would sit down in the dirt to examine a piece of pottery for value.

Well, I was hardly going to take on the orcs and ogres of the mountain pass solo, so I guess I was going on a side quest. I grumbled under my breath about the Forth Crusade then got down to business, listening as the mage told us the details about who had this scroll and where it was hidden. I foresaw many weeks of unexpected attacks, chests with poisoned locks and probably some undead. We might never get to Gauden to retrieve the Heaven's Shard, but at least we'd have a fun adventure not getting there.

Zac shot me a quick glance, one eyebrow raised. "Are you going?"

I pouted, just for show. "Might as well go kill stuff. It's got to be better than hanging out in this tavern waiting for any surviving members of my party to return."

He grinned. "Then go spend your coin, half dragon. We don't have all night here."

We didn't. Even though I didn't need to meet Dario, I was watching the clock carefully. Thankfully the game was due to wrap at about nine, because I had a few things on my agenda tonight—beginning with a long overdue talk with Zac.

We wrapped for the evening, everyone chatting excitedly about plans to retrieve this scroll then roll in the piles of money we were going to earn. I helped Zac clean up the plates and beer bottles, lingering until everyone had left.

He eyed me hopefully. Crap.

"I'm meeting Janice and Sean for a cup of coffee but wanted to talk to you first." I had no idea how to do this, so I just jumped in with both feet. "I've been really unfair to you in this whole 'us' thing. You've been patient, but I know you want us to be a romantic couple and I'm the one putting on the brakes."

"It's the cop, isn't it?" Zac interrupted. "I knew it."

Oh Lord. "No, it's not Tremelay. But there is someone else. It can't be. He and I are never going to work out, but I can't seem to put aside my feelings for him and move on with someone else. It's not fair for you to be hanging out on the sidelines waiting for something that may never come."

"An old boyfriend?" Zac pressed. "Someone at the coffee shop?"

This was getting uncomfortable, and I needed it to be okay. I wanted to continue playing in the Anderon game and being friends with these people. Somehow I needed to make this right.

"No, but I do need to see him every evening in a business-related capacity. I acted as a supernatural consultant for the police in the death mage killings last month, and as the city's resident Templar, it's my duty to protect the humans from supernatural elements that would cause them harm."

Zac's eyes widened in wary understanding. "Your family used to be Templars during the crusades, but that's history, right? Like how my family fought in the Spanish American War?"

"We were Templars during the crusades and we still are. We still fight the paranormal, guard the Temple, protect Pilgrims on the Path. The others do that under the direction of the Council of Elders. I do it on my own."

He thought I was crazy, some delusional vigilante Templar, only with a real sword and armor. It was one thing to indulge in fantasy every Wednesday night in role-playing games or participate in the occasional LARP, it was another to put on a spandex jumpsuit and run around Baltimore ridding the city of evil. It all flashed across his face—shock, disbelief, and relief that he'd found out what a nutjob I was before our romance had gone too far.

"And the guy you've got feelings for...?" he asked, waiting for confirmation of my psychotic state.

"He's a vampire. That's why we can only meet at night and why our relationship will never work."

"I see." He nodded. "Thanks for letting me know this. I totally understand. I mean, how could I ever compete with a vampire?"

"We good?" I hoped I hadn't gone too far and would find myself uninvited to all the activities I'd grown to love.

"Sure. You're our ace-in-the-hand when it comes to LARP, and everyone enjoys your Anderon character. Michelle talks with fairies, so it's not like you're all that different."

Great. I forced a smile, deciding a parting hug would probably be out of the question. "Next Wednesday?"

Zac nodded. "Next Wednesday. See you then."

For all his fantasy game fixation, Zac was a regular guy with a good job and a nice row house. He didn't need a girlfriend who had dead, skinned bodies topple out of closets on her, or who tracked down demons and killer mages.

I left, knowing there was one more unpleasant task before me this evening before I could crawl into bed. I had somewhere to be. Coffee with Janice and Sean. Yes, I'd rather have my teeth extracted than sit across the table from two lovebirds, especially given the uncertainty of my own love life right now, but Janice wanted me to meet him. She wanted my opinion on her new man before she got too invested in the relationship, and I did want to help. She'd had a dry spell nearly as long as mine, and with the self-esteem crusher of a divorce in her past, Janice needed reassurance that Sean was worthy of pursuit. I only hoped I could give her the thumbs-up.

CHAPTER 11

I T WAS UNBELIEVABLY awkward walking into a café solo and joining a couple. Janice and Sean sat on the same side of the table, their heads close as they spoke. Part of me wished I had invited a friend so I wasn't so obviously a third wheel. Part of me was glad I hadn't. The romantic overtones were thick enough to cut with my sword and anyone I brought along would have felt just as awkward as I did.

"Hi." I plastered a smile on my face and sat across from them. Janice turned to me, eyes shining. Her hand was intertwined with Sean's like they'd been Crazy Glued together.

"Oh, hi! Sean, this is my friend Aria. She was at the museum with me, but went off before I could introduce you."

Sean extended his hand across the table—the hand that wasn't attached to Janice's. "Nice to meet you. So you work at a coffee shop? And you're a history buff?"

I shook his hand, noticing how his eyes snagged on my Templar tattoo. Janice had said he'd mentioned it at the museum.

"History. Folklore and mythology. That sort of thing. I work at Holy Grounds off Pratt."

We all nodded, smiled, and scrambled for something to say.

"So you're divorced?" I asked. Might as well go for the jugular.

Sean nodded, looking somewhat embarrassed. "Two years. It wasn't anything either of us did. I just woke up one day and realized I was a different person, you know? It wasn't fair for either Heather or me to keep going through the motions, so we split."

Seemed reasonable. Seemed very responsible, actually. "And you're a developer? Harford County?"

Sheesh, I sounded like Janice's mom. He appeared to be a nice enough guy, but there were real jerks out there. I might not be able to dissuade Janice from dating him if I got bad vibes from Sean, but I sure as heck would try to make sure he didn't crush her heart.

"Mostly commercial development. Office buildings, warehousing. I'm looking into a few opportunities for residential development in the north part of the city, though."

"Which is why you're going to mayoral fundraisers." Made sense. He'd be the new guy in town when it came to revitalization projects, and less likely to succeed unless he got on the radar of the folks at the top.

"I figured it wouldn't hurt to start making connections. Even if the proposed zoning changes on our property fall through, we can sit on it for a few terms and try again." Sean raised his coffee cup in a toast. "That's the nature of development. Eventually the right political climate comes along for what you want to do. You've just got to wait it out, and make sure you're in the right place at the right time."

I sipped my coffee. Normal guy. Divorced. Good job. Savvy businessman. Goodlooking. What was the catch?

He smiled warmly. "So Janice tells me you're from Middleburg? Horse country, huh? Do you ride?"

"Since before I could walk." I didn't tell him that I usually rode in plate mail while carrying a lance.

"And you're from a family of Templars? You trace your family back to the Crusades?"

Oh sheesh. Did she tell him about the vampires and mages too? About demons and angels?

"Yes. We were around before the Crusades, but that's when we received our call to serve. My family has carried the cross ever since."

He leaned across the table, the friendly smile countered by the wary expression in his eyes. "So what does that mean in today's world? The Temple was razed to the ground. It's nothing more than ruins anymore."

There had been far more to the Temple than what had been visible to the naked eye. Stone might be long gone, but the Temple was still there for those with the authority to access it. Not that we made that fact generally known.

"The Temple lives on." I smiled and placed a hand over my heart, as though I were discussing metaphysical concepts. "And there are always Pilgrims to protect."

This time even the smile wavered. "Christians?"

"Pilgrims," I corrected. "Whoever strives to walk a righteous path regardless of what religion, or lack of religion, they follow."

Sean raised a skeptical eyebrow. "So who decides what a righteous path is? Sounds like something that syndicated radio host would say—the one who labels everyone who disagrees with him as sinful."

"Templars no longer judge right or wrong," I told him.

Templars didn't, but I did. I wasn't really sure where I was drawing the boundaries yet, but clearly I'd made a firm line in the sand when I'd judged Dark Iron and delivered my own, deadly form of justice.

"Aria's not one of those people who shoves her religion down other people's throats," Janice interjected with a nervous laugh. "Heck, I didn't even really know she was Christian. I mean, you *are* Christian, aren't you?"

"Episcopalian." This topic needed to go into the red zone along with immigration policy and universal healthcare. What to talk about instead, though? The weather? Sunday's Ravens game? "Do you LARP?" I asked instead. "I'm a half dragon in a weekly Anderon game."

Sean blinked. "A what?"

"So how are the police doing with that murder at the museum?" Janice chimed in, obviously realizing role-playing games were not a good conversation segue. I wasn't sure how acceptable this topic was going to be either since the police hadn't released the details on the murder, and I didn't want to be the one to break it to Sean over coffee that a killer in the city was skinning his victims.

"They haven't been able to identify the body yet. The M.E. found a knee implant, but when they traced the serial number it came up with some guy who is very much alive."

"Typo in the record." Janice wrinkled her nose. "It happens more often than you'd think. So no leads or anything?"

"Someone was killed in the museum?" Sean interjected. "Like a gang shooting in the parking lot or something?"

"No. Dead guy in the broom closet." Janice seemed rather cheerful about the whole thing. "Aria opened the door and the body fell right out on top of her."

I was glad she'd kept the gruesome details to herself, although Sean was wide-eyed at the mention of a corpse landing on top of me.

"What were you doing in the broom closet?" he asked.

Ugh. My face heated up, but before I could come up with something more plausible than the lame excuse I'd given Dario, Janice blurted it out.

"She was sneaking in there with her boyfriend to make out. Can you imagine opening the door to a closet and having a body fall on you?"

Sean seemed more disgusted by my attempted nookie in the broom closet than the idea of a dead body falling out of one.

"Anyway," I waved a hand, frantic to change the topic again. "No leads on that one, but remember that sister who called the priest to exorcise a demon from her brother? She's dead. Boyfriend said he saw the brother fleeing the scene, and the cops think the two cases are connected."

Janice's eyebrows shot up. "Amanda Lewis? Was she killed...killed in the same way as the museum guy?"

I got where she was going with this. "No, but there were similarities and apparently the brother is friends with a person of interest from the museum case."

"Wow. Just wow," Janice mused.

"Wait. There was an exorcism? And a woman died? And that's somehow connected to a dead body in the broom closet of the Walters Art Museum?" Sean was equally fascinated, although confused. He also appeared more worried about the idea of demonic possession than a woman murdered in her home.

"She didn't die at the exorcism," I explained. "She thought her brother was possessed because he'd been acting strangely the last few days. The exorcism was a bust, and twenty-four hours later she was dead on the floor with her brother as the prime suspect."

"Drugs," Sean conjectured. "Brother got in with the wrong crowd, got hooked on something, and the sister got killed in a robbery gone bad. I saw a television series on that sort of thing last week."

I shrugged. It was a possibility, but addicts and their dealers didn't usually skin their victims. And I couldn't see serial killers hooking up with drug addicts.

"Drat, I was going to run that human interest piece this week, too." Janice turned to Sean. "The exorcism? I was doing a story on mental health services. Father Bernard, the priest who did the exorcism, gave me some solid background on how the church is often the basis of referrals for psychiatric care."

Sean's smile reached his eyes as his fingers wrapped around Janice's. "Sounds like a great story. Maybe wait and see how the murder investigation concludes? Could be that there's a mental health angle instead of drugs. 'Brother snaps and kills his sister, in spite of her efforts to get him assistance'?"

"Oh, what a good idea."

And now both of Janice's hands were laced with Sean's, the pair of them looking into each other's eyes. I totally felt like a third wheel again. Totally.

But the mention of Father Bernard had given me an idea. "How did Amanda Lewis manage to find a priest who did exorcisms? I'd assume it's kind of a specialty."

Janice shrugged. "I think she asked around and one of the priests referred her to him. From what I can tell, he's the guy who gets all the demonic possession referrals. Doesn't that suck? Imagine you're trying to guide your flock, but every month or so some parish out in the county dumps a crazy in your lap?"

It did suck, but if this priest was the go-to guy for possession, even if the majority of those reported incidents were mental health cases, then he was probably the go-to guy for demon marks. I might not be Catholic, but the priest had seemed knowledgeable about the Templars in history as well as in the modern world. He would probably believe me when I told him about Balsur and the mark. And, although it was a long shot, he *might* be able to save my soul. It was worth a visit. And it was the only idea I had beyond waiting for my parents to come up with something or rereading my reference books for the nth time.

"Do you have Father Bernard's contact info? Can you share it with me?" I asked.

"Sure." Janice released her hands from Sean's and quickly shared the contact from her phone.

I slugged down my coffee then made my excuses, leaving the awkward threesome early after giving Janice an uncertain thumbs-up on Sean. He seemed nice, weird fascination with my Templar heritage aside. He clearly was smitten by her. She'd been wearing the bracelet I made for her, and it hadn't given off any warning signs about Sean's possible sleazy intentions. He was professional, attractive, available, but something about him set off my warning bells. I couldn't put my finger on it, but there was something about Sean Merrill that wasn't right. I got the impression, unfounded though it may be, that he wasn't *exactly* what he seemed.

Or maybe I was wrong. I hadn't been all that successful with my own dating life. And I clearly made a lot of bad choices when it came to men, otherwise I'd be snuggled up with Zac tonight and not about to call a certain vampire and see how things were going up north.

It was well after midnight by the time I got home. I hesitated, my finger over the call button, not wanting to interrupt him in the middle of something that might require his complete attention. Knowing Dario, he'd answer in the middle of a deadly battle just because it was me. I rarely called him unless it was an emergency, and I doubted he'd realize this was just a "checking-in" sort of call.

So I texted instead. *Doing okay? Found the group of renegades yet?*

He called right away. "We're in Townson right now. Haven't found anything but a couple of solitary vampires trying to lay claim to some pubs near the college. I'm heading over to an apartment complex where there's been a spike in assault claims to see if there's anything there. How'd your meeting with Janice's boyfriend go? Did he pass your exacting tests and gain approval?"

"Yeah. I guess. He seems like a nice enough guy.

I think I'm just being overprotective. So tell me about these solitaries near the college. What happened with them?"

The vampire grumbled something under his breath. "Leonora sent us out with a zero tolerance policy. She's paranoid without the scepter, and there was a time when we didn't allow any rogue vampires within five miles of our territory line. It's a reasonable course of action. It sends a message to anyone thinking of making a play for the territory that we're strong and ruthless."

"But...?" I got the feeling that Dario was more likely now to directly disobey Leonora than he had been in the past. It scared me. He was strong. He had a solid group who would side with him if there was a fight for leadership. But would it be enough? And would Dario, who'd never wanted to lead, actually take control of the *Balaj* as Master? Leonora would have to do something absolutely unforgivable for him to willingly step into the leadership role.

"These guys aren't hurting anyone. They get into a scuffle if one tries to poach in the other's area, but that's it. They're both so suspicious that they're barely taking enough blood to survive. They probably won't make it another month at this rate. I gave them a warning and let them be."

The longer I knew this vampire, the more I liked him. "So what happened with their *Balaj*? Why are they on their own?"

"We don't ask those sorts of personal questions, Aria. Usually they're on their own because they had a disagreement with the Master. They could have poached a brother or sister's blood slave, killed a few too many humans during feeding, brought unwelcome notice to the *Balaj* somehow. Lots of times it's just because of a general incompatibility.

We've all got brothers and sisters who don't really fit in. Usually the group works around them, but with some *Balajs*, a disruptive influence is cast out."

I thought of what Sarge had told me, about how their former Master had cast Dario out for turning Shay, for standing up to protest behavior he disagreed with. Maybe that's why Dario had more sympathy than Leonora for these solitary rogues.

"One guy was scared half to death before we even grabbed him. He said there was a human girl who he'd picked up the night before that attacked him. She tried to break his neck." Dario laughed. "Not that it would have killed him even if she'd succeeded. Can you imagine? What human girl trolls the bars for guys, then tries to break their necks with her bare hands? The vampire said he threw her into the wall and got the heck out of there as fast as he could."

"I doubt he filed a police report." It *was* kind of funny. Had the girl been watching too many action movies? Decided to take her rage out on random bar pickups? I couldn't imagine she'd have been successful even if her intended victim *had* been human.

"No, of course not. The guy hadn't eaten for two days he was so shaken."

"Maybe you should be hunting for killer co-eds instead of rogue vampire groups," I teased.

My words were greeted with silence. I heard a car honk in the distance. "Gotta go."

And disconnected. My heart raced and I stared down at the phone, worried about the abrupt end of our conversation. Had he found the rogue group? Did he have back-up? I envisioned Dario on his own, taking on five or six vampires.

He'd call back. He'd let me know as soon as everything was resolved. He'd know that I'd worry.

And worry I did. I sat up all night, trying to distract myself with research, television, anything to keep from obsessively looking at my phone every five seconds. Finally about an hour before dawn I got a text message.

Got one. Need to find a place to go to ground for the day. Talk to you tomorrow.

My fingers hovered over the keypad wanting to reply with... What? That I was glad he was okay? That I hated the thought of him sheltering in an unfamiliar place while the sun was up? That I had stayed up all night worrying about him?

I clicked the phone off and set it on the coffee table. That was something I didn't want him to know. It was bad enough we were meeting each night, that on the one night we hadn't met I'd still wanted to talk to him. He had a blood slave. I was dating. I could never have what I wanted from Dario, and he couldn't have what he wanted from me. It was best for me to reel this in, cool my jets, and start acting like just a friend—a business friend.

Business friends didn't sit up all night staring at the phone, waiting for a text. And if they did, they didn't admit to it. So instead I went to bed, hoping to get in enough sleep that when I made my way to church tomorrow I was somewhat well-rested.

CHAPTER 12

SLEEPING IN LATE made me feel like a princess. No work today. Nothing to do in the morning but laze around in my pajamas drinking coffee, eating cereal from the box, and watching talk shows. I managed to get showered and dressed around noon for my meeting with Father Bernard. I had no real confidence that the priest would be able to help me, but I didn't have anything better to do with my day off. When he'd suggested we meet this afternoon, I'd agreed. At this point I was willing to explore every option, no matter how farfetched, to get this demon mark removed.

I was just about to roll out when I heard a knock at my door. Opening it I blinked in astonishment. The man standing across the threshold from me was model-pretty, with high cheekbones and a perfectly angled jaw. Blond hair drooped dramatically over one of his sapphire blue eyes. Full lips curved into a nervous grin and the man shifted his weight, adjusting the stack of books he held in his arms.

"Reynard." I hadn't seen Raven's on-again,off-again boyfriend since I'd been thrown out of Haul Du, yet here he stood at my door, looking like he'd stopped by to cram for finals.

"Um." He shifted his weight again. The guy was buff. No way a dozen books were weighing him down. "Raven wanted you to have these. There's more down in the car."

He stood expectantly, waiting for me to invite him in. I was torn. I didn't want him in my apartment, invading my sanctuary with his energy, looking around at all my stuff. He was Dark Iron's second, and no matter his relationship with Raven I couldn't see him as any more than an accomplice to the man who'd been my enemy.

But I couldn't very well leave him standing in the hall, his arms full of books. Reluctantly I moved aside, opening the door wider.

Reynard walked in. Actually, he kind of loped. Or glided. He had an energy-efficient way of moving across the floor, gently setting the books on my table. The whole time he took in my room, a mixture of curiosity and caution flickering in his eyes.

His gaze landed on my sword and froze. I couldn't help it. I picked up the bastard sword and drew it from the scabbard, spinning the sword hilt along my palm.

"You actually use that thing?" he asked.

My mind instantly flashed to a memory of my sword sliding through flesh, red flowing along the blade.

"Yes, I do use it." The words came out harsher than I'd wanted. I'd spilled blood with this sword. I'd killed with this sword. And I wasn't happy about it.

Reynard obviously thought my displeasure was toward him, not myself. He backed toward the door. "I'll go get the other books."

And now I felt a twinge of guilt. The sword went back in the scabbard with a quick, smooth motion. "I'll give you a hand."

Reynard had parked me in, his Volvo angled perpendicular to the rear of my car. There were two boxes in the back seat. He handed me one, then took the other, shutting the door with a swing of his hip.

"Who has Rocket?" I asked, wondering about Raven's French Bulldog. This was killing me, having Reynard show up like this. My friend's death was still a raw wound, and this visit was ripping off the faint bit of healing I'd been able to do in the last month.

"I have him." Reynard stopped halfway up the stairs, turning to me. "I miss her too, Aria. When we were good, we were really good. And when we were bad...well the makeup sex was amazing. And we *always* made up. Always."

I understood, yet I still envied Reynard the time he'd had with Raven as well as every item of hers he still possessed. Evidently I now had her library, while Reynard had her dog. I was pretty sure he had what she'd loved the most.

His blue eyes met mine. "We lived together the last six months. I loved her. I love that dog."

I nodded. "You ever stop loving that dog, you let me know."

Reynard's mouth quirked up in a sideways, dimpled smile that never failed to break hearts. "I'll *never* stop loving that dog."

And with those words, I was suddenly okay with a man I'd always eyed with distrust. He might be a player, he might be Dark Iron's crony, but he'd loved Raven. That much I was sure of. We put the boxes down on the table and Reynard dug in his pocket, pulling out a red silk bag.

"These are some amulets, and a couple rings. They're not charged, but I thought you should have them."

I took them with thanks, setting the bag on top of the books. "So, how are things with Haul Du?"

We'd never been close, and I sucked at small talk, but curiosity was killing me. What did they think had happened to Dark Iron? Who was running things now that he was gone? Were they all sitting around waiting for him to show up, like he'd just gone off on an unplanned vacation?

Reynard shrugged, looking just as awkward as I felt. "Things are okay. I'm running Haul Du until the group can vote on a leader. It's been a month. If Dark Iron was going to come back, he would have at least contacted us by now."

I was sure guilt was written all over my face.

"Oh?" Yeah. Because I could think of nothing else to say. I'd killed Dark Iron, letting the vampires cover it up. He wasn't coming back—ever.

"I'm not surprised," Reynard went on. "The Conclave was getting pressure from some mage in South America to proceed with a theft charge. Even if you're innocent, nobody wants the Conclave sniffing around your business."

I knew nothing about this Conclave beyond the fact they struck fear into every mage's heart. I was envisioning they were like Templar Elders, enforcing some agreed-upon rules and regulations, only much scarier.

Besides, Dark Iron was hardly innocent. I wondered what the Conclave would have done if they'd discovered that in addition to theft he'd orchestrated the murder of four mages and personally killed another?

"Did you hear anything about what's going on with the Baltimore group?" I asked Reynard. "I mean, I know all the members of Fiore Noir are in jail, but are there other mages who are stepping into the void?"

He shrugged. "All I heard was that there's a group of psychics or something that have banded together, but they're not a certified group."

Again, I wasn't sure how a group became certified, and what role the Conclave played in that. Were groups *allowed* to be unaffiliated? I knew Russell was a solitary practitioner of necromancy, but I couldn't imagine any sizable group being able to practice without some kind of oversight.

I was such an outsider, and it hurt. I'd joined Haul Du excited to be working with others who shared my passion, only to be kicked out after eight months when someone had found out I was a Templar. After that, word had spread and suddenly I was a pariah to everyone practicing ceremonial magic. I looked at the boxes on my table. All this information, yet no one to help me learn it. I knew my limitations. I knew so little, and diving into these books without a mentor would be suicide.

Raven was going to help me. She'd promised to mentor me, to help rid me of the demon mark. I'd envisioned us working together, her teaching me what she knew about magic, me sharing with her the information we Templars knew, sharing the knowledge I had access to.

But Raven was dead. And I was standing in my apartment, looking at Reynard as if I were a lost puppy at the pound and he were a potential adopter.

Reynard pulled a card out of his pocket and set it on top of a box. "I know you don't know me, actually I always got the feeling you wanted to put that sword of yours through my back, but if you have any questions about any of this give me a call."

He opened the door, then turned to look at me one last time, his beautiful face serious. "I'm not Dark Iron. I might not be willing to let a Templar join Haul Du, but I'd be negligent if I turned my back while you summoned half of hell and let them loose in Baltimore because you didn't know how to properly secure a gateway through the veil."

It wasn't the most stirring speech of friendship I'd ever had, but I'd take it.

CHAPTER 13

ST. MARK'S WAS a little stone church in the Highlands. The gardens out back adjoined a neatly mown cemetery with tiny, crumbling markers. I made my way through the late-blooming roses and early mums to the rear entrance where Father Bernard answered at the first ring of the bell. The priest gave me a warm welcome, shaking my hand, inviting me into his office and giving me a hot cup of tea.

"Did you hear about Amanda Lewis?" I asked, figuring this would be a better conversation starter than jumping right into "I summoned a demon and he marked me."

"No," the priest wrapped his hands tightly around the mug, which had a brightly-colored, modern art cat on white enamel. "Did she find another exorcist? After you left she insisted I try a second time. I gave her the number of a therapist I know and urged her to come speak with me after the service this Sunday."

"She's dead." Abrupt, but I'm not used to delivering this kind of news. "Her boyfriend found her, and identified her brother Bradley as running from the scene of her murder."

Father Bernard stared, his tea halfway to his lips. "Dead? But why? Bradley didn't seem to be on drugs. He had plenty of money—a trust fund set up when their parents died. He seemed to be getting his life together. I've known that boy since he was in diapers. He's not a killer."

I shrugged. "He's a bit weird though, you gotta admit. And the police found evidence in his backpack and in the cooler in the garage that leads them to believe Amanda wasn't his first victim. I know you have a hard time seeing him as a killer, but people change."

"I guess they do. Poor Amanda. Seems she was right after all, although the demon that got into her brother wasn't the biblical kind."

"Which is kind of why I'm here, Father." I set down my tea and stood, lifting the edge of my shirt. "I want to show you this.

He came from around the desk, bending over slightly to look at the scar on my waist. "Skin cancer? Oh, my child! What is the prognosis?"

Well, that was better than assuming it was from kinky fire-play gone wrong. "It's a demon mark. I'm hoping you know some way of removing it."

Father Bernard went back to his chair and sat. He had one of those "not this again" expressions on his face. "Why do you think that's a demon mark?"

He didn't believe me. Evidently he figured Templars suffered from delusions, too. He was probably right, but not this time.

"A month ago I summoned a Goetic demon in order to gain information. Something far worse came through the veil, broke free from the circle, and marked me."

The priest nodded. "Do you have any history of drug use? How often do you drink alcohol?"

"No drugs. Well, none except for the two Percocet a co-worker gave me instead of aspirin one day. I'm too poor to buy much alcohol beyond my one beer, but I eat out each night and we do have a few glasses of wine."

Okay, that really did make me sound like an alcoholic. What was the cut off on that? I doubted it was fourteenish, okay maybe twenty, glasses of wine per week. And heaven forbid he ever visit my parents' house where decanters of whisky and brandy were in pretty much every room—bedrooms included.

"Was the demon summoning after a few glasses of wine?"

The priest's tone was kind and respectful, but I couldn't help but bristle at the implication. "No! I wasn't drinking wine with dinner then. I don't think I'd had a beer in six months when I summoned the demon."

He nodded, sipping his tea. "Has this sort of thing happened to anyone else in your family?"

He meant was there a history of paranoid delusions in my family. What could I do to make this guy believe me, beyond summoning Balsur right here into the church?

Wait, could I even do that? Probably not. There were some restrictions about demons and holy spaces, as I recalled.

"Father, we're Templars. No one in my family is foolish enough to summon a demon. My dad believes it's a lazy shortcut way to achieve knowledge. My mom is furious and ready to defend my soul at the point of her sword. *We* don't do this sort of thing, but *I* did. My intentions were good, but I screwed up. I took a shortcut and now a high-level demon has marked me. He wants my soul."

I could see a flicker of indecision in Father Bernard's eyes. "Aria, the devil cannot take your soul unless you relinquish it to him. You're a Templar. You're God's Warrior. You walk the righteous path. Of all us mortals, the devil will find it especially difficult to take your soul."

The loss of a soul didn't always happen by bargaining it away at a crossroads. Yes, some humans consciously gave up their souls for material or other gain, but damnation tended to be a slow, one-step-at-a-time process. Each decision moved a person closer to a fiery eternity, and that road to hell *was* very often paved with good intentions.

"I summoned a demon. I opened a door. That's enough for a demon to mark my soul if he gets the chance."

"But not enough to damn you," the priest countered. "Repent, surrender your soul to God, and that demon will have no hold on you."

Repent. I hadn't been to confession in...well, I'd never been to confession. We were Episcopalian. When we confessed, it was through prayer—a direct link between us and God. I thought about starting a nightly foot-of-my-bed prayer routine. Would it really be that easy?

No, it wouldn't. Because if I was honest with myself, I wasn't truly repentant. If I needed to, I'd summon a demon again. I wouldn't be forgiven the sin if I knew I'd repeat my actions. And there were other things I'd done that had tainted my soul far more than dabbling in ceremonial magic.

There were times when confession was a private thing between you and God, and times when it needed to be more of a therapy session with someone who was in-the-know about all things spiritual. This was one of that latter.

"Can I give you my confession? I'm not Catholic. Is that okay? As an Episcopalian you probably can't give me absolution, but your guidance would be very welcome."

Father Bernard gave me a quick smile. "Then we should probably discuss this here rather than in a confessional."

"I'm so sorry. I didn't mean to offend you or diminish your authority—"

He waved a hand to cut me off. "I'm not offended at all. You're a Templar. I'm honored you came to me. God gifted you and your ancestors with strength and power, gave you His blessing to secure the Temple and protect Pilgrims as they walked a holy path. Yes, some who answered that call did not have God's Word in their hearts, but most did. You are God's Warriors. Catholic or not."

I relaxed. Nine hundred years ago—on Friday the thirteenth—the Pope had declared us heretics, allowing secular rulers, mainly the King of France, to seize our holdings. Yes, there were Templars who'd been burned at the stake. Although many Templar families were still devout Catholics, we were English. Our family had shifted to the Anglican Church, and then the Episcopal Church, although that had more to do with regional politics than any bitterness over history. Our brethren in Spain and France had a good relationship with the Catholic Church. It was reassuring to know that we were still considered God's Warriors, even though we'd chosen a different spiritual path.

Father Bernard smiled. "The past is the past, and you sit before me, a Templar in need. What can

I do to assist?"

"I summoned a demon, Father. And I can't guarantee I wouldn't do it again. There are circumstances that necessitate quick information and sometimes you need to risk your soul to save others. The summoning that got me this demon mark? *That* I regret. I should have chosen a different option that time. But there may come a moment when lives are on the line. If it will save lives, I'll do it again."

Father Bernard steepled his fingers and rested his chin on the peak. "You say you should have chosen a different option that time, but you didn't. Who's to say there isn't a different, better option next time? You can't justify sin this way, Aria. As your father said, it's a lazy path. It's the easy way. And it's so easy to justify your sin by pretending to be the martyr, by throwing your soul on the fire to save others. There are always other choices. There's always a solution that keeps you from sin *and* saves your pilgrims, it just takes work to find it."

Man, this guy was tougher on me than my parents. "Okay. Point taken. I can't say I'll never summon again, but I won't rush into it and I'll make sure I examine all the other options."

He smiled, pleased. "Limiting your connection with the other side of the veil will weaken the demon's claim on you."

I squirmed. "But summoning isn't my only sin. I fear that I've already darkened my soul."

"You're a Templar. Modern Templars do not judge, and they no longer kill humans. What could you have possibly done to darken your soul? Gambling? Those bottles of wine you drink each night?"

"I killed a man." And it was glasses of wine, not bottles.

Father Bernard sucked in a breath. "I'm going to assume that you mean this metaphorically, because otherwise I'd need to report you to the police. So, metaphorically, what happened to make you kill this man?"

I took a deep breath. "Remember the occult gang last month?"

The priest shuddered. "Horrible. They were performing ritual killings."

"Not just ritual murder, the last two victims were used for soul magic."

I paused to let that sink in, watching the priest's eyes bulge, his mouth drop open.

"Yeah. Soul magic. They didn't have the appropriate item for this work, but a mage from D.C. did. He bargained the use of this soul trap for the death of three mages. At the end of the day, he contracted for the murder of the mages, chose one of the ritual murder victims. Four murders are on his head, two souls forever lost. Then he killed my best friend and tried to make it look like one of the ritual murders."

Father Bernard shook his head. "A horrible, evil man. But surely he would have spent the rest of his life in jail, to face his eternal judgement upon a natural death?"

I clenched my jaw for a moment, trying to gain control of the fury that roared through me. I'd been haunted by my actions the last four weeks, but thinking of all Dark Iron had done made me angry enough to kill him again.

"There was nothing, no evidence that would have led to a conviction. The mages he worked with never saw his face. The soul trap wasn't in his possession any longer. A search of his home would have revealed that he was practicing magic, but nothing more. He would have gotten away with it, gone on to kill again."

"You don't know that. And if there wasn't enough evidence to convict him, how are you positive he was guilty?"

"One of the death mages had set up a meeting with the killer, and this man showed up. Plus my friend knew what he'd done, but a dead woman can't testify."

"Aria, you need to have faith. You're a Templar. Justice will prevail. Sometimes that justice isn't on our timetable."

Others would have died. I couldn't stand the thought of Dark Iron walking out of that room, smugly thinking he'd gotten away with murder. I couldn't stand that he'd thought me too weak to stop him. Pride. And murder. And evidently laziness and impatience. It was all a lot of sin for my soul to bear.

Father Bernard was right. I had no faith. I couldn't turn the other cheek and watch a murderer walk away to kill again. I couldn't let five people's deaths go unavenged. I couldn't let *Raven's* death go unavenged. And for all that, I was on the road to damnation.

"Thank you for your time, Father." I stood, realizing that confession and penance wouldn't help me remove this demon mark. The priest had said I was God's Warrior. Well, if God needed a human with a sword, then He certainly intended me to use it. As Templars we were expected to have blood on our hands, we were to have faith that God would guide our swords. We were more Old Testament than New.

And if I burned for protecting my Pilgrims, for ridding the world of evil, for avenging those innocents who had been murdered, then so be it.

CHAPTER 14

RUSSELL FINDAL HAD changed in the last month—changed in a good way. The necromancer still had wary shadows about his eyes, but the tight lines in his face had eased somewhat. His brown skin had taken on ruddy undertones, as if he were spending regular amounts of time outside in the sunshine. His salt and pepper hair was still cropped close, but a short, tight-edged beard of gray made him look more the distinguished scholar than a summoner of the dead.

I probably would have been better off going to one of the mediums downtown, but I knew Russell, knew he was the real deal. Who knows how many women with a palm on their door I'd need to go through to find someone who honestly had a connection with the spirit world.

"How have you been?" I took the sweet tea he handed me with a smile, declining the plate of lemon wedges.

"Good. It's taken me a while to find my feet, but good. I see Shay, I mean Bella, once a week." A fond smile creased his face. "I always bring a toy for her. You know, a doll or a Lego set or something. This week I found some sculpting supplies and we spent the evening making little clay animals."

His sister had been fourteen when she'd been

murdered, and unfortunately she'd lain dead for over an hour before Dario was able to turn her. As a result, the young vampire had suffered irreparable cognitive damage. She was a fifty-four-year-old vampire trapped in a fourteen-year-old body with emotions and intellect somewhere around a child of four. She was all Russell had left of his family, and the reason he'd made his peace with the vampires and had decided to remain in Baltimore.

"Sounds fun," I replied. It did. The idea of clay animals made me want to go hang out with my nephews for the weekend. "You still working at that warehouse?"

"Part time. Mostly I'm running a food truck down on Baltimore Avenue." He grinned. "This guy owns six of them. Barbeque. He does all the meat smoking, and sends us out with the trucks. I like it. I get to meet a lot of people. It's day work, which leaves nights I'm not at the warehouse free for my practice."

And by practice he meant necromancy. Russell had hung a sign outside his row house, the familiar psychic palm along with his hours. "Business good?" I asked, wondering how much clientele he'd get in this residential neighborhood. He was pretty close to Camden Yards, so who knows? Maybe all the Orioles fans stopped by for a glimpse into the future of the team's season.

"Mostly out-of-towners, although I've got some customers locally. Things have really stepped up now that all of the spirit workers and psychics are working together."

Reynard had mentioned this, but it still surprised me. Psychics were an independent lot, not as likely to form big groups like other mages. They were friendly with each other and sometimes chatted over a glass of tea like Russell and I were doing, but there was never a leader, never a structured organization to their practitioners.

"So, I gotta ask, is that woman down by the Inner Harbor for real? The one who walks around the Constellation dressed as a gypsy, handing out cards?" I must have a dozen of her cards. She was quite a sales person, and very dramatic. I'm sure she made a fortune from the tourists, even if the cops were constantly running her off for soliciting.

Russell laughed. "See, that's where things have improved. I've got nothing against people with minimal talent making a living, but they need to know who to refer people to when a client needs real help."

"So all those people running the séances and ghost tours...?"

He shrugged, stirring a spoonful of sugar into his already sweet tea. "There's good money in that, and a lot of them have reasonable skills. But if there's a poltergeist tearing up someone's house in Franklin Terrace, or a guy's aunt in Federal Hill died without telling him where she hid the stock certificates, then Mr. Séance needs to know to step aside. And who to call."

He nodded, a look of calm satisfaction on his face. "Doesn't have to be me. There are some talented mediums who aren't as public and work on the side. We all just need to know who specializes in what and feel comfortable making that call."

It made sense. I sipped my tea and we continued chatting about the neverending construction on 895, whether that developer was really going to tear down Old Mall and turn it into upscale condominiums in the middle of the slum, and how the Ravens' prospects looked this year. Finally, once a suitable amount of socialization had taken place, I pulled the fox figurine out of my pocket and set it on the table.

Russell's gray eyebrows flew toward the ceiling. "Nice work. Old World work, I can tell from here. Does this practitioner have an eBay store? Because I'd love to order one of these."

I waved my hand. "Family connection. I'm not sure if she takes orders or makes them for anyone outside the family, but I'll check. It's a *lelek raktarban.* I have a few of them, but this one seems to have attracted a spirit."

His eyebrows threatened to vanish into his hairline. "May I?" he gestured toward the fox.

I nodded and Russell picked up the resin figurine, exclaiming softly as he examined it inches from his face. "There is indeed a spirit residing here, although he appears to be angry."

Crap. I'd assumed based on my conversation with Gran that this was a helpful spirit. "Angry? What can an angry spirit in a *lelek* do to me? Do I need to ditch it down the sewer drain or something?"

"Not angry at you, just angry. It's often the case. Anger is a powerful emotion—one that is powerful enough to bind a spirit to this world and energize it to seek a vessel."

I still didn't like the sound of that. "So let's say this spirit was killed by a drunk driver. Does that mean he's only going to help me prevent drunk driving? Or hide my beer and wine? Or pester me to take revenge on the driver that killed him?"

Russell shook his head, setting the figurine back on the table. "Oh no. There might be a specific scenario that motivates him more than others, but he's here to help *you.* And he chose you specifically.

If he wanted to prevent drunk driving, he'd have attached himself to an addictions counselor or a bartender, or a member of MADD. There's something specifically about you that attracted this spirit."

Well, that was a relief. "Someone told me that the spirit is struggling to adjust to using the *lelek* as a vessel. How long do you think it will be before he's able to do more than fall off the shelf and sit on top of books? What can I expect from him?"

"Sadly some never do master the use of their vessel. The fact that yours has managed to move around is a good sign. I can give you some ideas and exercises you could try that might help the spirit, but there's no telling how much he'll be able to do. Ideally he should be able to communicate with you, verbally or through other means, move about on his own, act as an intermediary between you and the spirit world. I've heard a few legends of spirits who could move back and forth across the veil. Whether any of this will happen in your lifetime or not, I don't know."

This was all so depressing. No wonder the spirit was angry. I'd be pissed too, trapped in a vessel and unable to communicate properly.

"Let's try something right now." Russell got up from the table and pulled a battered cardboard box off a nearby bookshelf. "If we're lucky, we'll be able to find out who this spirit is. Calling him by name will strengthen the bond between you both and help him learn to communicate with you."

The necromancer opened the lid, unfolding the board and placing the triangular planchette in the center.

"A Ouija board." Obviously this wasn't

something we'd ever had in our house growing up. I'd never seen one while in Haul Du either since all the mages in that group studied Goetica. Ouija was a tool of mediums and divinatory mages, of necromancers and those who dealt with the spirit world. The hair on my neck stood up just looking at it.

"It's a tool, just like a pendulum, cards, or a scrying mirror." Russell sat and laid the fox figurine on the plastic pointer. Then he reached across the table and took my hands in his own.

"Aren't we supposed to put our fingers on the thingie?" That's how I'd seen it done in the horror movies.

"What, so one of us can accuse the other of moving it ourselves?" he scoffed. "If the spirit can't manage to move the indicator on its own, then I'm afraid he might not be of much help to you. I even placed the figurine in direct contact with it, to give him a little additional assistance."

I looked down at the Ouija board, my heart sinking. My little fox was game, but he hadn't been able to do much more than fall over and roll across the ground. I wasn't sure moving a pointer was within his abilities. Hoping for the best, I closed my eyes.

The lights dimmed. Russell's soft chanting was barely louder than the hum of the refrigerator. Magical energy sparked along my skin and I shivered. He was doing all he could to help my little fox communicate. It was hard to believe that a month ago I'd regarded this man as an enemy, although a sympathetic one. And here he was helping me.

"The spirit is very frustrated that he can't

speak," Russell announced. "I get the sense that he's determined and not about to give up. That's good. Now, let's see if he's strong enough to move the planchette and tell us his name."

I opened my eyes and stared, disheartened. The fox and the planchette were exactly where they'd been before. Nothing had happened. I got the feeling nothing was going to happen.

"Patience." Russell gave my hands a squeeze, his eyes practically willing the pointer to move.

It jerked to the side. I caught my breath and watched while the poor fox trembled, jerking the planchette one tiny fraction of an inch at a time. Finally it stopped.

Russell sighed and released my hands. "That's it. He's either gone where he wanted to or he's too tired to continue."

We both stood, looking down at the pointer. It had paused over the letter" "V".

"Victor? Vinny? Do you know anyone no longer living whose name began with a 'V'?"

I shook my head. "Maybe it's 'V' for vampire?" There had been quite a few who had died at the hands of Russell's specters last month before both sides had called a truce, but I really didn't know any of those vampires well enough to think they'd stick around to help me.

The necromancer shrugged. "Could be, although these vessels are generally only available for human spirits. I can't think a vampire spirit would be able to use one. I'm not even sure there *are* vampire spirits. I've never encountered any who hung around after death, but it's not like I've been asked to communicate with any of them. I just get the feeling they go straight to their final destination once they die."

Which would be hell. It was the ultimate price paid by vampires for their immortality.

I tucked the little resin fox into my purse and left after thanking Russell for the tea and the help. It was nice to know someone in the magical community who didn't regard me as a pariah, although necromancers were highly specialized. So were Goetic mages, though. I thought again about Reynard's unexpected visit. *That* was a friend I needed to cultivate. We both cared about Raven, and he'd opened the doorway to communication and an exchange of information. Maybe, in time, he'd be able to put me in contact with someone who could tell me how to remove this demon mark.

In the meantime, I had a hodge-podge of friends that included a necromancer, a reporter, a detective, a vampire, and a group of gamers. And a three-inch fox figurine whose name started with a "V".

CHAPTER 15

THE COFFEE SHOP was unusually busy this evening due to a special event at the Inner Harbor. I looked out the front door, craning my neck to catch what was going on down-street, but couldn't see anything from the crowds of people.

Usually I was one of the day shift employees, since the 5:00 p.m. onward part-timers were the ones with regular day jobs. I missed Brandi and Anna, but was tickled to see I was working with Chalese. The middle-aged woman had an indescribable job at Public Works during the day, but claimed they didn't pay her enough to cover the cost of her hair stylist. Then she'd gently pat her 'do, claiming that hair that gorgeous didn't come cheap.

I believed her. The hair in question was meticulously curled and colored a warm honey brown, with extensions that brought the overall length to just above her waist. Beyoncé would have been green with envy. Heck, *I* was green with envy, self-consciously running my fingers through my snarled dark-brown mess and wishing I'd taken a bit more care this morning with my appearance.

Chalese was a blast to work with, and that wasn't completely due to her careful grooming and wry sense of humor. The woman could work. I'd never seen anyone so quick on the machines. It was like she had six hands or something. And when she called out an order, I swear they could hear her all the way to Dundalk.

By nine that evening things had slowed down and we were both watching the clock, waiting impatiently for closing time. I was just about to start cleaning the pastry case when the door chimed. I peeked around the espresso machine and saw Sean Merrill heading my way.

Odd. He wasn't with Janice, and I couldn't recall if I'd told him where I worked or not. It could be a coincidence that he was here. I mean, some nights you just needed a latte, and from last night I'd seen that Sean liked his caffeine late. Yeah. It had to be a coincidence, because my friend's boyfriend going out of his way to come to my coffee shop would have been kind of creepy.

"Hey." I greeted him with my best, friendly smile. "Double shot with a twist?"

He grinned back. "Yep. I am a creature of habit. I'll take one of those brownies, too."

I relaxed and scooped a brownie into a white bag. No big deal. The guy was probably at the Harbor for whatever thing had been going on tonight, and just popped in for an espresso before heading home. I handed him his brownie while Chalese took care of the espresso, balancing a lovely lemon twist on the edge of the cup before handing it to him. He smiled and sat at a nearby table, grabbing a discarded newspaper and looking through it as he sipped.

"Friend of yours?" Chalese jerked her head sideways toward Sean.

"A friend of mine just started dating him. He's a developer up in Harford County, but he's in the city a lot for business. Seems nice."

Too nice. There was something about him that bothered me. Maybe I just liked the bad boys and any nice, normal, non-vampire man seemed wrong.

"He's too old for that body," Chalese sniffed.

"What?" My heart stuttered. Sean wasn't a vampire, but there were plenty of other creatures who looked human but didn't age like one.

"You know. Some guys just seem old." She narrowed her eyes and glared at him. "Looks mid-thirties on the outside, but I'll bet he's all prune juice and bran muffins on the inside."

Oh, she meant he was boring and old-fashioned. Maybe, but I think Janice liked that sort of predictable and Steady-Eddy kind of guy. I finished with the pastry case while Chalese cleaned the machines. It was nine-thirty and I went to lock the door, noticing that Sean still had quite a bit of espresso left in his cup. It was bound to be cold by now. Normally I would have assumed he didn't like the drink, but Chalese knew how to make a double with a twist. Chalese knew how to make everything.

"We're closing up," I told him apologetically.

He looked up in surprise. "Oh. Sorry, I got sucked into this article about the occult murders last month. Do you know the one guy, Charles something, just got sentenced to twenty at Jessup?"

Chuck. I'd kind of actually liked him. "I'm glad they caught them. It was pretty horrible, snatching people off the street and killing them like that."

He tilted his head in surprise. "They? Janice said you were involved with the investigation, that you assisted the detective in charge and were responsible for the arrest of nine of the mages."

Oh Lord, Janice had been talking me up. I squirmed. "I'm a Templar. I acted as a consultant, sharing information on ceremonial magic with the local police." I also banished demons and killed a man. But that was better kept to myself.

Sean folded the paper, drinking down the rest of his espresso. "So what are your thoughts on vampires, demons, werewolves, and all that? Kill them on sight? Or do you think it's possible for humans to co-exist peacefully with the paranormal?"

That was the weirdest question from a civilian I'd ever fielded. My gamer friends asked this sort of thing all the time, but they rolled dice and killed orcs every week, too. Fantasy was part of their lives. I hadn't expected it to be part of a developer from Harford County's life.

"Demons can't be killed." There. That was a good avoidance answer if I might say so myself.

"But the rest?" he persisted. "Let's say there really are vampires and werewolves. Exterminate, or let them live?"

"It depends. I've got no prejudice against other creatures as long as their existence doesn't threaten humanity. Ideally, they'd be judged individually by their actions. So unless they were predisposed as a race to slaughtering humans left and right, I'd give them the benefit of the doubt."

"But you'd judge them. As a Templar, you'd feel comfortable making that judgement call and delivering justice?"

This conversation was edging out of hypothetical scenarios and uncomfortably close to my actions last month. "Only God should judge, but I find that I can't stand by and watch my pilgrims die, killed by someone who has no sense of the value of human life. Templars may not judge, but I do."

His eyes met mine and I got the feeling he was

the one judging me, like he was trying to decide how he felt about me. I didn't mind since I'd been doing the same thing to him the moment he started dating my friend.

"So say there are vampires, and they prey on humans. Sometimes they even kill humans. How would you weigh in on that?"

I hesitated, thinking of my anxiety-inducing indecision when it came to vampires. "I'd have to consider each case individually. Humans kill by accident, and we don't subject those who are guilty of manslaughter to the same level of punishment as those who commit premeditated murder."

He nodded. "So let's say there's a regular pattern of assault, one that supposedly has no lasting damage on the victim—in fact, maybe the victim isn't even aware of it. That would be tolerated? How about the occasional accidental death where the human knew the risks and accepted them?"

Did he know about vampires? It wasn't an impossible idea. They did reveal their presence to humans who worked with them in various enterprises. Perhaps the *Balaj* was involved in Sean's development project. Or perhaps this guy was just feeling out my moral compass. Which was weird since *I* wasn't the one dating him. Did he always screen his potential girlfriend's friends in this fashion?

"I don't know," I admitted honestly. "I'm less worried about the assault with no damage than I am about the accidental deaths. I mean, can someone really give consent, fully understand the risks involved in such an exchange? What if there was some glamor involved on the part of the vampire? Or something addicting in the act? Drunk people cannot legally sign contracts. I'd presume the same here. No consent is possible if the human is impaired or under the vampire's influence."

Sean smiled and got to his feet, tucking the newspaper under his arm. "You should have been a lawyer. It was nice running into you tonight, Aria. Thank you for staying open past closing for me. And thank you for the interesting conversation."

He left and I watched him go, well aware that I'd left Chalese with the lion's share of the closing activities. Sean was an old man in a young body. He was smart, friendly, well-mannered. And I still didn't trust him.

CHAPTER 16

I WOKE UP early, grabbing my phone and wiping the sleep from my eyes as I peered at my texts. I'd had one from Dario right around sunset last night that had informed me he was busy and off-the-grid. It was immediately followed by another one that I cherished like it had been a love letter.

Miss you.

I missed him too, but for him to say that hit right to my heart. It wasn't the sort of thing you'd say to a business associate. Maybe something you'd say to a friend, but hardly one you'd only gone forty-eight hours without seeing. No, this meant something more. I just knew it.

The prior night's sleep deprivation had caught up with me, and I knew how useless it would be to sit up staring at my phone when Dario said he'd be unavailable and unable to contact me. So I'd gone to bed and slept like the dead until morning.

And now I was panicking, worried that something had happened to him and, since it was daytime, I wouldn't find out until nightfall.

I breathed a sigh of relief when I saw his last text, sent just before sunrise.

Okay and going to ground. Literally. I can't wait to be home so I can spend daylight hours in an actual bed. Waking up covered in dirt and worms is not dignified.

I laughed, sending a reply before I even realized what I was doing.

Sweet dreams, my prince of worms.

So cheesy. And I was pretty sure vampires didn't dream during the day. I remember Dario once telling me that he truly was dead at that time. I couldn't imagine that, losing eight to fourteen hours each day, unable to be awakened at all, vulnerable to anyone who might drag me out into the sunlight and my true death. Was that life really worth immortality? Because it wasn't *really* immortality when the slightest ray of sunlight could kill.

But this was just as philosophical as my discussion last night with Sean. And I couldn't lay abed any longer. I might not have a shift at the coffee shop today, but I did have an exciting invitation that had come late last night from the good Detective Tremelay. Brian Huang had not been located. His family said he hadn't returned home from the police station after the last interview. Tremelay didn't have enough to scare up a warrant, but Huang's family had asked to come in and speak with the police.

Finally, there might be some information that would give us—I mean the cops—motive and possible whereabouts for a man who inexplicably bore the same knee replacement implant as a dead body, who'd been seen in the company of a murder suspect. Hopefully there would finally be some answers.

Tremelay met me in the lobby, disappointed that I didn't have cookies this time. The dude made more money than I did. Time for *him* to buy the cookies. Plus, as intrigued as I was about this case, I wasn't his "subject matter expert" this time. I think he just liked bouncing ideas off me, and honestly I loved being involved. Templar. Barista. Wannabe detective. That was me.

The Huang family was in one of the larger interview rooms, extra chairs brought in to accommodate the fact that every single family member was in attendance. There was a woman I assumed was a wife, an older couple that could have been Huang's parents. An adult male. Two teenage kids, their faces worried. The wife twisted her hands together, while the elderly couple stared stoically at the wall.

"The parents don't speak any English. You wouldn't know Mandarin, would you?"

I shook my head. My linguistic studies had been in ancient as well as modern romance languages. I probably should think about learning an Asian language, though.

We walked in and Tremelay made the introductions as we all bowed and shook hands.

"I haven't seen Brian since he came here," Lisa Huang stated, her voice flat and emotionless. "He's been strange since the day the body was found in the museum, though. It's like that morning he woke up a completely different person."

Tremelay glanced at the children, then back at the wife. "How was he different?"

She swallowed a few times, reaching out to touch her son's shoulder. "He didn't like his favorite foods anymore. His taste in music changed from classic rock to rap. He stopped spending time with the children. He used to love to go to Jack's soccer games, but I had to drag him to the one this week."

"He was sneaking out at night," the girl spoke up, eyes glistening with tears. "I was up late texting some friends, and I saw him. I stayed up waiting for him, and he didn't come home until close to dawn. Same thing the next night, too."

"I saw him with this young guy," the boy added. "College-age white guy. Backpack, baggy jeans, T-shirt from some local band. Twice I saw Dad with him, and once they were with a girl. She looked younger, high school maybe. Caucasian with pink and blue in her hair. Lots of make-up."

Lisa put her head in her hands. "The Brian I married would never cheat on me, and especially not with a teenage girl, but the last few days he hasn't been the Brian I married. When he came home and said they found a body at the museum, he seemed panicked. I mean, it's got to be unsettling to have a murder at your workplace, but Brian was scared. I got the feeling he knew the dead man. Or maybe knew the man who killed him."

The father spoke rapidly in Chinese, ending with an emphatic slam of his fist on the table.

Lisa winced. "Maybe these other two got him involved with the murderer. Maybe the murderer is a friend of his, and it's got nothing to do with whether he's having an affair or not. Either way, I'm sure Brian knows something."

"What did his father say?" I asked.

The wife's eyes met mine. "That Brian is not his son. He said that a monster has taken Brian's body, because that man is not his son."

A chill ran through me and I turned my attention to the father. Had he meant that metaphorically? Maybe the supernatural events last month were clouding my judgement, but I thought he meant that literally.

What monster takes over a person's body?

Immediately I thought of demons, then remembered the failed exorcism of Bradley Lewis. Amanda had been convinced of the same. She'd been sure that whoever had been walking around in her brother's skin wasn't actually her brother. But if not demons, then what?

Skin. I remembered the odd coincidence of the implant, the skinned corpse in the museum. The guy's skin in the backpack. Had the college-guy been Bradley Lewis? Were all three killers? Three non-human killers who took a person's skin and walked around in their bodies?

Norwicki stepped to the table and placed a sheet with a grid of photos in front of the boy. "Can you identify the guy you saw your Dad with? Are any of these photos that man?"

The boy scanned down the list, placing a finger on one picture. "This one. Only his hair's a little shorter now."

Bradley Lewis. The detective had him put his initials next to the photo, then swapped the sheet for another, this one with rows of female head shots. "Are any of these the girl he was with?"

He shook his head. "No."

I pulled out my cell phone, scrolling through the pictures. "How about her?"

Jack winced at the photo of his dad hugging the teenage girl. "Yeah, that's her."

"Where'd you take that?" Norwicki demanded.

"Outside the police station," I told him smugly. "She was waiting for him." I saw the pained look on Lisa Huang's face and quickly added, It wasn't a passionate embrace. They were both crying."

I don't think that made the woman feel any

better about the situation. I ached for her, really I did, but there was a connection between Bradley Lewis, Brian Huang, and this girl. I thought back to when I first saw her at the Inner Harbor and wondered what happened to the boy she'd been with, the one who I'd assumed was a verbally abusive brother.

"Do you have a photo of, um, of the contents of Bradley Lewis's backpack?" I asked Tremelay. I spoke in hushed tones, but didn't want to risk letting the Huang family know that the murders involved skinned bodies.

An expression of revulsion crossed the detective's face. "No. I have a picture from when the kid went missing at six years of age, but not his...um, his current situation."

Not that it would have helped. I doubted I could have recognized anyone from an oddly tanned skin. Still, I wondered if the boy at the Harbor had been a victim. If not, where was he in all of this? He'd called the girl Becca or something, and the missing friend had an odd name—Lawson?

Lawton. And the skin in the backpack had belonged to Lawton King, a sixteen-year-old boy from South Carolina. Like Tremelay, I was beginning to think there was no such thing as a coincidence. The girl was involved, the missing friend was found dead. I had no idea how Bradley Lewis tied in to this, or who the rude brother from the Inner Harbor was, but somehow all five of these people were involved.

Tremelay turned back toward Lisa Huang, asking her further questions about her husband's behavior and associations. I tuned them out, thinking about the three, possibly four or even five individuals involved.

Putting aside the teen girl, her friend/brother from the Inner Harbor, and the mysterious Lawton kid, we had two suspects. Brian Huang and Bradley Lewis, both of whom had experienced sudden personality changes last week. Both of whom family members described as being a sort of doppelganger, an imposter in their son or brother's body. If I hadn't witnessed a failed exorcism, I'd be thinking demonic possession.

As it stood, I was just as baffled as the police. More baffled, actually, since they were looking for a team of serial killers and I...well, I wasn't sure *what* I was thinking at this point. The police could be right, but I was beginning to wonder if this killing spree was at the hand of a non-human murderer. Or murderers. If I was right, then Tremelay was really going to need my help. And fast, because any paranormal creature that killed and assumed their victim's identity, who tore the skins off their prey was not going to be stopped by the Baltimore PD

Which was why I needed to get my butt back home and do some research.

CHAPTER 17

THE PETERSON BOOK was open on the couch, but it was what I saw in the kitchen that had me shaking my head. Flour covered the counter tops, spilling in a heap of white powder on the floor. The broken bag lay in the sink. It looked like someone had yanked it from the cabinet, ripped the bag open, and shook it all over my kitchen.

I shouldn't even *own* flour. I couldn't cook anything beyond heat-and-serve. When I'd moved in, I'd stupidly bought what everyone told me were kitchen staples—flour, sugar, spices, baking soda, yeast. I wasn't sure the yeast was still good by this point. The flour certainly wasn't, now that it was mostly on my floor.

Grumbling to myself, I got the dustpan and broom. Dario was north of the city, and it was daytime. Even if it *were* night, I couldn't imagine him sneaking into my apartment and having a field day with baking supplies. My apartment was warded against entry by anyone else. Obviously this was an inside job, which meant my fox named "V" was the culprit.

Why would "V" do this? Was he trying to tell me something? Something to do with kitchens or flour, or baking? Maybe ghosts? In cartoons, people dumped flour over themselves and were mistaken for ghosts.

I realized what was going on when I went to throw my first dust pan full of flour away. By the trash can was another mess of white powder, the fox figurine on its side at the edge. He'd drawn a "V", but once I got a good look at it I realized the mark in the flour wasn't truly a "V" after all. It was a checkmark with the extensions at each end jutting outward at a perpendicular angle.

The equivalent of a stick figure bird.

"Raven?" My voice shook as I picked up the fox and cleaned it off. The eyes glittered at me, but there was no confirmation of my theory. "Raven, is that you?"

It had to be her. I didn't know anyone named "V". Raven had died violently with unfinished business. She'd vowed to help me with the demon mark. My friend was so stubborn, so strong-willed, that I could completely see her sticking around this world, forgoing the afterlife to help me as she'd promised.

But how could she help me when she couldn't do much more than roll around, knock books over, and write a checkmark in flour? How the heck were we going to communicate if she couldn't speak? Or even write.

I placed Raven on the kitchen counter and ran to my room, digging into a box of miscellaneous stuff that I'd brought with me when I'd moved from my parents' house. Yarn. A photo album. One of those adult coloring books with crayons. Slippers. And a white board. Sadly only two of the dry-erase markers were still working, but it should do. I brought them out and placed them on the dining room table.

"At night I'll put you next to this and hopefully

you can leave me messages. I'll even uncap the markers each night to make it easier for you."

Even then, she might not be able to do much. The fox figurine had no movable parts, no opposable thumbs. How Raven was going to hold a marker steady enough to write, was beyond me. Although there had to be some way she could manipulate her surroundings. Poltergeists could write, could pick up and throw objects. If those spirits could do it without corporeal form, Raven should be able to. Then Russell's words came back to me. It might take her time. It might take her longer than my lifetime.

I refused to believe that, so I grabbed the fox and plopped down on the sofa, Peterson's *Monsters of the New World* on my lap. "Okay, I know you've been insistent about this book. Does it have to do with the skinning murders? Because the Huang family gave me the idea that this might not be a serial killer who has a sick thing for taxidermy, but something else entirely. What type of creature skins their victims and then assumes their identity?"

I flipped through the book, stopping at Native American Skinwalkers. They were a type of magic user who used animal skins to assume that form and gain the powers of that particular animal, as well as cross the veil. More than just the normal animal abilities of the wolf, panther, or bear, the mage would gain the symbolic powers that the animal held in the spirit world.

Wow. I wondered how long it took them to be able to do that. If they mastered one animal, were they able to master another or only remain proficient in transformation to the one? I looked further, noting that the majority of documented practitioners were of Navaho descent, although others had claimed to have achieved this level of skill over the past few centuries. There were also conflicting claims as to whether the person who performed this was evil or not. Navaho legend said the magic user had to kill a close family member in order to gain the ability, and then used the animal skins to go around killing other humans.

I closed my eyes and envisioned two or three Native Americans running around Baltimore and killing people to assume their identity. A museum employee. The deadbeat brother of an investment guru. A high school girl.

I couldn't see it. Assuming an animal form like an owl? Yes. Assuming the identities and forms of *those* three humans? No. Well, maybe the investment guru if they hadn't been interrupted and Amanda Lewis had been skinned. One of them might have wanted to play the market and win, but why her jobless brother?

And all that was assuming the technique even *worked* with human skins. Things weren't interchangeable in the magical world. Plus some accounts claimed these people were practicing their magic for a higher purpose. Murdering people and assuming their identity wasn't in keeping with that higher purpose.

So, theory one was that the murderers were the evil version of the Native American skinwalkers.

I picked up another book, determined to explore all options. Selkie. Nope, they were human with a seal skin. A Chinese fox-spirit was said to be able to assume human form, but there was nothing I could find about them wearing their victim's skin. In fact, the fox-spirit seemed to use its victim's heart to maintain its human appearance.

I wasn't willing to rule out demons, although

that would mean that Father Bernard's exorcism wasn't correctly done. It *was* a possibility.

Theory two: demonic possession.

Shapeshifters? But they shouldn't need a skin to assume a human form. Still, I glanced through *Transformative Beasts*. Most shapeshifters, including werewolves, changed back and forth between their primary human form and their animal one without any external aid. These creatures weren't able to shift into other animals or humans— just the two. But there *were* several types of shapeshifters who could shift into a variety of animals as well as humans. One reportedly killed and took the victim's identity, but there was no mention of it needing the skin for this.

I wasn't going to rule that out either. Maybe the shapeshifter was just using the skinned body as a way to delay identification and the skin was a sort of focus in transforming into that appearance.

Theory three: shapeshifters.

Perhaps aliens? Like in that pod-people movie? Oh sheesh, I just couldn't go there. So basically I was looking at shapeshifters, demons, or evil skinwalkers who had crossed the line and started wearing human instead of animal skins.

"What do you think? I asked Raven. There was no reply, but I could swear I saw the figurine wobble. "I think I better call Dad and see what he has to say about this."

I picked up my phone and nearly jumped from my seat as it rang in my hands. It wasn't my father with some psychic awareness that I needed him, it was Dario.

"Hey! Better night tonight?" It was just after sunset, so I doubted there had been enough time for things to go south yet. He was probably just calling in response to my cheesy text.

"Depends on your definition of 'better.'" His tone was light and teasing, but I caught the underlying stress. "Can you come up here? I'm in Hampton. It's north of Towson, just outside the beltway. There's something I need you to see, to get your opinion on."

If this serial killer really was non-human, then I needed to research it as quick as I could. Part of me kept remembering what Father Bernard as well as my father had said: demon summoning for information was lazy. And if time was of the essence, I couldn't let it run out and put me in a corner where I'd have to further sully my soul.

But Dario had always been there for me. Always. At the drop of a hat he'd come when I'd asked. The vampire had never let me down, and that sort of friendship was something to be cherished. I wanted to be the same kind of friend for him. I wanted to be there when he needed me, without question, just as he'd done for me.

"Where in Hampton?" I wrote down the address as well as his comments on landmarks. "At the Target? Should I meet you in housewares, or in women's fashion?"

"Meet me behind the building, by the dumpster."

Well, that sounded ominous. I had visions of human bodies in the dumpster, drained of their blood by the rogue group of vampires Dario and his family had been chasing.

"I'm on my way."

I grabbed my sword and the spelled butter knife, and added my charm bracelet just in case. I'd only bothered to spell three of the charms since we'd been free of supernatural crises the last four weeks, but it would do. Right before I left I paused and looked at the fox figurine. Should I take her?

"I'll fill you in when I come back," I told Raven, uncapping the dry erase markers in the hope that there would be a message for me upon my return. Nothing burst into flames, fell off the table, or flew across the room, so I assumed she was down with this plan.

Then I jumped in my car and set my phone GPS to the address in Hampton, hoping between that and Dario's directions I could manage to get there without too many detours. The call to my father would have to wait, as would any further research on the murderer and my demon mark. A friend needed me, and I wasn't about to let him down.

CHAPTER 18

B Y THE TIME I'd managed to find the correct exit
and navigate the unfamiliar area, it was closing
on ten at night. Cars still filled the parking lot and
shoppers rattled by with their carts full of plastic
bags. I parked out front so I'd seem to be a regular
shopper and not some robber driving around back to
case the joint. Before I could lock my door, Dario
appeared beside me, scaring me to the point that I
nearly peed my pants.

"What took you so long," he grumbled as I
stilled my franticly beating heart. "Did you drive to
Hampton via Frederick or something?"

"I missed the exit and wound up heading to
Philadelphia." Which had been a toll road. I was still
pissed about that.

"Well I've been babysitting a body for the last
hour and a half. It's cold and stiff at this point."

Grumpy vampire. It was kind of cute, actually,
to see him like this.

"Human body?" I was surprised he hadn't said
"bodies." His past descriptions of renegade groups
led me to believe they were killing machines. Living
with a feast or famine cycle tended to make a
vampire want to gorge when they managed to grab a
victim.

"No, a vampire body."

Dario turned and led the way while I followed, still shocked at his words. Had one of the *Balaj* been killed by the rogues? The dead had to have been one of theirs. I couldn't imagine I'd be called in each time they killed one of the renegades. Then I remembered our conversation about the Towson rogues and wondered if a *human* had possibly killed a vampire. A determined, knowledgeable, Van Helsing sort of character wouldn't find it impossible, but I imagined a college girl trying to break a vampire's neck and had to stifle a giggle.

Dario and I blended in with the shopping public until we rounded the side of the store, past silent loading docks and around to the rear. Two women stood by a back door smoking, their smocks still tied around their waists. They watched us with a wary curiosity, one edging her foot toward the propped-open door.

I'm sure they wondered what the heck we were doing. Dario headed left, jumping onto an embankment and edging along a narrow path between overgrown shrubberies and the side of a gigantic dumpster. Looking up I saw the back of a low-rise apartment complex a few hundred feet away. No wonder the two women on their smoke break hadn't been overly alarmed. This was clearly a short-cut from the store to the apartments.

It was also the dump site for a body. I had no clue how the vampires had managed to find it with the thick bushes still holding on to their fall foliage. If they hadn't, there was a good chance this body would have lain there until winter, when some poor human cutting through to his home saw it.

Or not. Vampires turned to dust in the sunlight, their bodies would, too.

I leaned in, pushing aside the stubborn thorny

limbs to get a better look at the dead vampire. It was there I got my second shock of the night. The vampire was completely devoid of skin, legs and arms sprawled outward from a twisted torso.

"The other victims were in the city," I mused. We were in Hampton. It wasn't far, but it definitely was a break from where the killers had previously been active.

"And all the others were human." Dario reached down and grabbed the corpse's head, turning it to face me. I don't know if I was more shaken that he grabbed the horror-movie skinned head with his bare hand, or at the sharp set of vampire teeth in her mouth. Big, pointy teeth. I knew they had fangs, but the absence of lips made those gigantic canines look all the more lethal.

No wonder Dario had called me. He knew about the serial killer in Baltimore, but I hadn't had a chance to tell him my theory about the killer not being human. This particular choice of victim would make a whole lot more sense if the killer was a demon, or demons, with a signature style of killing than if the killer were a human. Human serial killers *were* pretty darned scary, but to take down a vampire required knowledge—knowledge of how to make sure they stayed dead as well as how to quickly incapacitate them. Vampires were fast. The slightest delay and the killer would be the one with a snapped neck, sprawled dead in the thorny brush.

"How...?" I couldn't even formulate the question I was so busy envisioning how a human, psychotic though he might be, could overpower a vampire and manage to skin one. We might be dealing with a team of two or three, of which at least one might be some type of supernatural, but still... My mind boggled at the idea of even three demons *skinning* a vampire.

"She was killed no more than four or five hours ago," Dario commented, casually wiping his hand on his jeans. "Otherwise the body would have combusted."

It would have been daylight five hours ago. It got me to wondering if the killer's trophy, the skin, would also need to be safeguarded from daylight. He *had* to have known the victim was a vampire. What was driving his choice of victims, though? And why a vampire?

"How did you find her?"

Dario seemed pretty emotionless about the whole thing, so I was assuming the victim was a rogue and not a member of his *Balaj*. Although Dario *did* seem to turn emotionless whenever it was time for business.

"Remember the vampire in Towson with the wild story about the college girl trying to kill him? Well, last night a rogue I spoke to mentioned an encounter with a zombie. She said she'd picked up a woman for an evening meal, had even gone so far as to bite her. Evidently she tasted horrible, like a long-dead corpse."

"The woman was an orc?" It's all I could think of, remembering my Anderon game and how I'd been told that orcs tasted terrible.

"If orcs look like humans, then it's a possibility. This vampire was completely convinced the woman was a zombie. She said after she bit her, the zombie stabbed her in the back of the neck with something that felt like a sharp awl, then bit down on her arm."

"Ghoul?" They were technically dead, and *did* like human flesh, although there were no reports of them eating live victims. They ate corpses. The older the better.

Dario shook his head. "Ghouls have fangs. This vampire showed me the bite mark. Dull, flat, human incisors. Clear pattern where the teeth had broken the skin and bruising all around the edges. They weren't sharp. It had happened six hours prior and the rogue still had the marks. That's one heck of a bite."

That led me back to demons. If they possessed a human, they'd have the same old teeth as I did.

"Another rogue said a woman of the same description went off with a vampire friend of hers and never came back. She was panicked, thinking maybe we killed her friend. But by the description she gave us, that vampire wasn't one we'd killed."

Was that vampire dead like this woman? Or dead because she'd stayed out too late and couldn't get underground in time? Or maybe she'd moved on, ditching her "friend" for a different town? Either way, this body *must* belong to a different vampire or it would have turned to ash by now.

Unless the killer hid the body during daylight hours, bringing it out tonight. If so, then they wanted it to be discovered. As a warning? Sheesh, the whole thing was just so sick I couldn't even imagine a motive.

"That was last night. You said this happened tonight?" I asked Dario. "That's a potential for two vampire victims. Isn't it odd for someone to be hunting vampires in the same area two nights in a row?"

That took balls of steel. Yeah, these guys were rogues and unaffiliated, but they clearly communicated with each other, and formed short-term alliances. Word would have gotten around. I was now more convinced than ever we were dealing with demons. Either that or a human female really had a death wish.

Human female. No, it couldn't be. But she'd said something at the Inner Harbor about wanting a vampire. I'd thought at the time she'd meant want, as in to date and have sex with, not skin and assume their identity.

"Was the human female young? High school age? White, with pink and blue streaks in her hair and lots of black eyeliner?"

Dario nodded. "That's how both vampires described her."

And now I was rethinking whether the girl seen with Brian Huang and Bradley Lewis was involved or not. Was she also a paranormal creature, or could a human teenage girl possibly have done this?

Then I remembered Russell, and acknowledged that I couldn't rule out a human killer. The necromancer had been able to take down more than a dozen vampires using vengeful spirits. There was no saying a crazy girl who'd watched too many Buffy episodes wouldn't be equally motivated to risk her life this way. But there was the whole skinning component. I couldn't see a vigilante vampire hunter skinning one, *or* killing and skinning innocent humans.

Demons. It *had* to be a group of demons, but something about the theory just seemed off.

Dario nodded. "So there's probably *another* victim like this one somewhere around if what the rogue said last night is true and all were the same attacker. Although we'll not find any proof of what happened to the other victim since her body has most likely turned to ash at this point."

The two dead, well one presumed dead, as well as the vampire who'd been bitten were all women. The female victim who'd survived had been the one who was convinced a zombie had attacked her and the guy in Towson, although I wasn't sure that attack was related to these. The attacker had adapted, going from trying to break a vampire's neck, to stabbing and biting, to...this.

I looked down at the corpse with her bulging eyes and fangs, quickly turning my head away from the gruesome sight. I'd seen far too much of this sort of thing in the past few days. "Do you have any idea who this vampire is? Was?"

Dario shook his head. "Not one of ours. I can ask any other rogues we catch, but there's usually not much of an opportunity for conversation. I've only run across six since I've been up here who were decent vampires just trying to survive. The others are like berserkers. It's all we can do to catch them and put them down. This has got to be the most vicious bunch of renegades I've ever encountered. It's not normal, even among vampires who are starving. I can only hope we can catch and kill them all by the week's end."

I winced. The *Balaj* didn't take prisoners, and I couldn't see a rogue vampire consenting to a question and answer session before execution. Thankfully Dario was willing to ignore Leonora's orders and let the "decent" solitaries go free.

The whole thing was just bizarre. I mean, the idea of a taxidermy-inclined demon team was strange enough, but a demon who went after not just one, but *four* vampires? "How did the woman kill her?" Our usual methods included beheading or destroying the heart, neither of which appeared to have happened to this victim.

"Her heart is gone, but it happened after the skinning." Dario shot me a wry glance. "Don't ask me how I figured that out."

Ugh. "So she incapacitated her somehow, skinned her while she was still alive, and then destroyed her heart?"

Skinning while alive... I didn't want to really think too much about what that must have felt like. The humans had been dead first, exsanguinated, no doubt to make the skinning a cleaner process. The humans had all been left with internal organs intact, too. The fact that the killer had taken this vampire's heart meant she knew about them—and knew how to kill them. That fit with the demon theory.

Dario ran a hand over his short dark hair. "I don't know how the killer incapacitated her. Vampires don't go down easy. This vampire clearly fought with her attacker and lost, but I'm not sure how. Oh, and another thing—I've got no idea why, but the attacker took quite a bit of the vampire's blood as well as her skin."

"The human victims were drained of blood, but we're not sure if the murderers are doing anything with it. The M.E. thought it was to make the skinning process easier."

Dario reached down and turned the woman's head again, pointing to a hole at the base of her neck. "Did the others have this?"

I nodded. "Yeah. That's the same mark the humans had. The killer had to have known this was a vampire though. I mean, even before she attacked her. There's no way either a human *or* a supernatural creature would go into a fight with a vampire unaware and walk away, let alone actually manage to kill one."

"Well, kill one she did, although I'm not ruling out that there may have been two attackers. Perhaps the female lured the vampires in, tried to incapacitate them, then the other joined her once the vampire was down."

I took a deep breath, trying to sort through all this. "So if this is the girl then she's not the innocent accomplice we thought. All three took skins and, if the girl is doing the same as the two boys, all three assumed their skin's identities."

I squinted and thought through my research. There was still a chance this was a really freaky demon possession, but I was leaning toward either a skinwalker or a shapeshifter. If they were to collect enough skins, they'd have myriad disguises and a variety of skills—and powers in the case of this dead vampire.

Three theories was two too many. I felt like throwing my hands in the air and walking away from the whole tangled mess.

Dario turned and jerked his head to the side for me to follow him. I made my way carefully down the dirt path, noticing the two vampires left behind were wrapping the body in a tarp. Normally I'd insist on the police being involved so this latest victim could help provide evidence that might lead to the killer, but the vampires wouldn't want the medical examiner seeing those fangs. I wasn't sure I would either. Some things were better left in the dark, in the realm of nightmares.

"So it looks like the intriguing not-paranormal serial-killer case has landed in your lap after all." Dario paused once we were clear of the dumpster, the two employees still watching us as they smoked. How long *was* their break time?

"Yeah. Now I just need to figure out what these things are. I wonder if the blood means anything? Although from what I've read of demons, skinwalkers, and shapeshifters, none of them drink or do anything associated with blood."

"We're not the only bloodsuckers," Dario commented. "Maybe these three are something else—something that drinks blood as well as takes skins."

The world was filled with supernatural beings who enjoyed a liquid meal. The skin taking and assuming the victim's identity was the most limiting factor in all of this. I needed to concentrate on that and assume the blood thing was irrelevant, or an anomaly.

I rubbed my face. "Guess I need to do more research. Do you think the skin wearing...whatever who is wearing this vampire's skin would try to team up with the other renegades or form her own *Balaj*?"

"Not likely." Dario glanced behind him up the trail. "Solitary vampires are suspicious. She might try to find a partner, but other vampires would notice the slightest thing that was off about her and run for it."

It would take forever for the rumors of an "off" vampire to reach Dario's *Balaj*, especially on the outskirts of their territory. It might be easier to track through the other two killers instead.

"What *about* the skin? Will it survive sunlight exposure? Can you all locate it somehow through smell?"

"Yes, if any of us meet someone posing as this vampire by wearing her skin, we'll know. And no, the skin will not survive sunlight exposure. The vampirism mutation is at a cellular level. I'm assuming if the killer knew enough to take the heart, then she knows enough to preserve the skin appropriately."

But what the heck *was* she? The other question running through my head—what would have happened had she not removed the vampire's heart—was far too gruesome for me to even ask.

"She would have recovered if the killer hadn't taken her heart." Dario shot me a grim smile. "We regenerate. Limbs, most organs, skin. It would have been a long and painful week, but she would have recovered had she kept her heart."

Ew. I really didn't need to have that visual, but it did make me think about something else.

"What about the blood? Let's assume that the killer is drinking it and not just draining the body to make skinning easier. Is there any reason to drink a vampire's blood?"

"Skinning a vampire would be just as much of a bloody chore as skinning a human. If she's drinking the blood..." He shrugged. "There are some healing properties transferred to humans who drink our blood, but they're not substantial. I can't imagine any creature choosing to drink vampire blood. It doesn't have the same life-giving qualities of human blood. Technically we're dead. There's no life-force to transfer with the blood."

Yet another mystery to add to the pile. Dario walked me to my car and I looked at the horizon, calculating about six hours left until sunrise.

"How much longer are you going to be up here?" I grumbled.

He smiled, opening my door for me, bypassing the lock as usual. "What, Ramen noodle dinners not doing it for you? You're wanting me to hurry this up so you can eat decent food once again?"

Yeah. It was the food, not him I missed. Right. "If you don't get back soon, I'm going to start losing weight. It's taken me a month to get some hint of curves going on here. Don't put me back to square one, malnourished and without my daily red wine."

Dario wedged me against the door, his hands in his pockets. I could have edged around him, scooted aside, but I froze, enjoying the feeling of having him so close. We stood there, silent. Each breath I took brushed my breasts lightly against his shirt. Every cell tingled. If only he'd bend his head down and kiss me, press himself against me, run his hands down my body.

"Hopefully just a few more days." His breath was cool on my forehead and I swayed against him. "Think you can hold out until then?"

No. I swallowed and tried to get my traitorous, sex-starved body under control. "Extra cannoli when you get back?"

I felt the rumble of his laughter against me. "Of course."

He stepped back, but not before placing his lips on my forehead for a quick kiss. "Try not to wind up in Philadelphia this time."

And with that he was gone, vanished with a blur of vampire speed while I stood against my car door. I managed to make it home in record time, for once not losing my way and circling the beltway multiple times. It was quiet at my apartment, the parking lot vacant as other tenants enjoyed their night out. I was the only one home early, climbing the steps and thinking of my tangled mess of theories instead of drinking and partying with friends.

I was so engrossed in thought that I almost

missed the white box right in front of my door. A hastily penned note sat on top of it.

Boss said to bring this by, but I can't get in your house. Did you magic it or something? These are for you, so you don't starve to death in the next two days. Please call if there is anything you need and I will provide. Aaron

Below the name was a phone number. I carefully lifted the box, untied the twine and peeked inside, even though I knew what it held. Cannoli, neatly in a line on top of parchment paper.

Dario had sent a Renfield to bring me cannoli. And he'd told the man to put himself at my disposal. All thoughts about our doomed future, about Giselle, about Zac, vanished. He missed me. All the little, as well as the big, things he'd done for me suddenly fit together like pieces of a puzzle.

I unlocked my door and walked in, carefully placing the cannoli in the fridge. It wasn't just the food and the wine, it was everything. This was more than business, it was more than friendship, and it sure as heck was more than just lust.

I wasn't falling in love with Dario, I already was in love with him. And as tragically as this might end, there was no turning back.

CHAPTER 19

THERE WAS A message on the whiteboard when I woke up. I wasn't sure it was in English, but it was definitely a message.

Peterson's buok. Soot in mybxk. Lolgru.

"Your penmanship is disgraceful," I told the fox figurine. "Seriously, Raven. I can't make any of this out beyond 'Peterson's.'"

My cup shattered in a flying whirlwind of pottery, the air around me crackling. I quickly moved books out of the way of the spreading coffee and grabbed a roll of paper towels. "All right. I get that you're frustrated, but I'm trying to bring some humor to this situation. We'll work it out. Just have a little patience."

Words bloomed in lime green on the white board. *Suorg*

Sorry. Okay, so G's might be Y's and U's might be O's and O's might be R's. That made her previous statement even more confusing.

"I've got a better idea." Out came my laptop. I opened the word processing program and put the resin fox in front of it. Typing had to be easier than trying to write without movable hands.

The curser blinked, but no words appeared—either on the laptop or on the whiteboard. Had she worn herself out? That burst of temper had been pretty impressive.

I finished cleaning up the coffee, and made myself a fresh cup, but there was still no further communication upon my return to the table. The little fox's eyes seemed a duller red. I reached down and rubbed my thumb across the resin head. "Rest. Try again when you feel able to. I'll leave the laptop here and if it's in sleep mode or something when you're ready, just bust up another coffee cup to get my attention, okay?"

The eyes glittered red before dimming once more. I smiled, knowing that my friend was starting to regain her usual humor. This was progress. From rolling around the floor to this? She'd managed to identify herself to me, and although the words on the whiteboard were gibberish, I had a feeling they soon wouldn't be. Just a few more days, and I was certain Raven would be able to communicate in at least short, choppy sentences.

But did I have time to wait? Russell had said she was angry, and I had just experienced her frustration. There had to be something important she was trying to tell me—something that could be life or death. Or she was telling me I was leaving the stove on. Or that I had black mold in the kitchen.

Just to be sure I pulled my Peterson's book onto my lap and leafed through it, just as I'd done pretty much every day since the little fox had taken to perching on it. Nothing. At least nothing I hadn't been reading in the last few days.

I sighed and went to set the book on the table, realizing that with the white board, the laptop, and a bunch of boxes there wasn't any room. This place was a mess. Again. I was up early. Raven clearly needed to rest before any further attempts at communication. Might as well clean up a bit before starting in on further skinwalker/shapeshifter research.

Starting with the boxes. They were filled with Raven's books, and given her specialty with Goetic demons, there might be something in one of them about possession and skinning victims. I grabbed the edges of the cardboard and tore at the tape, gently lifting out the contents and sorting them. Within minutes I was lost in the delight of books—old and new. There were references filled with demon names, attributes, and sigils, grimoires that had been published as well as battered copies that looked like she'd scooped them up at a garage sale. There was even a collection of personal grimoires from modern magicians—no doubt deceased. The handwritten pages were yellowed and stained, but a fascinating window into the practice of mages from the last century.

The next box held a wider variety of tomes. Herbal and other naturalist identification reference books as well as spells and incantations from other disciplines. As I reached the bottom of the box, I smiled to see a few books on the history of Templars. Raven had read up on me.

There was one more at the very bottom. It was brand new, with a glossy cover and an uncreased spine. It was a book I never would have thought to find in a Goetic mage's collection, one Reynard or any of the other members of Haul Du would probably never open.

It was Peterson's *Monsters of the New World*.

Why in the world would Raven have this book? I glanced over at my copy, and then back to the pristine version I'd just removed from the box. Maybe *this* was the Peterson's she'd been trying to get me to look at. Was it a different edition? Was there something in this particular book that wasn't in mine?

Peterson's buok. Soot in mybxk. Lolgru. It was what Raven had written on the white board. *Peterson's book. Look in my box? Lolgru*—what the heck did that mean? I sat cross-legged on the floor and hefted the big book onto my lap. Lorelai? Solgrun? I fanned the pages, stopping at one that was a slightly different texture.

Loup-garou. Only after the first page, the following one wasn't Peterson's dry, informative narrative, it was a handwritten page that had been carefully inserted in place of the original. I squinted, recognizing Raven's tight print. As I read, my heart stuttered, tears welling up in my eyes. It was the ritual to remove the demon mark. That's why Raven had delayed in D.C. rather than heading straight to my parents' house. She'd copied Dark Iron's ritual and secreted it away in this book, taking the original with her. If something happened, no one would think to look here—no one but me, eventually, after Reynard delivered the books she'd willed to me.

Oh, God. My friend had come through. Even after death, she'd come through for me. I wiped away the tears and carefully read the ritual. It wouldn't be easy, but I could manage this. The only hitch was it needed to be done at a specific date and time—Halloween, midnight.

Luckily that was only a little more than a month away. One month, and I'd be free of this demon mark. My soul might never be clean after what I'd done to Dark Iron, but without Balsur breathing down my neck, I might be able to stay on a righteous path.

CHAPTER 20

THE RELIEF I felt at finally having a solution in sight to my demon mark meant I was able to turn with renewed energy to the problem of our local band of killers. They had blood that tasted like a rotted corpse, and wore the skin of a human to assume their identity. Skinwalker? Shapeshifter? A stealthier-than-usual demon with a really twisted sense of humor? Or some sort of zombie? Either way, I'd exhausted pretty much every book in my own research library. It was time to turn to someone with a far more extensive collection, who'd spent decades devoted to information on the supernatural. I set the fox figure in front of the computer, just in case Raven was able to communicate again, and picked up my phone.

"Aria." I heard the click of the phone switching to speaker, because that's how my parents' rolled. Dad sounded cheerful. I could hear noise in the background, like something frying on the stove. Unbidden, the scent of French toast and bacon surfaced in my mind.

"I've got good news," I announced. "I found the ritual to remove the demon mark. Raven had hidden it in one of her books. If all goes well, after Halloween the only marks I will have on my body are scars."

"That's wonderful!" Mom's voice sounded as if she were across the room. "Do you need supplies or any help with the ritual? Anything we can get for you or any way we can assist?"

"I'll let you know. I haven't studied it very much yet. I've got a few other things I need to concentrate on right now, then I'll start working on prepping for the ritual."

It was six weeks out after all. I doubted there was anything in there that I couldn't manage to acquire in six weeks. If Dark Iron could get his hands on it, I, with my Templar resources, should be able to.

"No more demon summoning, Aria," Dad warned. "If you need help with something, you call me. I don't like you messing around with the underworld."

I wouldn't...unless it was an emergency and the only option. But I wasn't about to tell my father that.

"Actually that's why I'm calling, Dad. I need to pick your brains about some stuff. Can I rain-check the in-person visit? I've got to work this afternoon and can't come down right now."

I heard him sigh. "Of course I'll help, but we'd really like you to come down next weekend, Aria. Roman and Athena and the kids will be here and we're doing a family weekend. Plus, you know how Gran loves it when you visit. She's not getting any younger, honey."

No one was, but I had a feeling Essie would outlast my parents and probably me, too. "I promise. I'm supposed to work Sunday night, but I'll switch with Chalese. She's wanting something called 'balayage' on her hair and it evidently costs about the same as a used BMW, so she's eager for the extra hours."

"What's balayage?" I heard my dad whisper. I could practically see my mother shrugging in the background. Her natural blond hair had only become more beautiful with the increasing streaks of silver. I doubt she'd ever been within twenty feet of hair color.

"There was a murder here earlier this week—a dead body was found skinned in a museum broom closet." I didn't tell them that I'd been the one that found it, or that it had toppled out on me from said closet. Or that I was going into the closet to make out with a guy.

"Skinned?" Mom's voice rose in pitch with the word. "What kind of monster does that?"

"Exactly. At first we, the police and I, thought it was a human serial killer with a weird taxidermy thing going on, but recent events have caused me to believe the killers might be non-human."

"Killers? As in plural?" My dad sounded intrigued, which was a good thing. Even if he didn't know what the murderer was, interesting him in the case was a way to assure he'd spend a sleepless night in the vault checking information in manuscripts only he had handy access to.

"We think there are three. One of the suspects has the same knee replacement serial number as the dead body found in the museum. Another was seen fleeing the scene of his sister's murder with the first suspect. His backpack left behind contained a human skin and a cooler in his garage contained a skinned body."

"Two." I could practically hear the gears turning in my dad's amazing mind. "Could be any number of creatures who utilize human skin, or could still be a human murderer. What makes you think the killer is paranormal?"

"Both of their families insisted that they suddenly changed this week, that they were imposters inside their loved ones' bodies. The dead woman even called a priest in to exorcise a demon from her brother. That's how convinced she was that whoever was walking around in his body wasn't him."

"Okay," Dad mused. "Could still be humans. People snap. There are triggers that can cause a psychotic break that would make family members feel they no longer knew their loved ones."

"Last night a dead vampire was found skinned up north of the city. Dario says a vampire bit the suspect and she tasted like a rotted corpse. The victim was somehow subdued, her neck broken and blood drained before she was skinned. After skinning her, the killer ripped the vampire's heart out to ensure she remained dead."

I heard my parents muttering in the background and waited for them to talk among themselves before continuing.

"It would take a lot to subdue a vampire like that and keep them down while they were skinned," Dad mused. "Sounds like the killer is either non-human or a mage with a spell that would freeze or knock a vampire out."

"Which fits with a skinwalker," I interjected. "They're mages. If they're powerful enough to use a human skin to assume the victim's identity then they're powerful enough to spell a vampire unconscious."

"But why a vampire?" Mom asked. "A mage that skilled should be able to lengthen their lifespan without the constant hunger and sunlight limitations of being a vampire."

"I think the skins are temporary," I said. "Like a disguise. If they collect enough, it would be almost impossible to track them. The skinned bodies will take forever to identify—if they *can* be identified at all. We lucked out with Huang and his knee replacement device. Otherwise he'd still be a John Doe at the morgue."

"So there has to be a reason she wants to be a vampire," Dad mused. "Are these three trying to take over the city? Are they consumed by a need for vengeance, like your necromancer friend was?"

A vampire, a middle-aged museum employee, a deadbeat college drop-out, a teenager from South Carolina, a girl who wears too much make-up and "wants" a vampire... It was an eclectic batch of individuals.

"I have a hunch they're not thinking that far ahead. It's like they're children turned loose in a candy shop after hours, taking whatever catches their eye. The girl expressed a fascination for vampires. Except for the museum victim, the others are young guys."

"But how could kids have that sort of magical ability?" Mom asked. "Unless they're old in terms of years, but emotionally still children."

"Which is a strike against skinwalkers," I reasoned—so far my best match in terms of paranormals who take and wear human skins.

"Not necessarily," Dad cautioned. "What if they are part of some cult, taken and sequestered at a young age to learn their magical skills? Maybe their mentor died and this is the first time they've been out in the big world on their own. It's got to be a heady feeling. And it would explain the odd victim choices and lack of restraint. Just an idea."

"Or shapeshifters," Mom added. "They age very slowly compared to us. I don't know if any of them use human skins, but there are types who can kill and take on a human's identity."

"What about demon possession?" I asked, throwing yet another of my theories into the mix.

"I don't know," Dad mused. "I'm leaning toward skinwalker. It's the best fit in terms of the human skin and the unconscious vampire. Perhaps there's something in the skinwalker magic that rots their insides, metaphorically as well as physically?"

"I wouldn't completely rule out shapeshifter," Mom cautioned. "Demonic possession is probably not what's going on here. Three of them would be running around trying to kill as many people as possible, not impersonating their victims. Skinning would be dramatic for a demon, but they'd make sure to present the body for the biggest shock."

A skinned corpse falling out of the closet of a museum in the middle of a posh reception was a big shock, but concealing bodies in rarely-used coolers and skins in backpacks, stuffing a skinned vampire body in out-of-the-way bushes—none of that matched with what I knew about demon personality. Mom was right.

I heard Dad stirring something in the background. "I'll look into it, Mavia, but I don't believe the shapeshifters you're thinking of require a human skin. They kill their victims so they can easily assume their identity, and I believe they have a method to collect their thoughts and memories, but I don't recall any past incidents where they've skinned victims."

"So skinwalkers or shapeshifters, but probably not shapeshifters?" My parents had been a huge help. I was down to two theories instead of three.

"Navaho or Cherokee skinwalkers are where I'm leaning in this one," Dad continued. "The Cherokee ones are called spearfinger, because when they kill one finger extends into a sort of long hollow knife to stab their victim and drain the blood."

"Wait." That sounded oddly familiar. "Do they stab them in the back of the neck? Because the M.E. said that's where some type of awl or knife was inserted in order to drain blood from the victims."

"I believe my notes say they've always stabbed in the chest. Mavia? What have you seen?"

Seen? My mother had actually *seen* a spearfinger?

"Only one case in Georgia," Mom chimed in. "The stab wound *was* in the chest, but I don't know if they always kill that way or not."

Crap. "Skinwalker, either Cherokee style or Navaho style. Shapeshifter, although that's less likely. And one of them either has a vampire fetish or has watched too much Blade."

"Or." My heart sank at that one word from my father. "Or it could be something else. I'm not as knowledgeable about American legends outside of the U.S. and Canada, but I believe there's an Aztec god who also has something to do with skinning his human victims. And I seem to recall another god from South America who also collects human skins. Let me check with Javier. He'll know better than me. It's pretty farfetched, but I'd be negligent not to throw it out there."

I had no time to wait for my father to have a face-to-face meeting with this Javier. Templars didn't exchange information over the phone or via the internet, even though my dad seemed to be making an exception in that rule for me.

Theory three was now: A south-of-the-border god skins humans and vampires in the Baltimore area. Details at ten.

I needed to cross some of these off my list. Shapeshifter seemed less likely after talking with my father. The shapeshifter didn't fit based on what he's said, and the demons? I'd expect them to cause more chaos, to be more into a spree of mass killings rather than this onsie-twosie stuff. If this was three demons I'd think the body count would be higher, and they'd be more prominently displayed. Demons had nothing to fear from human law enforcement. Why hide the body in a broom closet when you could perch it on an exhibition of medieval jewelry? Why run from the scene of Amanda Lewis's murder when you could just kill her boyfriend and add one more corpse to the mix?

Mom was right, this just didn't feel like demons. Which left me with the skinwalkers, or this new, disturbing idea of my father's that the killer might be an Aztec or Incan god.

Oh, Lord, don't let it be a god. With scant worshipers they'd been dormant for millennia. If one of them awoke, it would take every Knight of the Temple to conquer them. I don't think they could even be banished. The best we probably could do was contain them.

Contain. The worry that had gnawed at my insides since last month had been fading, but now it was back in full force. The death mages had been trying to contain some horrible unnamed thing from Baltimore. They'd needed human sacrifice as well as soul magic to hold this monster in check. What if that monster was loose now that the rituals had stopped? Chuck as well as the others in Fiore Noir had said it was only a matter of time.

Soul magic to stop a god. My stomach churned at the thought. Could this be what was plaguing Baltimore? If so, it was only going to get worse. Gods had servants, and I envisioned more and more of these murders with skinned corpses, all dedicated to the glory of whoever. A god with minions who killed for him, who assumed the victims' identities and searched for additional sacrifices.

I needed to see Chuck. Sean said he'd just been sentenced to twenty at Jessup. I said goodbye to my parents, promising to see them next weekend for family time, then immediately pulled up driving directions to the prison as well as visiting hours and protocol.

I'd call Tremelay to facilitate the meeting, then get on the road. If I hurried, I could talk with Chuck and be back in town in time for my shift at Holy Grounds. Hopefully.

CHAPTER 21

Jessup was going to have to wait until tomorrow morning. I'd asked Tremelay to coordinate an interview with Chuck, and was just about to update him with my three theories when he interrupted.

"We got Huang."

Huh? "What do you mean you got him?"

"Caught him at the bus station trying to get a ticket to South Carolina. He didn't have enough money and was acting suspicious, so security called in his name. He's at the station now."

"I thought you didn't have enough to charge him with anything."

Tremelay snorted. "We don't, but we can hold him for twenty-four hours. Want me to sneak you in to watch while I talk with him?"

Did I ever. I needed to make sure the detective was safe while in a room with what could be a dangerous paranormal creature. A skinwalker. Or something else. I'm sure Tremelay was smart enough to take precautions, but he was assuming Huang was either a human serial killer, or an equally human accomplice.

"I don't think Huang is human." I told him. "I mean, he once was human, but he's not now. That body in the broom closet at the Walters? That's Brian

Huang. The guy you've got in custody is someone else who is wearing his skin."

There was a moment of silence, then a sharp intake of breath from the detective. "Ainsworth, sometimes you scare the holy fuck out of me. This guy is wearing a dead man's *skin*? Like that Hannibal dude or something?"

"Well no, not exactly. He's not a human trying to escape prison by slapping another guy's face on top of his, this is a type of mage—a skinwalker. At least I think it is."

"Wait. *More* evil mages? You're shitting me, Ainsworth. The last ones kill and steal souls. These ones kill and steal skins?"

"I'm not a hundred percent, but that's where I'm heading. One killed a vampire, Tremelay. Do you know what it takes to kill a vampire? She killed and skinned it. That's not normal human stuff."

The detective sighed. "Get in here. I want you with me when I interview this guy. The Lieutenant is gonna have my nuts in a vice for this, but if Huang's not human, then I need you by my side."

I hung up, thrilled. Well, not thrilled that people were being murdered and skinned, but thrilled that I was a resource to the Baltimore PD, that I was the person Tremelay needed by his side when interviewing a possible skinwalker. Yeah. Ego boost big-time.

Brian Huang was in the interview room when I arrived, curled up on a chair with his head in his hands. He was crying, and at that moment I didn't see a forty-year-old father of two, but a child. I walked in and sat next to Tremelay, well aware of Norwicki on the other side of the two way mirror.

Our suspect looked up at me, his brows

furrowing as his eyes traveled down my face and body, snagging on the red cross tattoo on my wrist. "You're the Templar."

Not, *the* Templar. Just *a* Templar. Still, I wondered how he knew to look for the tattoo, and wondered at the rising note of panic in his voice.

"We need to know about some recent murders," Tremelay told him. "Not just the one at the museum, but the murder of Amanda Lewis. You've been seen in the company of Bradley Lewis who is a suspect in his sister's murder."

"You've also been seen in the company of a girl who killed a vampire in Hampton last night," I added.

Huang had remained stoic in the face of Tremelay's comments, but he'd blanched at mine. "There are no such things as vampires," he said in a wavering voice.

"Your friend has a different opinion." I pulled up my cell phone and showed him the picture of their embrace in the station parking lot. "She wanted a vampire. She got a vampire. And your other friend, Bradley, killed his sister."

Tremelay scowled at me and I winced, realizing that I was co-opting his investigation. I better shut up and let him take the lead, whether Huang was a skinwalker or not.

"I didn't kill anybody." Huang's voice was reaching the upper octaves. "I've *never* killed anybody. Never. Becca either. Yeah, she has a thing for vampires. She's read too many of those romances with dark princes biting necks and all. Still, she's not a killer. She's just...confused."

"Tell that to two women in Hampton," Tremelay said, eyeing me with a scowl. "Tell me about your friendship with Bradley Lewis and this Becca."

Huang's breathing increased to the point where I thought we may need to call for a paper bag. "I don't know any Bradley Lewis. Becca is...she's someone I've known from when I was a kid."

"Becca is all of sixteen," Tremelay said. "What, did you baby sit her or something? Who are her parents? Do you know them?"

"No! She's...we were raised by Grandmother." His eyes darted back and forth between us, wet with tears. "I just want to go home. Can I go home? It was all a mistake. I thought I'd be happy, but I'm not. I just want to go home."

"There's no going home, Brian. Not until we catch the murderers." Tremelay leaned back in his chair. "Bradley Lewis was seen fleeing from the scene of his sister's house while she lay dead in the bedroom. There was the skin of a boy from South Carolina in his backpack—Lawton King. There was the skinned body of another man in a cooler in the garage."

Huang began to sob. "He took it. He took the skin. I'm trapped. I can't be anything but this unless I kill and I don't want to kill. Please. I just want to go home."

Tremelay's eyes widened, looking to me with a mute appeal. Yeah, Huang sounded crazy, and I tried to figure out what was going on with the skin situation. Was he a victim too? Had a forty something year old man been taken in by a young man and a teenage girl?

"How do you know Bradley Lewis," Tremelay insisted.

"He'll kill me. You gotta understand, he'll kill me. I just want to go home."

"You're not going home." The detective leaned forward. "You're going to jail. Cooperate, and we'll think about a deal. Otherwise at the very least you're an accomplice to three, if not five, murders."

Huang buried his head in his hands. "I want a lawyer. You said I could have a lawyer, well I want one. And I want Grandmother."

Who the heck was Grandmother? I thought of Huang's elderly parents and wondered how old his grandmother could possibly be. Heck, she'd have to be almost Essie's age. And was she in China?

That is, if he really was Huang. If I was right and the dead body in the closet was Huang, then this was somebody else wearing his skin—someone who was desperate to get back to South Carolina and his grandmother.

Wait. Hadn't the skinned body of the boy been from South Carolina? I thought again of the snarky boy with Becca at the Inner Harbor. Had that been where they were from? Were they once four and they killed one and took his skin? With the ability to assume other's identities, I had no idea who these skinwalkers really were.

Or even if they truly were skinwalkers.

The detective raised his hands and waved toward the door. A uniformed officer came in and escorted Huang out. The man was hunched over, sobbing the entire time. I felt for him. Either this was a family man, a loving husband and a father of two who'd somehow been embroiled in these murderers, or a monster who'd assumed the innocent man's identity and was an amazing actor.

I just couldn't believe the actor part. But I equally believed that this man who'd just left the interview room wasn't the Brian Huang his parents had raised, that his wife had married. Still, he was oddly sympathetic and in spite of the evidence, part of me wanted to believe that he really didn't kill anybody.

Which left Bradley Lewis. And this Becca.

I kept thinking of the man in Huang's skin my whole shift at the coffee shop. Becca and the other boy had been young. From his actions, I was thinking whoever was impersonating Huang was young, too. And Bradley Lewis wasn't much older. Had three of them journeyed up from South Carolina, met Bradley and sucked him into their schemes? I found it hard to believe that Lewis could have mastered the magic involved in skinwalking in such a short time, but the murder of his sister did fit with the theory. She'd be the close relative he'd needed to murder to gain the skill.

Had three teens managed to become adept at it? Who had trained them? And what about Huang's insistence that he hadn't killed anyone? I got the impression he was telling the truth, but all my research said he'd needed to kill a relative to gain the skinwalker ability. And *someone* killed Huang. I didn't know the details of the magic, but I assumed only the murderer could wear the skin. That meant the teen impersonating Huang had to have at least killed twice.

Which made him a liar. And me terrible at scenting out the truth.

I was wrapping up my shift, eyeing the gray of dusk and the sudden burst of gold from the streetlights when Tremelay called.

"He's gone."

"Mmm," I replied, giving the pastry counter another wipe. "His lawyer made you release him?"

"No. When the lawyer got here and we went to get him from the holding cell, he was gone. Well, most of him was gone."

Most of him? He'd left behind a rope made of clothing or a lock of hair? "What do you mean?"

"Brian Huang's skin is in the cell, but the rest of him isn't."

I thought back to the horror movie the detective had referenced, where a prisoner escaped by slapping a dead guard's facial skin on top of his own and riding out in the ambulance. This was reversed, though. The skin was still in the cell, and the body was gone. I doubted a skinned corpse walked unnoticed out of the prison. So where *was* the body that had once walked around in that skin?

CHAPTER 22

"YOU SURE YOU want to go to Jessup today?"
Tremelay's voice was rapid-fire with
excitement—more excitement than last night when
Huang's gruesome disappearance had rocked the
entire police station. How in the world were they
going to explain that one? Someone somehow gets
into a holding cell, kills their person of interest and
takes the corpse, leaving the skin behind?

I wasn't even sure how to explain it, even with
my skinwalker theory. Did Huang, or whoever he
was, shed the human skin and turn himself into a
bird or mouse to escape? Because that was pretty
much the only way I saw him getting out of that
holding cell and a station with armed officers all over
the place.

My trip to visit Chuck at the prison wasn't
urgent. At this point I doubted we were dealing with
an Aztec god. I just wanted to cross it off my list, and
to try to pry out of the Fiore Noir member what it
was they'd been performing death and soul magic to
guard against. The killers that I'd begun to believe
were skinwalkers were a more immediate problem
than whatever unknown situation loomed on the
horizon.

"I can push it to this afternoon or tomorrow.
What's up? Have you found Huang again, or

whoever Huang was under the skin?"

It was going to be impossible to find him now. I had no idea who, teenager or not, had been impersonating Brian Huang. The only ones I'd seen in what I assumed was their regular form was Becca and that boy at the Harbor. Somehow I doubted Huang with his tears and his desperate pleas to go home was the same kid as that jerk with Becca.

"No, and I don't think we're going to find Huang. We've got his skin. We found what I assume was his body at the Walters in the broom closet. At this point we're just looking for Bradley Lewis as our murder suspect."

"So you found *him*? Or Becca?" Although I had a feeling Becca would be underground right now if she'd clung to her vampire fixation.

"Nope. I had a guy call me who said he heard about the murder at the museum and has information for me. He doesn't want to come down to the station. Wants to meet me at a park in downtown. Thought you might be interested in tagging along given that we're most likely dealing with a supernatural murderer and not the run-of-the-mill serial killer."

I weighed the risks of delaying my meeting with Chuck and the potential information I'd miss if I didn't attend this interview. The interview won. Chuck's information could wait.

Tremelay met me as I locked my car, walking with me to the park bench where a thin man with a strawberry-blond flat-top and a day's growth of golden whiskers on his chin and cheeks sat. He smiled nervously at me as I walked up, nodding politely when the detective made the introductions. We sat on the bench across from him. And waited.

"You had something you wanted to tell us?" Tremelay prompted. "About the murder at the Walters Art Museum?"

Stu Moorman rocked on the wrought iron seat, the squeak-squeak of metal loosely bolted to pavement driving me to the edge of insanity.

"This is gonna sound crazy," Stu said. "I didn't want to tell anyone, but when I read about the psycho-skinner in the paper, I knew I had to say something."

What, what, what? Janice usually gave me a head's up before she ran an article on something we'd discussed in private. I looked back and forth between the detective and Stu until Tremelay pulled a folded paper out of his pocket and handed it over to me.

It wasn't The Sun, and it wasn't Janice. Somebody had leaked information on the skinned body at the Walters to the *City Paper*, and they'd gone with it. I skimmed the article and grimaced. Janice would be pissed that she'd been scooped.

Tremelay ran a hand through his hair. "This is the second guy we've had today with supposedly firsthand information on the killer," he told me. "Norwicki just came back from the last lead, which had turned out to be a man performing home-tanning with deer hides he'd gotten from butcher shops that catered to hunters."

Ugh. I'll bet his neighbors loved that.

As if reading my mind, Tremelay nodded. "Evidently his basement looked like a house of horrors with hides tacked to boards suspended from the ceiling. Whole place stank of decomposition and chemicals. But no, he is not our killer."

"This isn't about someone tanning leather in

their basement," Stu said, rocking the bench again. "It was something else. Something worse. I think I know the people who killed that man at the museum."

"What did you see, Mr. Moorman?" Tremelay asked.

Squeak. Squeak. Squeak. "I was down in South Carolina, looking at a few things. I'm a picker, you know, like those guys on TV?"

I'd seen the show. Two guys who roamed the country visiting elderly collectors, and searching flea markets and estate sales for possible antiques.

"I sometimes do museum transfers or pick up donated items. Usually small stuff like a pair of forceps that the Museum of Civil War Medicine in Frederick wants. This time I was bringing up a set of knives for the Walters."

I sat back in my chair, already feeling like this was a waste of time. Cursed knives that skinned victims on their own, that killed that guy I found in the closet of the museum? Whatever wild story this guy had, I might as well enjoy it.

"On the way back I saw these hitchhikers just outside of Spartanburg. It was raining, and they didn't look much more than teenagers in age. Two boys and a girl. I figured they were runaways because they didn't care where I was going as long as it was north."

And now I was on the edge of my seat, envisioning the plot to a slasher horror movie. *Cursed knives skin three teenage hitchhikers.* Or *three teenage hitchhikers steal cursed knives that turn them into psycho skinwalkers.*

That actually fit. Becca and the two guys steal a knife that turns them into...something, then they hook up with Bradley Lewis and go on a killing spree. Made as much sense as skilled teenage mage skinwalkers.

Stu shifted nervously on his bench, the squeak in double-time. "I couldn't just leave them in the rain like that, but I was a little worried with three of them and just me, so I made them ride in the bed of the truck. It's got a cap on it, so it's out of the rain. I didn't have anything back there but a neon sign I'd gotten in Greenville and some lunchboxes from the 60's I'd grabbed on my way down. Nothing three teenagers would think worth stealing or could use as a weapon or anything."

The guy sounded pretty safety-conscious so far. Well, as safety conscious as a man picking up three hitchhikers could be. I waited for the gruesome part of the story, and wasn't disappointed.

"We stopped for gas in Roanoke. They got out and stretched, said they wanted to keep going with me. I felt kinda bad for them back there in the bed of the truck for hours, wet as they were, so I bought them some coffee and snacks at the quick mart. We didn't stop again until that rest stop on 70 between Hagerstown and Frederick. I had a few phone calls to make and the three of them went into the rest stop. It had been a while, so I went in to check on them, tell them I needed to get going. That's when I saw it."

Squeak, squeak, squeak. I held my breath, waiting for dead, skinned teenagers at the rest stop.

"They had some guy on the floor of the handicapped stall, naked with his clothes in the sink. I could see the blood on the floor, hear cutting noises, like they were slicing them up. I looked around the corner, just to see what was going on. The one boy had this long curved knife that looked like it came right out of his finger. He was using it to peel the skin from the man and was yelling at the others, telling them that they needed to get with the program, that they needed to grow up and start getting their own skins because he wasn't going to do it for them like Grandmother did. The other boy was crying and gagging like he was going to puke. The girl kept saying she didn't want this guy, arguing that the one boy didn't have any reason to kill the man or need for his skin when he had a perfectly good one he was wearing right now. That's when I ran."

"You got in your car and drove off." I added. It's what I would have done.

Stu shook his head. "I ran into the bushes and threw up. Then I hid there for a while. My phone was in the car, and I was scared that they'd seen me, that they were after me. After half an hour or so, I got up my nerve and bolted to my car. They were in the bed like nothing happened, chatting with each other, sharing a soda. None of them had a spot of blood on them, and I wondered if I was crazy, if I'd imagined it all. I didn't know what to do so I got in and kept going. Parked the car on Charles Street, took the knives to the museum. The kids weren't in the truck when I got back, so I got the heck out of there and went home."

"You drove an hour with three murderers in the back of your truck?" Tremelay's voice was as squeaky as the bench, his eyes huge as he leaned closer toward Stu.

The man nodded. "I'd been driving for twelve hours, hadn't slept in days. I'd been living on Slim Jims and Red Bull. There was other people at that rest stop. Nobody screamed. I was the only one who seemed to have seen anything. And when I got back to the truck, there them kids sat, chatting away like nothing happened, not a spot of blood anywhere... I thought maybe I imagined it. Then I read that there's this crazy running around the city skinning people and I thought maybe I *hadn't* imagined it."

Tremelay sighed. "Can you come down to the station and describe them enough for a sketch artist?"

"I took pictures." Stu pulled out his cell phone and handed it to Tremelay. I looked over his shoulder at the blurry photos, taken through the back glass of a pick-up window.

They might have been blurry, but between the five snapshots, I had enough to make out their faces. Becca with her thick eyeliner and colorfully accented hair. The Goth-looking boy that was with her at the Inner Harbor. And a third boy with dark brown skin and wide, terrified eyes.

There was something in those eyes that reminded me of Huang.

"I'll bet that's Lawton King," Tremelay told me, pointing to the picture of the frightened boy. "I'm not positive. The only picture we've got was from when he was six. That and...you, know. The backpack."

The skin in the backpack. But where was Lawton King's body? Or maybe Lawton King hadn't always been Lawton King.

"The girl and possibly King, but that's it. None of these three are Bradley Lewis," Tremelay said, disappointed. Still, he forwarded the pictures to both his and my cell phones.

"I think Bradley might be a victim," I told him. "This boy took his identity, and this other boy, maybe-Lawton, took Huang's."

"They called him Gary," Stu pointed to the Goth-looking boy. "He was clearly in charge. I think maybe he was older or something. He was the one doing the skinning in the bathroom."

Gary. Becca. Maybe-Lawton. "Did this boy have a name?" I pointed to the one with the haunted eyes.

"Landon or Lawson or something. Felt bad for that kid. Seemed like they'd dragged him along and he was in over his head."

I squirmed with excitement. Although we had a long way to go to catch these guys, at least we had a clue where they'd come from and who they were. Gary, the jerk from the Harbor, the one who'd said he needed to "change" and get some money from his bitch of a sister. He had become Bradley Lewis. Lawton, the one who'd missed the meeting because of his kid's soccer game—the one his wife had forced him to go to, he'd become Brian Huang. And Becca, the vampire obsessed girl. Well, she'd gotten her vampire. Whether she was still alive or had caught a ray of sunlight and burned to death was still unknown.

"So, where do you think they put the skin from the rest stop?" I asked Stu.

"Probably a backpack. They each had one. They were dark green, so I couldn't tell if there was blood on the packs or not. I didn't see any blood in the back of my truck when I was unloading. That's why I thought maybe I'd imagined the whole thing."

"Was this guy working at the museum the night you dropped off the knives?" Tremelay asked, sliding a picture of Brian Huang in front of Stu.

"Yeah, he was there. There was the woman who signed for them. She's in charge of the armory and weapons exhibits. Elsa Cartwright. There was another guy who was a security guard. I think this guy in the picture was cataloging something. I remember as Ms. Cartwright and I were leaving, he called out that he'd probably be another hour before he could go home. She reminded him that he needed to be in early the next morning for some special function. Calligraphy or something."

"And the kids weren't in the truck when you came out of the museum?" the detective asked.

Stu shook his head. Tremelay thanked the man, handing him his card as he stood and motioned for me to follow him.

"I don't know what to think," the detective grumbled. "Three kids. Do you think they hooked up with Brian Huang and later with Bradley Lewis? Are we looking for five instead of two killers?"

"No, we're looking for three." I told him about my suspicions.

"Huang was pathetic." Tremelay leaned against my car as we spoke, flicking through his notebook. "Think that Gary guy killed him and made Lawton wear his skin?"

"I don't know. I want to believe Lawton/Huang when he said he hadn't killed anybody, but skinwalkers need to kill in order to gain the power. Plus I don't think that one can wear a skin they haven't taken themselves."

The detective shook his head. "Either way, he's killed *someone*. And this Gary kid killed Bradley and Amanda Lewis. Although where Bradley Lewis's body went to is anybody's guess. We've got Huang's body and skin accounted for. Lawton's skin but no body. And an as-yet unidentified body from the cooler."

"That could be Bradley Lewis," I told him.

"Maybe. It takes forever for the damned DNA lab. Wish we had a quicker way of doing this."

Another thing I'd need to research. If Chuck could identify the owner of an object by killing a few chickens, I should be able to figure out a non-death magic spell to do the same with skins and bodies. Kind of a magical DNA test.

"Walk with me," Tremelay pushed away from the car. "Let's get coffee and go over all this."

I followed him. "It's looking like skinwalkers, even though that leaves a few loose ends. It's the most logical conclusion to all this."

"Then what's the girl doing?" The detective asked. "No one saw or mentioned her since she was hugging Huang in the station parking lot, then she's suddenly in Hampton killing vampires?"

"She's got a fixation with them and Gary wouldn't help her," I told Tremelay. "He was making fun of her. I saw the pair of them at the Inner Harbor the morning after the Walters murder and eavesdropped because she was talking about vampires and he was being such a jerk. I recognized her when she was with Huang at the station and started connecting the dots. But I think they've split for good. At least, Becca and the two boys have. Lawton is obviously trying to get back to South Carolina, and who knows what's on Gary's mind."

"Lawton will probably go back to Gary. He's scared and he doesn't have any money or way to get home. Gary is all he knows. Wait. There really *are* vampires?" Tremelay stopped so quickly I almost ran into the back of him. "And that black guy who was in your apartment when we arrested the mages last month, *he's* a vampire?"

"Yeah. But these skinwalkers are more important right now." I'd purposely kept this from Tremelay, not wanting to overwhelm him. Demons, angels, and mages who sacrificed other humans was enough to digest in the course of a month. I'd hoped to wait a bit more before revealing all this to him.

And I wasn't sure I wanted to deal with questions about the vampires either. Tremelay had to have watched the movies, read the books, heard the legends. He'd want to know how they fed, how humans played into their lives.

"This is all starting to come together," I told him. "If these three kids that Stu picked up in South Carolina are skinwalkers, then in addition to their regular teenage identities, they've got Bradley Lewis, and a vampire north of the city. I don't know if they've taken any other skins, so we'll need to act fast."

"If they keep changing their identities, we'll never catch them," the detective mused, stopping at a food truck and ordering two coffees.

"Exactly. Luckily the vampire one will probably be the easiest to catch. She can only go out at night, and she'll be easily picked up if she comes close to any of the other vampires."

"If they catch her, then she might be able to lead us to the other two," Tremelay said.

I nodded. "The catch is I'm not one hundred percent positive what sort of monster these three are. Most likely, they're skinwalkers, but they *might* be shapeshifters. Also, it's a long shot, but I don't want to rule out the Aztec god thing too soon."

"A god?" Tremelay handed me a coffee. "Seriously? And I thought demons were bad. Why couldn't we just have a crazy serial killer? Why an Aztec god?"

"Probably not the Aztec god," I tried to reassure him. "I'm leaning toward skinwalker, but I need more information to narrow it down. That's why I wanted to go up to Jessup."

"Charles Kennedy Jones." Tremelay nodded. "You've got it, Ainsworth. Be at Jessup at two this afternoon, and I'll make sure he's ready and waiting."

CHAPTER 23

T HERE WAS NO note from Raven when I got home, either on my laptop or on the dry erase board. I tried hard to hide my disappointment and worry, chatting cheerfully with her about the Stu interview and my pending visit to Jessup as I got ready to go. The little fox figurine hadn't moved from the table, its eyes still dull. Had breaking the coffee cup taken that much out of her? Raven never was able to manage her temper, and she was a bit of a control freak. Her current state had to have been driving her nuts.

Setting her closer to the laptop, I set my wards and headed out. My phone rang just as I was pulling out of my parking lot. I grimaced when I saw it was Janice and reluctantly answered her call.

"Did you *see* that article? Did you see it?"

I imagined her wild-eyed, froth flying from her mouth like a rabid animal. What surprised me wasn't her anger, but the fact that the article had been out for twenty-four hours before she'd seen it.

"I never read that rag. *Never*, "she ranted. "Someone at work handed it to me, wondering why I wasn't up to speed on this, why we'd been scooped by the damned *City Paper*."

I winced. "Is he still alive? The guy who handed you the paper, I mean. Will your next article be about how a reporter snapped and killed one of her coworkers?"

"It's *not* funny, Aria. This is my job. I held back on it and now I look incompetent. Do you know how that makes me feel? He even stole the name I came up with for the killer."

"Sorry. I didn't mean to tease you when you're upset." Although, to be honest, *I* was the one who came up with the name Psychotic Skinner, not Janice.

"Did he get his information from you?" Janice accused.

"No! I don't even know the guy. The only reason I know about the article is Tremelay showed me a copy this morning." Janice had to have been really upset to even think such a thing of me.

"Sorry." She seemed to be calming down. "I just hate to get scooped, then to have Tony rub my nose in it like that..."

Teasing aside, I was honestly surprised Tony was still among the living. "Besides, if the reporter had gotten his information from me, then he would have known that there are three serial killers, not just one. He also would have known that they're not human."

"Woohoo!" And now Janice was excited. "Demons? Please say it's demons so I can work in the exorcism in Canton. Lay it on me girl. I've got to get something in to redeem myself, here."

"I'm not positive what it is yet, but it seems that three something-or-others posing as two teenage boys and one teenage girl hitchhiked their way to Baltimore from South Carolina. They kill their victims, take their skin and assume the victim's identity. One of them seems to have a vampire fetish because she attacked several north of the city and managed to kill and skin at least one of them."

Silence met my words. I heard Janice suck in a huge breath and let it out. "That's probably the most frightening thing I've ever heard. More frightening than occult mages sacrificing humans."

"Makes it hard to catch them when they could be anybody," I complained. "Unless we find the skinned body and can quickly identify it, we've got no idea who they're impersonating."

I heard Janice scribbling in the background. "Can't they speed up DNA testing? Make it a priority?"

"No. There are only so many labs that do that sort of thing and with murder, everything's a priority. Plus DNA testing doesn't do us any good if the victim didn't have theirs on file. If the monster is walking around in their skin impersonating the victim, we might not even have a missing person's report. Nobody reported Brian Huang missing. Or Bradley Lewis."

"I can dig around and see if there are any other reports of demonic possession. Most of them are probably bogus, but could be another Bradley Lewis out there," Janice offered.

It would help. "Thanks, I'm on my way to check out one of the theories on these guys, then I'll call you back. The vampires might be able to help, too. They got a good read on the one dead vampire, and should be able to recognize if someone's walking around in her skin."

"Mmmm." Now there was rapid typing in the background, along with a beep. "Call me this afternoon?" Janice asked, her voice distracted. "I gotta get on this, and Sean keeps texting me to call him. I hope he's not cancelling tonight."

I promised to call her and hung up, musing over the fact that she'd seen the developer every night since they'd met. Personally that would drive me nuts to see someone every single night, to have them texting and calling me when we weren't *really* a couple.

Oh. Dario. Okay, maybe with the right person, that amount of contact wouldn't be irritating. I might be suspicious of Sean, but deep in my heart I was hoping that he *was* that right person for Janice. She deserved someone who was crazy about her, someone she was crazy about. And unlike in my doomed situation, Sean wasn't a vampire.

***

JESSUP CORRECTIONAL CENTER had a dark past. It had been designed over a hundred years ago and the tight corners and narrow staircases weren't suitable for a maximum security prison. With a reputation for riots, fights, and escapes as well as attacks on officers, the final straw came when two guards were stabbed in 2007.

The main building was demolished, over eight hundred inmates moved to another high-security facility. The remaining buildings housed medium security offenders and a separate women's prison. Still, security was tight, and it took me quite a while to go through checks, sign-ins, and metal-detectors. Turns out there was a visitor dress code that thankfully I had unknowingly complied with. Several people were turned away for short skirts, leggings, or tank tops.

I felt sorry for them. Visiting days were based on a prisoner's ID number, and thus were once per month. Those with inappropriate clothing would need to run home and change, or risk not seeing their friend or family member for another month.

Luckily Tremelay had pulled his police strings and gotten me in outside of the normal visiting day. Still, after making my way through all the security checks, I sat in a room that reminded me a lot of a bus station and waited.

Finally they called my name and I walked into a large room, divided with plexiglass, half-height cubicle dividers separating the individual booths. I sat and waited yet again. A few moments later a guard escorted a jumpsuited Chuck in. He sat and picked up the phone receiver like he'd done this a million times.

I did likewise. "Did you get the Fisher's caramel popcorn?"

It had been our deal. He gave me the info on Dark Iron, I sent him a gigantic bucket of the Eastern Shore staple four times per year. It was a deal well worth making.

He nodded. "I'd expect this isn't a social visit. You here for magical information? Need to pick my brains about a ritual or something?"

His voice was full of longing, as though he'd hoped every day for a practitioner to talk shop with. I doubted many in prison were mages, and I'm sure he kept his extracurricular practice to himself.

"I'm here about skinwalkers. At least I think they're skinwalkers. They might be an Aztec god or or shapeshifters, or possibly demons."

He blinked, his head jerking to the side in surprise. "Skin whats? And did you say Aztec *god*?"

Either Chuck was ready for an Academy award, or these monsters killing and skinning humans weren't the Big-Bad that Fiore Noir had been using sacrificial magic to protect the city against.

I was here. I was in the company of a skilled ceremonial magician. Might as well use my time wisely.

"We've got three killers going around Baltimore killing people and skinning them. At first we suspected a human serial killer, but we're now thinking all three are some sort of paranormal creature. They take the skins of their victims and assume their identity."

Chuck looked horrified, which was odd given that he'd participated in sacrificial magic. "They *wear* the skins of dead people? Do they tan them first or something?"

It was gross either way. "The M.E. says they've been preserved somehow, but it's not a tanning method he's familiar with."

He shook his head slowly from side to side. "Are their victims important, powerful people? I assume they'd have to be to warrant going to all that trouble."

"Not exactly. A college-age slacker. A museum employee. A renegade vampire. And we found another skin that belonged to a teenage boy."

"That's four." Chuck wrinkled his brow.

"There's only three of them, but it seems they're collecting these skins and can swap around who they're impersonating."

Chuck swallowed, looking rather ill. "Ugh. I don't know of any mages who do that sort of thing. I've never even heard of it before. What did you say these things were again?"

"I don't know. I thought maybe they were related to skinwalkers although I've never heard of them using human skins, just animals."

His eyes narrowed. "Aren't skinwalkers just human mages who specialize in a kind of shape-shifting?"

"Yeah, but these taste like a rotted corpse so I'm not convinced they're human. Would a mage who participated in that kind of magic change at a molecular level?"

"How do you know what they taste like?" Chuck again looked horrified.

"One killed a vampire, but before that a renegade north of the city said she'd picked the girl up and when she bit her, the girl tasted like a rotted corpse."

"I don't think the magic user in his original form would be changed in any way that would make him taste like that to a vampire." Now Chuck was beginning to look intrigued. "Perhaps something in the transformation process gives him or her the flavor of the dead body that used to wear the skin. Or a mage that skilled might have a life-extension spell. Some of them involve becoming like the living dead. Of course, a decent illusion spell is necessary because rotted corpses walking around isn't socially acceptable."

If so, it was probably the first theory. I just couldn't see the man who'd cried in the interrogation room as an ancient. "I'm pretty convinced we're dealing with skinwalkers then. Unless you tell me that there's an Aztec god somewhere around Baltimore."

Chuck recoiled. "God, I hope not! So besides the bodies and preserved skins, what have you got? Any witnesses?"

"Just one. A buyer for the museum. He said he saw three teens skinning a man at a rest-stop off I-

95 and when he read in the paper that we found the dead guy in the closet, he called in to tell the police."

Chuck pursed his lips, scowling at the phone receiver. "You sure it's not him? What did he buy? Cursed object? Maybe at night he turns into psychoskinner man and he's trying to throw you off the trail."

"I didn't get that vibe from him at all." I bit my lip in thought. "He was down in South Carolina picking up a piece for an exhibit. Guy fancies himself one of those pickers, going around to flea markets and estates scrounging for a Fabergé egg in Aunt Mable's dresser drawer. Cursed object is a good theory, but we've got witnesses that have them in the same place at the same time, so it wouldn't be a cursed picker guy switching between a bunch of skins."

The mage rested his chin on one fist and leaned forward, phone tight to his ear. "So tell me about skinwalkers. What do you know?"

Not much. Not until I got home and read more. Now that I'd narrowed it down, ruling out Aztec gods, this made the most sense.

"There are a few Native American tribes who have legends of individuals claiming to be skinwalkers. They're human—at least they are at the start—and they were mostly likely magic users who turned evil."

Chuck snorted. "Evil is such a subjective concept. Taking an animal skin and using it to gain power and knowledge? How is that evil?"

"Well, according to the Navajos, the skinwalker needs to kill an immediate family member to gain the skill."

"Every gift of magic requires a sacrifice," Chuck

commented calmly. I glared at him until he squirmed. "*I've* never done it but I could see if there was a family member you really disliked—say that brother that bullied you growing up—there might be a temptation."

"Anyway." I frowned at him as I continued. "Once they gain the ability of a skinwalker, they use their animal forms to kill and injure others."

Chuck snorted. "Seriously? Why bother? You can do that from a distance with all sorts of other magic—most of which doesn't require you to off one of your own family."

The mage was starting to get on my nerves, but I still had hope he'd have some insight for me. "I don't know why. Maybe killing someone up close and personal as a scary animal is a thrill for them. Maybe they concoct blackmail schemes and rake in the dough. You know, 'pay me or a giant bear will maul you.' Or maybe they just like being animals."

"Or they like being other people." Chuck rubbed his chin. "That *would* be kind of fun, running around as someone else. There's no accountability. Rob a bank, then ditch that skin and wear another. It would be like one giant high school prank."

High school prank. I envisioned three teens running away from home and their Grandmother, hitchhiking their way to the big city, stealing people's identities and living their lives. It did seem juvenile, if you took away the murder component.

Teenage skinwalkers. Whatever their true age, I needed to get back and research this further. What were their habits? And, most importantly, how could I stop them.

And what the heck was I going to do *after* I stopped them? Could they be sentenced to a prison for the criminally insane, one where the three teens could be in solitary confinement so they wouldn't skin their roommates? But that would be Tremelay's problem, not mine. *My* problem was bringing these three in.

I had one more thing I wanted to ask Chuck before I left. "Okay, so whatever Fiore Noir was spelling against, it wasn't an Aztec god, and it clearly wasn't three teen skinwalkers. Tell me, Chuck. Tell me what I'm going to have to kill in the near future?"

He grinned. "You know what's been fun? Having you visit me and tell me about your skinwalker problem. I'd love someone to come by regularly and talk shop. I might even be able to help. I'm quite eclectic in my practice as compared to the others in Fiore Noir."

How did I ever think I liked this guy? "You cared enough about the city to kill to protect it. Tell me what's coming."

"Once a month, on my visiting day. Each time you come I'll give you a clue—after we talk shop for at least an hour, that is."

"I don't have time for this," I snarled. "Baltimore doesn't have time for this. For all I know there might already be a basilisk or some other monster terrorizing the city. I'm already sending you popcorn and now you want to be besties?"

"It's September. If the Big Bad, as you call it, doesn't appear by first frost, it will wait until spring. That's plenty of time to visit me and put the puzzle pieces together."

This was Baltimore, first frost could be in October or it could be in January. I had no idea how long the last two soul magic spells would hold. I had no idea what the heck they were holding back. And I really didn't want to visit Chuck monthly in addition to sending him popcorn.

But I had to. He'd just given me a clue. Whatever this was, it didn't like the cold. If we had an early winter, there was a good chance I could figure it out before spring. Six additional clues. And, unlike most people, I had a brilliant father to help me.

"Okay. I'll see you next month."

I slammed the phone on the receiver and stomped away, but not before I saw the smirk on Chuck's face. It made me think that twenty years at Jessup was far too light of a sentence.

CHAPTER 24

I'D BARELY CRACKED open *Native American Magic* when my phone beeped with a text. It was Tremelay, sending me an address.

The Powerplant? Was he asking me to go clubbing? Maybe. If there was a good band or a decent D.J.

I glanced over at the fox figurine, still resting on the book shelf with dull red eyes. "What do you think, Raven?" Then my phone chimed again.

Hurry.

I might not know much about the detective's personal life, but I doubted he was in a huge rush to have me meet him at a drunken dance-fest. Tremelay wouldn't demand my presence if it wasn't important, so I threw my sword over my shoulder and ran out the door.

Parking in that section of the Inner Harbor was impossible at night, so I walked. Or rather, I ran. It wasn't as easy as it had been a year ago when I'd been working out regularly. By the time I arrived at the huge building which had formerly housed a coal-burning electric plant, I was sweaty and puffing hard. And I was horribly underdressed.

Instead of eyeing my sword, everyone eyed my faded jeans and worn T-shirt. It was a far cry from the miniskirts and barely-there dresses most of the women were wearing. I shifted away from the crowd that was waiting for the concert venue, and looked for the address Tremelay had sent.

The Powerplant was a monstrous conglomerate of bars, clubs, and businesses as well as the concert site. Everything had been built onto and around the original building, which still had the iconic smokestacks. Well, iconic except that they were now adored with a giant guitar advertising the Hard Rock Café.

I went into the club he'd indicated, finding it packed with a plethora of people wearing black clothing.

"Where are you?" I texted him, looking around. I couldn't imagine Tremelay in this sort of place, but who knows what the guy did for kicks in his spare time.

"Bathroom. Meet me here."

I stared, open-mouthed, at my phone. He was in the *bathroom*? What the heck did he expect me to do, give it a shake when he was done?

I pushed my way through the crowd, fairly certain that people were fondling not only my rear end, but my sword as well. Finally I arrived at the very back of the bar where the bathrooms were located only to find myself refused entrance by a stern, uniformed police officer. A few texts to Tremelay and I saw him pop out of the silver-painted metal door and wave at the officer to let me through.

"What's going on?" I asked the detective. The burly officer had been smack outside the men's room. Whatever was going on, it had to be big to shut down the only place for guys to pee in a bar at full occupancy. Was there a celebrity in there doing number two? Because I couldn't imagine any other reason for the cops to be guarding a bathroom.

Guarding a *stinky* bathroom. I wrinkled my nose as Tremelay opened the door. And I quickly realized that the stench wasn't from someone who'd suffered burrito-induced food poisoning, but from a body which had been dead long before the band took the stage.

"Bodies." I'd never seen Tremelay look so pissed. "Two skinned bodies in one of the stalls. Fuck knows how long they've been there. People have been complaining about the smell since the place opened, but no one thought to check in the stall until just now. And these ones were posed. They look like they're having sex. And yes, they're both skinned."

I peeked in the doorway of the stall and wished I hadn't. The bodies were posed in a position that held sexual innuendo. I thought back on Chuck's and my conversation about teenage pranks. The dead body falling out of the closet on top of me fit with that theme, too. Perhaps the one in the cooler had been destined for a prank along with Amanda Lewis's corpse, if only her boyfriend hadn't interrupted.

But two bodies meant two more skins. Assuming the one was only hunting vampires at this point, I was looking at two murderers who could assume any one of five identities—six if I counted the teenager's Gary was in when they arrived.

And we'd never find them. Not when we had no idea who these bodies were. My only chance was to catch them in Gary's or Bradley Lewis's skins. Although murderers with any sense would have ditched those by now.

But I wasn't dealing with adults. I was dealing with teenagers—teenagers who'd argued in a rest-stop bathroom and at the Inner Harbor. They'd not give them up. Not unless they had to run for it and leave a backpack behind.

Whoever these teens were, they needed to be prosecuted as adults. It wasn't just the multiple murders, it was the absolutely psychotic desecration of these two bodies in the bathroom stall. It was vomit-inducing. Red bodies, tendons and muscles all on display like in an anatomy textbook, eyes bulging, teeth bared. The whole thing was like a scene from a slasher horror flick.

"Now you can see why we have the bathroom cordoned off," Tremelay commented. "We didn't want to clear the bar and alarm the public. We're hoping to sneak these two out the back on stretchers, like overdose victims."

"Who found them? And how the heck did the killers get them in here? You'd think someone would have seen them."

"This place is locked down tight until the band arrives to set up. No one saw them. No one saw anything. The roadies did tell management the bathroom stunk something horrible, but nobody thought to look until they'd been open for almost an hour."

I looked over at the stalls. If this had been the women's bathroom, it would have been found right away, but with a line of urinals and two other open stalls, nobody would have thought to pry open the locked one and see what was going on in there.

I scrunched up my nose. "You can sneak out the back door, but this is gonna leak out, Tremelay. Like it or not, it's gonna hit the morning paper."

Mainly because I was going to call Janice. I owed her, and the woman needed to get a decent story after being scooped by the *City Paper*.

"I know it's gonna leak out," Tremelay snapped. "No news crews have shown up yet. I'm sure some asshole with a cell phone has gotten pictures, though. More skinned bodies. Everyone just got settled down from the occult sacrifices, and now we've got three teenage skinwalkers killing people."

"Skinwalker is better than an Aztec god," I reassured him. "I wouldn't have the foggiest idea how to stop an Aztec god. Not that I have any idea how to stop a skinwalker, but that at least I can find that out in a timely fashion. I've got research material on them and so does my Dad. Aztec gods...not so much."

"What have you found out so far? What do I need to know about these kids?" Tremelay asked.

"They're a sort of Native American witch, an evil person who gains the powers, skills, and memories of whatever skin he is wearing. It's usually animals, but I'm thinking if I dig a bit I can find incidents where skinwalkers have taken human skins. They transform into whoever they're wearing at the time."

"So these people are draping skins of their victims over themselves and walking around? Is that how Huang escaped? He shed his skin and turned into...I don't know, a rat or something?"

"That's what I believe. It's a kind of magic," I tried to explain. "They put on the skin and they actually become whatever. Coyote, owl, bear, Brian Huang."

"Why? I'll admit it might be kind of cool to be a bear for a day or two, at least until they darted me and stuck me in a zoo, but not other humans. At least not a lazy kid and a museum employee with a huge family crammed into a four bedroom rancher in

Glen Burnie. If I was going to assume another person's identity it would be the Mayor, or Bill Gates, or Brad Pitt."

I wrinkled my nose, thinking that Tremelay should aspire to be a younger movie star than Brad Pitt, but who was I to judge?

"I really don't know. They're kids, like Stu Moreland said. Maybe they're skinwalkers-in-training and out on a sort of lark. An evil joy ride."

Tremelay shook his head. "The name Moreland mentioned matched up with the name of the skin in the backpack—the kid who'd gone missing at age six from South Carolina. Do you think a skinwalker stole these kids and trained them?"

It was a chilling thought, but one I'd had in the back of my mind. They had to have learned the magic somewhere, and given that Lawton had vanished from his home when he was only six years old, only to turn up a skin in a backpack ten years later…. Was that six-year-old boy trained along with the others, or had another trained skinwalker come upon Lawton King recently and taken his life?

"All I know is we've got a possibility of five identities to look for if we rule out the girl up north and her vampire skin. Five, including these two." I waved a hand at the corpses as a tech loaded them carefully onto gurneys and covered them with sheets.

"Gary, that we have pictures of, these two unknowns, a rest-stop guy, and Lewis." Tremelay's mouth set in a grim line. "I'm gonna try to fast track the DNA on the cooler body and these two. With this many murders, we've got a crisis. We're also going to probably have the feds knocking at our door the next day or two. This kind of thing is right up their alley, and we've got four dead including Amanda Lewis and body and skin from her house."

Feds. Crap. If this had been a human serial killer, I would have welcomed their presence, but with a supernatural element...

If only there really was a branch of the FBI that dealt with supernatural phenomenon. What I wouldn't give for Scully and Mulder right now. I'd team with those two in a heartbeat. But unfortunately I'd wind up with a bunch of suits who shuffled me aside and put every officer to work looking for three human psychos.

Skinwalkers. I watched the bodies being wheeled from the bathroom and out the emergency exit at the back of the building and knew this was going to be up to me. If the feds arrived, they've grab Tremelay as their lead detective on the case, tying up all of his time.

Me. Again I felt a wash of loneliness. I liked working with Tremelay. I liked working with Raven. And I liked working with Dario.

I needed to cut the self-pity crap. Feds or not, Tremelay would always find a way to make time for what might become our side investigation. Raven would help once she regained her strength. And Dario—he would find that vampire imposter, I just knew it.

"What are you thinking, Ainsworth?" Tremelay asked. And I knew then that he was with me, no matter what his job demanded of him.

"I'm thinking I need to research skinwalkers more—how to detect them, how to catch them."

How to kill them? Admittedly these three had done their share of murder. I'd killed Dark Iron but I didn't want to kill again. These were kids, even though they were murderers on a spree. This was different. There was plenty of evidence to put these kids away for life. There was no need for me to take justice into my own hands.

But the skinwalker who'd posed as Brian Huang had escaped prison in a matter of hours. Like Dark Iron, I wondered if human justice would possibly be enough for kids with this level of magical ability. My soul was smudged already. It was about to become even darker.

"So you're nose-deep in books tonight while I'm filling out reports." Tremelay sighed and ran a hand through his already messy hair. "Do you have a sec before you go home? I've got something I wanted to give you, but it's at my apartment."

I blinked in surprise. Not that I thought Tremelay would try anything sleezy, or that I had anything to fear being alone with him in his apartment, I'd just never thought about where the detective lived. He seemed to be either out investigating a case or at the station.

"Sure. I've got time."

We stood for a moment, as if both of us was waiting for the other to do something, then Tremelay finally turned, gesturing for me to follow him. "It's not all that. My place. I mean it's kinda cheap and small. And I just moved in a few months back and have been too busy to unpack much. I haven't even put the bed together yet. I'm sleeping on the mattress on the floor."

We walked through the same emergency exit as the bodies had gone and toward his unmarked car, double parked next to the ambulance. Being a detective had its privileges. Parking was evidently one of them. "Well, hopefully I won't be seeing your mattress," I teased.

"Hardly," he shot back, tempering his word with a quick grin. "I'm just warning you that the place is a mess."

"You've been in my apartment. People who live in glass houses and all that." He unlocked the unmarked car and I slid into the passenger seat, waiting for him to come around and get in. "Besides, I'm eager to see where you live. Do you actually own an iron? Are your clean clothes twisted up in a heap in a laundry basket in the living room? Are there dishes stacked up in your sink with dried food crusted on them?"

"Now you're describing your place." The smile stayed on his face as he pulled away from the curb. "It's not that bad. Mostly unpacked boxes. And yes, I tend to live out of a laundry basket. Hanging and folding clothes has got to be a torture technique. I'd rather be suspended by my toes than try to match socks."

His socks didn't match? I tried to sneak a peek, but his pants came down too far and the floor of the car was too dim to tell. Even so, I got the feeling he had on one navy and one black.

Chuckling, I sat back in my seat and relaxed. I was so glad I'd met Detective Justin Tremelay, glad he'd trusted me, believed me, glad he was my friend. My quirky friend with his rumpled shirts, rumpled hair, and mismatched socks. What a character. And what a Templar-at-heart this man was.

"What are you grinning about, Ainsworth?"

I couldn't help it. Skinwalkers, dead people. I shouldn't be happy, but somehow I was. I had friends. I had good friends. And Raven might be dead, but she wasn't lost to me.

"Your socks," I told the detective. "I swear sometimes you look like a toddler dressed you."

He grinned back. "I'm a toddler at heart, Ainsworth."

Tremelay pulled along the curb and parked on a street full of brick row houses, putting the car in park and unlocking the doors.

"Here we are."

We were two blocks from the MLK. It wasn't the best section of town, but it wasn't the worst. I looked over at the line of houses, identical except for window treatments and front-door ornamentation.

"I thought you said apartment?"

He nodded, swinging his legs out of the car. "Two one bedroom apartments in the house. I've got the downstairs, and a single mother of three has the upstairs. She's thrilled to have a cop living in her building."

I'll bet. I shook my head at the thought of four people in a one bedroom apartment, but I wasn't exactly in a position to judge. After this month's rent, I wasn't sure how I was going to pay the next. In a few months, it might be me living with three other people in a one bedroom apartment.

I followed Tremelay up the steps through a door. The lock squeaked, and when the detective flicked on the light I saw boxes. A lamp sat on a tower of three. Others were lined against the wall, black marker on the sides proclaiming them to be "living room" or "misc." I milled about the room while Tremelay disappeared into what I assumed was the bedroom. Sofa, recliner, a couple of end tables, and a shelving unit against the wall.

"Three months and you haven't unpacked all of this?" I asked.

Tremelay gave an affirmative grunt from the bedroom. I immediately jumped to the usual conclusions as I looked around the apartment. Divorced middle-aged guy, kicked out by his wife. Cops were stereotypically cheaters, so my mind wandered to the worst. I browsed the living room and kitchen, hearing the sound of ripping boxes and thumping from the back room as I tried to get a better idea of the man who'd become my friend.

The shelf by the window housed a pile of books, mostly classics and a few military thrillers. Next to them was a stack of framed photos. A woman about my age, stylish dark hair, her smile nearly engulfing her heart-shaped face. A group of people I couldn't make out in kayaks going down a small rapid. The girl again in a graduation gown.

"Is this your daughter?" I shouted, feeling nosy.

"Kyra. She's in medical school. Third year."

He sounded so proud. He should be. I pursed my lips and nodded, impressed. The next picture was of a woman in her thirties, her skin tanned, her black hair in a long braid over her shoulder. It was one of those casually posed pictures, with jeans and a pristine button-down shirt while sitting on lichen-coated boulders in an autumn woods. Pretty, although there was something haunting about her dark eyes.

"That was my wife, Anaya."

I jumped to hear Tremelay's voice so close behind me. He reached out to take the photo, setting it with great reverence on the shelf.

I was dying of curiosity, but heard the raw grief of love lost in the detective's voice. Maybe *she* left *him*. Either way, this was an open wound for him and I just couldn't pry further.

I didn't have to pry. He reached out to touch the face on the picture. "I met her when I was a wet-behind-the-ears rookie and she was a defense attorney. I'd been called to appear on a domestic violence trial that I'd responded to. She kicked my ass." Tremelay smiled nostalgically. "I asked her out before we left the courthouse."

"Love at first sight." I couldn't help but feel warm and fuzzy at the thought.

He shrugged. "For me. Took six months before she finally went out with me. She was so out of my league. I couldn't believe my luck."

I looked at the picture again, at the woman's almond-shaped eyes, lined dark. Even in jeans and a button-down she looked exotic. "She's beautiful."

Tremelay's face twisted. "Yes. She is."

The detective turned away, picking up a box off the kitchen counter. By the time he'd turned to face me, his expression was once again serene. "Here. I want you to have this."

My brain raced wondering what in the world the detective could possibly be giving to me. A book on the occult? A grimoire he'd found in a used bookstore somewhere? A magical item?

It was a flak jacket. And a gun. I held up the vest, my eyes questioning as I looked at Tremelay.

"Figured it would be a bit harder for a demon to stab you if you were wearing that. Don't know how effective it's going to be against skinwalkers, though."

It wouldn't exactly be stealthy. The jacket was definitely my size, but the plates were freaking huge. This was way more protection than my thin Kevlar vest from home. I could probably take a heat-seeking missile to the chest and survive in this thing.

"Thanks." How the heck could I wear this anywhere? A guy in a jacket this bulky would just look buff. I'd look like someone had shot me up with a truckload of steroids. It might not be great for day-to-day wear, but it would have its uses. In fact, I could have used it last month when Dark Iron shot me. Although since he'd shot me in the arm, maybe not.

"Did you see the pistol?" Tremelay asked. His voice had an edge of excitement to it, like he was delivering Christmas gifts to me.

"Yes." I pulled it out and cleared the chamber, clicking to drop the non-existent clip out of habit. "Sig nine. Very nice."

It was a sweet pistol, and it had obviously been well maintained.

"There are four clips and a handful of bullets in the box," Tremelay told me.

I looked down in the box, then up at him, perplexed. "Why are you giving me this?"

A small flak jacket. Yeah, I could see that maybe he'd had one from whenever and thought to give it to me, but a pistol? A really nice Sig? That wasn't the sort of thing you just handed off to someone.

"I have my .40, so I don't ever use it. There are going to be times when your sword isn't going to be enough. No one will expect a Templar to be carrying a pistol, not that I'm advocating concealed carry without a license." He squirmed, shifting his weight from foot to foot. "These guys are skinning people, Ainsworth. I know you're going to go after them, and with your luck, you'll get to them before I do. Whether they're human or skinwalkers, I don't want to find your body next."

I'd been meaning to get a gun, but with the

handgun license laws and the actual purchase, I couldn't spare the cash. This was...sweet.

"It's a loan," I insisted. "You need it back, and it's yours. And as soon as I can save up some money to buy my own, I'll return it."

"Fair enough," he nodded.

Something else struck me. "How do you know I can shoot? You've only seen me use a sword."

Tremelay smirked, taking the gun from me and carefully putting it back in the case. "You joust. You have shot two types of RPGs. I know you have a shotgun back home, and you've done the trap shoot thing. I was pretty sure in all your Templar training they taught you to shoot a pistol. And from the way you cleared the gun when you first picked it up, I'd bet my life savings I'm right."

He was. I wasn't a sharpshooter, but I wasn't a danger to society with a gun in my hand either. I bent down and picked up the box. "Thanks. I appreciate it."

Tremelay nodded sharply, suddenly looking uncomfortable. "Don't mention it."

He drove me back to my apartment, where I thanked him again before heading inside. I had a lot of research to do, but the first thing I did after stashing my new pistol in a safe place was to Google Anaya Tremelay.

I couldn't help but wonder about the woman who haunted my friend's life enough to remain a picture on his bookshelf. My browser exploded with professional pictures and articles. Lawyer. District Attorney. A few high profile cases. Anaya had raised thousands running in charity marathons and had organized several races to benefit a local food bank. Her pro-bono service was noteworthy. She was a freaking saint.

And she was dead. The stream of press-mentions ended abruptly only to be followed by an obituary three months later.

I felt like shit for all my stupid assumptions about Tremelay's marriage and fidelity. I'm sure they'd encountered a few rocky points in their time together, heck, even my parents had their rough spots. What mattered was he clearly loved her, still loved her. She'd died far too young, and after two years he still grieved.

I went and looked at the flak jacket and pistol with fresh eyes. That jacket was way too small for Tremelay. Had it been hers? Was this her Sig? It warmed my heart to think my friendship meant enough for him to part with his wife's things. I needed to be nicer to Tremelay. We both lived for our work. We both had family we loved. We were both from Templar backgrounds, even though his had evidently gone underground after the purge. But beyond all that, the detective was a good guy.

Yeah. I needed to be kinder to Tremelay. And maybe once in a while, if finances allowed, I could bring him some cookies.

CHAPTER 25

I WAS TWO hours into Hakan Garza's *Native American Magic* and I was ready to throw the book across the room. It wasn't just the weird, archaic prose that frustrated me, it was the way the author danced around the fact that he didn't know squat about how to catch or kill these creatures.

One idea he put forth was to learn the skinwalker's real name, then basically "out" them, thus rendering them unable to use the skins to change form ever again. That sounded promising except for the fact that I had no stinking idea who these people were. Tremelay said he'd been wading through missing and endangered children reports out of South Carolina, checking Amber alerts nationwide in case the three teens had hitchhiked their way from somewhere else before Stu Mooreland had picked them up. Who knows if he'd even get a hit. They could be from the sort of family situation where their disappearance wasn't noted, let alone reported. Lawton King was the only name we knew, and searching a decade for missing children named Gary and Becca was proving a daunting task.

And that was if the teenagers were their real identity. Lawton's skin had been the one in the backpack, making me wonder who these three skinwalkers really were under all the aliases. I noted the name solution, just in case, but kept reading and hoping for a more reliable method of subduing these killers.

Another idea was to use bullets coated in ash. What sort of ash, Mr. Garza didn't say. Wood? Bone? Did the type of tree or animal matter, or did the ash need to be from human remains? There were just too many variables for me to feel confident in this method. Then the author went on to say that I'd need to shoot the skinwalker in the neck, because even with the unspecified ash coating, hitting them elsewhere wouldn't kill them, it would just piss them off.

With my luck I'd hit the guy in the neck only to find out I'd used the wrong ash. Besides, the idea of shooting teenagers bothered me enough that I decided I wasn't going to pursue that option. I really wanted to neutralize their magic and bring them in for Tremelay to prosecute, not kill them.

The next extremely vague idea that Garza put forth was to turn the skinwalker's curses back upon himself. Fat lot of good that would do me. From what I'd seen, they hadn't been using magic at all, they'd been breaking their victim's necks, draining their blood, then skinning them. Kinda hard to turn a curse back on the skinwalker when there was none.

Or maybe there was. Outside of Amanda Lewis, the victims hadn't shown any defensive wounds. Were the skinwalkers using some type of magic to knock them out? Not a curse precisely, but some type of spell to freeze or bind a victim. It made sense. That way there'd be no struggle that would mar the skin. Magically render them unconscious, kill them quickly by breaking their neck, then get to work. Dario had said there must have been some kind of magic to subdue the vampire victim. This fit.

Except that hadn't happened with Amanda Lewis or in the first two vampire attacks. Perhaps their sleep spell was only effective on some individuals? Or maybe the teenage practitioners weren't skilled enough to obtain reliable results? Either way, Amanda Lewis had been sliced repeatedly, then had her legs dislocated. And the other two vampires—one had said the woman tried to break his neck. Of course the other one didn't fit at all with the attacker trying to bite the vampire.

Whatever. It was all I had. Of course, to turn a spell back upon the caster, I'd need to not only *have* a rebound spell, but manage to make myself the victim. And becoming one of the skinwalkers' victims was going to be pretty difficult when I had no idea where to find them. I couldn't exactly put myself in their path when I didn't even know where their path was.

I was at a dead end. And I didn't even have any cannoli to eat as comfort food. I was in the middle of such a pity party that I was contemplating breaking out my Emergency Beer when Tremelay called.

"God, I love the FBI. I'll never say another bad thing about the feds ever. If I do, slap me, because they are the best thing since sliced bread and microwave ovens."

His excitement was infectious. I held my breath waiting for him to tell me what breakthrough on the case the FBI had brought to the table.

"We got the names of Stu Moreland's three hitchhikers, *and* the lab got back to us on the body from the museum, and the body in the cooler. I'm hoping we'll have something soon on the two dead at the Powerplant. Right now all I've got is the M.E. saying they're two young Caucasian males, early twenties and fit."

"Lab reports first," I told him. This was like Christmas morning, and I wasn't sure which present to open first.

"I'm not going to go into the excruciating details, but between the lab data, the fed's database, and their amazing ability to get hospital and juvenile records, we've discovered that the body in the cooler is Bradley Lewis. The body at the museum *is* Brian Huang."

"And how are the feds explaining that we interviewed Brian Huang days after his death?" I wondered. The fact that Gary had hidden Bradley's body in his own house bothered me, too. That was ballsy.

"No idea. They'll probably go with the secret identical twin thing like in the soap operas. They're conjecturing this is a group of teens who joined up with some Baltimore people they most likely met on the internet, but now they've begun to turn on each other."

"Killing Lawton King and Bradley Lewis." I finished the line of reasoning. "And the creepy jail break was the evil twin who left Brian Huang's skin behind as a sort of calling card to go with the skinned body in the museum."

"With the 'death' of King and Lewis, the Feds have concluded the two remaining members of the gang are Becca Campbell and Gary Jarvett. They've narrowed it down to Gary as the killer based on Stu Moreland's account and that he was seen with both Brian Huang and Bradley Lewis. They are thinking Becca ditched the group once they got to Baltimore and is an accessory after the fact."

The other two hitchhikers. It didn't bother me that the Fed's had overlooked the Teen Formerly

Known as Lawton King and Brian Huang. I was beginning to agree that Gary was our main man. Catch him and we'd eventually find Lawton and Becca. Well, the vampires would probably find Becca and woe to her if they did.

"Anything else on the Powerplant dead?" Those two bodies bothered me. Lawton would need a new skin to conceal his true identity, and Gary seemed to be in collecting mode. If they were impersonating those two dumped in the bathroom stall, then I'd have no way to recognize them.

I wish there was an Identify Skinwalker spell. It sounded like something from my Wednesday night Anderon game, but that sort of spell really needed to happen. Maybe there was a ritual in Raven's books that could help me.

Or Chuck. These monthly visits might prove more useful than I'd originally thought. Although right now I didn't have time to wait for a month to find an identification spell.

"The usual broken neck, stab wound stuff. The manager said the rear entrance was unlocked when he came to let the band in to set up, but one of the other managers was there at the same time. They each thought the other unlocked the door. Weird band. A group called Midnight Visitor. They were a one-hit wonder back in the grunge era and something of a local favorite. They didn't see anything, but had me talk to the opening act which is a local garage band. Rabid Rabbit. Nice kids, although they seem a bit antiestablishment. They don't usually do big venues, sticking to impromptu raves in abandoned buildings and shit like that. Lead singer, Travis Dawson said they were huge fans of Midnight Visitor and couldn't turn down the chance to open for them." Tremelay made a *hmm* sound. "I think I know these Rabbit guys. The name sounds familiar, but I don't listen to that sort of music."

"Bradley Lewis." I was so excited. "He had a Rabid Rabbit T-shirt. It's got to be a connection." Three teens, of course they'd be into that sort of music. And Gary did seem to be an antiestablishment guy. Finally I had a lead on where I could manage to find these kids, and possibly lure them in. I just had to find a Rabid Rabbit concert, and show up. I'd stick out, being a bit older than their target demographic, but I was close enough to pass for a fan of their music.

We had a lead, and I had somewhat vague ways that I might be able to catch these three. I just needed to get going on a rebound spell, coat bullets in a variety of ash, then memorize the kids' names. The only problem with the name angle was that I had no idea which kid was wearing which skin, or if Gary really was Gary. Ugh.

"So we're probably looking for the skinwalkers to be impersonating whoever was dead in the bathroom," I conjectured. "Becca is out of the picture at this point. It's Gary who's the focus, and as you said, Lawton is probably with him."

"One could be wearing rest-stop bathroom guy," Tremelay added. "I'm going to assume this Gary is smart enough to ditch the Bradley Lewis skin. He's got to know we're looking for him as Amanda's killer, and he won't know we've ID'd the body in the cooler yet."

Three skins, two boys. Only problem was we had no idea how to recognize those three skins.

"I've got a few ideas on how we can disable or restrain them once we manage to find them." I went ahead and outlined the three methods Garza had advocated.

"I'm not coating my bullets in ash," Tremelay complained. Trust him to zero in on that one. "Do you know how much that's going to gum up my gun?"

"Only if you shoot it. Have a clip that only has ash-covered bullets and use that whenever we encounter the skinwalkers."

"And you've got a crystal ball to tell me when that is? Or am I going to be in the middle of a firefight, fumbling for whichever clip happens to have the ash-covered bullets?"

"Well, I'm hoping not to shoot them at all," I shot back. "I'd like to use one of the other methods to screw up their skinwalker abilities so you can prosecute them."

Tremelay made an *mmmf* sound. "Fine. Make sure they can't poof out of a prison cell like Huang did, or we're back to square one."

He had a point. Garza better be right about this name thing, or the skinwalkers would be slipping out of jail as a mouse or bird just as quick as they got in.

"What happened to these kids?" Tremelay mused. "They went missing from their homes in South Carolina at six years old, only to turn up here ten years later as killers with the magical ability to assume their victims' identities. What kind of sicko snatches three little kids and turns them into murderers?"

Six years old. I thought of my nephews and felt sick. I'd watched enough crime shows to know that young kids didn't always wind up dead in the woods after they were taken. I immediately thought of an adult skinwalker, wanting to pass his knowledge along to another—especially another who could be trained young enough to perhaps surpass him in skill. Kidnap three kids, groom them, train them. If that was the case then after we secured these three, I'd need to find the adult who did this to them.

But why were they hitchhiking across South Carolina? Had their mentor died, leaving them hungry and adrift? It made me feel a bit sorry for these kids—even more so if they'd been brainwashed into this from a young age. But there was one more detail I needed to check.

"So in Becca, Lawton, and Gary's families, was there a murder in the last ten years? An unexplained death? Because in order to fully become a skinwalker, they'd need to kill an immediate family member."

"Crap, I forgot about that." I heard Tremelay scribbling. "I'll ask the feds. Tell them it's a theory about an initiation rite their kidnapper may have put them through."

In the meantime, I was just going to assume they had, and that we were dealing with three brainwashed kidnap victims who'd developed magical powers and gone on a killing spree. Time to get started on a rebound spell. And to coat bullets with a variety of types of ash.

"So, you wanna go see a band tonight?" There was a note of humor in Tremelay's voice.

"Um, I've got more research tonight, plus that spell to work on. Unless there are more dead bodies at the concert, count me out."

"You sure?" Yes, he definitely sounded amused. "Rabid Rabbit is playing."

Oh, hell yeah. "You found them? I thought they were a stealthy, impromptu rave kinda band."

"I knew I'd heard the name before and not just

from the Bradley Lewis connection, so I sent a quick text to Norwicki. His daughter knows them. She's on a text list and gets notifications when a concert is going down."

I wasn't exactly prepared to take down two skinwalkers tonight. All I had was possibly their names, no way of telling which was which. Or if that technique even worked. Still...

"I'm in." We couldn't pass up this opportunity. I'd need to wing it.

I had a few hours to coat bullets and to see if I could come up with a quick rebound spell. Was a flak jacket appropriate attire for a Rabid Rabbit concert?

CHAPTER 26

"REMEMBER WHEN YOU said I could call with any questions I might have on spells?"

My words were greeted with silence, making me think that Reynard had extended the offer in a burst of sentimental feeling for the friend of his dead girlfriend—a sentimental feeling that had faded over the last few days.

"Yeah?" The word was drawn out and hesitant, like Reynard wasn't sure he wanted to know what I'd gotten involved with this time. I didn't blame him. After the mess with the Fiore Noir mages, he must think I was nothing but trouble.

And I did get his girlfriend killed. It was in trying to help me out that put Dark Iron's target on her back.

"We've got three skinwalkers in town. They're teenagers and on a killing spree. One is impersonating a vampire, but I don't know who the other two are. I'm trying to figure out a spell to identify them."

I was cradling the phone against my shoulder, rolling bullets around in pulverized, burned chicken bones from dinner. Identification was my biggest obstacle tonight, though. I couldn't exactly go around shooting every attendee at the Rabid Rabbit concert in the neck with ash-coated bullets just to see who suddenly lost their magical skills. It was slightly less impractical for me to shout names at every concert goer in hopes that I'd hit upon the right one.

Basically, this whole night would be a bust unless I had a way to determine who the skinwalkers were, to set them apart from all the humans in the crowd.

"I don't know what skinwalkers are," Reynard confessed. "You should be able to identify demons through holy water or a religious incantation, since you're a Templar. Would that work?"

I hadn't thought of that. I was so used to looking for a magical application that I didn't always think of Templar solutions. It wasn't totally my fault. I hadn't taken my Oath, and most of those prayers hadn't been in use for over a hundred years. The Temple Guardians knew them, but I doubted any of them had actually used what amounted to a "detect evil" spell.

"I could try that, but it's more of a prayer to guard against evil intent. I'd really like to find something that reveals non-humans."

"You and everyone else," Reynard complained. "Do you know how much I'd pay for something like that? I can never tell if I'm dealing with a vampire or not. I've got an amulet that lights up in the presence of demons, but it wouldn't do squat for anything else."

At least I could sense vampires. I wish it was the same with other paranormals or with magic. Honestly, I wasn't even sure a non-human detection spell would work. Technically skinwalkers were human, or at least they used to be. Maybe the evil intent would work? But only if one of them was actively plotting to harm someone. If they were just milling about, enjoying the concert, my "evil intent" prayer wouldn't reveal anything.

"Scan for magic? Something that shows the presence of an active magical spell?"

"Hmmm." Reynard was stalling. I could hear him paging through something in the background. "I do have an amulet for that but it only lasts for a few minutes. They'd need to be casting a spell pretty close to the time you activated it for the amulet to pick up on the energy. I've mainly used it to detect spells with long effects—like illusions. It's not a good choice if you're looking to catch an attack before it comes your way. You need a ward with a wide range of effect."

Skinwalkers weren't using illusion to change their appearance, they were actually becoming that person using their skin. Reynard was right. Unless I caught them in the middle of a transformation, that amulet wouldn't detect anything.

"The only wards I know how to do are to prevent people from entering a room, and to give me a heads-up if they break the ward and force their way in."

"The spell I'm thinking of is kind of like that," Reynard explained. "It's a broad area of effect without the 'lock' to keep people out. Basically residual magic would trip the ward. The only thing is I don't know how much magic needs to be present for it to activate. Or if these skinwalkers have an ambient magical signature. Most mages don't. And in that case, we're back to the situation where it only triggers if you happen to catch them in the middle of casting a spell."

The chance they'd cast a spell at the concert was too slim to spend the time crafting the spell. I didn't have much time. And with my luck the person who triggered it would be a teenage girl with a love charm.

"How about an ownership spell?" I didn't want to reveal too much, but I was thinking of what Chuck had done to trace the soul trap back to Dark Iron. "Maybe something that will reveal a disconnect between the skin on the outside to the person on the inside?"

Reynard snorted. "An ownership spell will just reveal that the person on the inside now 'owns' the skin he's wearing, not the former owner of it. Maybe something that traces the spirit energy. A violent death would leave previous spirit energy clinging to the skin that wouldn't match with the spirit energy of the person, or thing, wearing it. But that's way out of my area of expertise."

It was way out of mine too, but I knew a skilled Necromancer, and he knew a whole city of spirit workers. Someone had to be able to pull a spell like that off. The big question was could they do it in the next few hours.

"Wish I could help you, Aria. Sorry." He didn't sound all that sorry. He sounded relieved. But as much as he might regret his offer to me, I knew Reynard would honor it. And I was going to make sure he did honor it, no matter how awkward these conversations might be.

"No problem. Thanks anyway." I hung up and immediately called Russell.

"Well. People killing others and wearing their skins. I thought I'd heard it all." Russell made a tsk noise. "And they think necromancers are evil. We're not murdering people for our magic. We're not stealing their souls or their identities. Compared to these mages, resurrecting the dead is downright moral."

I didn't want to get into that argument with Russell. There were things necromancers did that didn't sit right with me either—using spirits to further your need for revenge, for instance. And zombies, if that's what he was referring to, were soundly on my not-moral list. Just because one magic was heinous didn't make all the other black magic good in comparison.

"The problem is these two could be anybody in the room and I won't know," I explained. "Is there something that will let me know a person has assumed another's identity? Is wearing their skin? Reynard said maybe a spell that showed the disconnect between the residual spirit energy of the skin and the spirit of the wearer."

"Nope." The reply was fast and definitive. "People have objects from their parents, grandparents, children. All of those hold residual spirit energy and they'd all show up. Half the people in the room would light up with that spell."

I was striking out here, and I had one hour before I was supposed to meet Tremelay at the concert site. "I'm desperate, Russell. Got any ideas?"

"If those two boys were recently murdered, there's a chance their spirits are still hanging around. They might be following the skinwalkers who killed them and stole their skins."

Ghosts. "Do you have something to detect their spirits and talk to them?" If so, those dead boys, those ghosts could show me who the killers were, even if they'd taken on other skins and identities. It was a great idea.

"No, but you do. That spirit in the little fox can see and communicate with other spirits and act as a medium for you. Heck, he might even be able to tell who these skinwalkers are without ghosts present."

"She," I corrected Russell. "We had a breakthrough and the spirit in the fox is my friend Raven. She overexerted herself a few days ago and hasn't been able to communicate any further. My big chance to catch these guys is tonight. There's no way she'll be able to help me."

"Then you'll need a medium who can sense spirits and communicate with them."

I had a vision of a dark-haired woman with a crystal ball, set up in the middle of an impromptu rave. "She'd need to be stealthy. This is a concert with a bunch of young people and loud music. So not the appropriate venue for a séance."

Russell sighed. "What kind of music?"

"I'm thinking industrial? Grunge? Or something similar. The band is called Rabid Rabbit and they opened for Midnight Visitor last night but they usually play in old garages and warehouses."

"Could be worse," he grumbled. "Okay, I'll go. But you'll owe me one Aria. I know you ain't got money, so just return the favor when I'm in a pickle and need a Templar to give me a hand."

"Absolutely." He'd helped me with the fox figurine. I couldn't expect him to continue to be my on-call necromancer without being available to him in return.

"Text me the address and I'll meet you there."

"It's in an hour." I looked at the clock. "No actually in forty minutes, so you'll need to hustle."

"Not a problem. If there's a ghost there, I'll find him."

I hoped so, because Russell was my last chance

to find these guys.

CHAPTER 27

I DECIDED TO go for the battered military look, since I'd be sporting a less-than-figure-flattering flak jacket. I found an old pair of cargo pants in the back of my closet that had seen better days. There were unidentifiable stains in streaks and splotches along the sides, and several holes scattered throughout. A huge bleach stain decorated my left ass cheek. They were perfect.

As was the threadbare, long-sleeve, Charlottesville Cheetah Run 10k shirt I wore under the vest—faded blue with a series of silhouetted big cats running across my chest. I completed my look with a canvas belt full of grommets, and biker boots. The only concession to my mission was the neat braid I'd bundled up in a granny bun against the nape of my neck, out of the way of grasping hands if I wound up grappling with a foe. I also kept the earrings to tiny, not-grabbable studs. With two nephews and a niece I'd learned the pain of having hoop earrings yanked from my ears.

No jewelry besides that. I stuffed Tremelay's Sig in a pocket of the cargo pants, wincing as it banged heavy against my thigh. Hopefully they didn't pat us down, or have metal detectors. If so, I was relying on Tremelay to get me in the door.

As I left I strapped on my sword, praying that

the look-away spell would let me carry it within the club. Nothing I'd read said anything about swords being effective on skinwalkers, but this was my Templar weapon—my *consecrated* Templar weapon. I felt naked when I was without it.

It was weird driving my car with the pistol pulling at my right pants leg and the flak jacket adding an addition twenty-five pounds to my weight. I needed to start running with extra weights to get used to it. Actually I needed to start running again. Outside of the LARPs and the occasional sword practice in my apartment, I was becoming woefully out of shape. I couldn't afford a gym membership, but there was no reason I couldn't do push-ups, planks, and sit-ups in my apartment. Or run a couple miles per day with a backpack full of rocks or something.

The band was in an old service station nestled under a highway overpass. The convenience mart area had been demolished to make one open space with the four garage bays. The counter had become a tiny bar with no seating and a limited variety of beer in tubs of ice. There was no line, no doorman, no bouncer, only a girl with half a dozen facial piercings snagging the five dollar entrance fee and packing us in like sardines.

"You can't bring that in." She pointed at my sword. Others behind me looked at my back, perplexed. Drat this look-away spell. It worked ninety percent of the time, but there was always the occasion when someone saw me walking around with a huge bastard sword strapped to my back.

I grudgingly trotted back to my car and stashed it in the trunk, making sure I activated the spell that would deliver a painful electric shock to anyone who tried to pop the trunk. Thankfully the woman collecting money didn't notice the pistol nearly pulling my cargo pants off my hips, so at least I had one weapon in case things went really bad.

The temperature in the garage was to the point where I was regretting the flak jacket. Sweat pooled under my braided bun and ran down my back. I wasn't the only one perspiring. The dancers in the bay areas were soaking wet as they jumped around to the canned music. The band would start soon, if they started on time, that is. I was assuming at these informal venues, promptness wasn't exactly necessary.

Not that I could even see if the band was setting up. People were wedged in tight, making it difficult to navigate around. It was like trying to make my way through a maze. I looked at each person I passed, thankful that the crowded club meant I could at least get a close look at people. With the dim lighting and flashing strobe effects, it would have been impossible to recognize anyone at a distance.

"Aria." I hand touched my shoulder.

I jumped, my heart racing as I spun around. Russell looked completely out of place in the garage packed with teenagers, but then again, I'm sure I did, too.

"See anything?" I asked.

He nodded. "I do see a spirit, but it's insubstantial and hovering around the stage. I'm going to try to get closer and see if he, or she, will communicate with me, but it's a long shot. When they're blurry and gray there's no distinct features to recognize. And ones that won't fully materialize usually lack the presence to do more than float aimlessly around."

A long shot was the only shot we had. "Thanks.

Let me know if you can get anything out of it, anything at all."

Russell edged his way slowly through the packed crowd, reaching the corner of the stage just as a group of kids started wheeling amps into place and taping cables to the floor. One picked up a guitar, moving it from the side to front and center, placing it on a stand and plugging it in. Russell's eyes followed, focusing slightly to the right of the guitar.

The guitar? Or the roadie? Judging from Russell's reaction, I was guessing the ghost was somewhat attached to either one.

Just as the band was beginning their warm-up, I spotted Tremelay, working the room as I had been doing. I had to laugh at how incongruous he seemed, a middle-aged man among all these young people. It wasn't just his age, though. Tremelay walked like a cop. He might as well have had a sign stapled to his forehead that announced he was police. I was rethinking the benefit of his presence here. If the skinwalkers were at all nervous, they'd vanish the moment they saw him.

Although teens were generally cocky and overconfident. They'd managed to hitchhike their way to Baltimore from South Carolina. They'd killed at least seven people without any repercussions. There was a good chance that at this point they felt invincible.

So I ignored Tremelay and made my way to the stage, catching Russell's eye as I approached. The canned music dropped in volume, and sound checks began, the voices echoing loudly in the room in between stretches of silence. The crowd buzzed in the background, kids literally hopping in excitement.

"I can't quite make out what the spirit looks like, but he says his name is Travis Dawson," Russell told me, leaning close to be heard without shouting. "He's quite agitated that someone else is taking his place leading his band."

The shapeshifter. I looked down at the crude band advertisement on my phone and saw that Travis Dawson was indeed the lead guitarist and singer of the band. This might be a local group playing in abandoned buildings, but judging from the packed room they had a significant following. I could see where a spirit would be upset, losing not only his young life, but the band he'd fronted. It was one thing to be dead, another to watch an imposter in your skin take your place before an adoring group of teens.

The crowd erupted as the band took the stage. Travis looked just like the ad picture. The tall lanky guy with a fuzzy poof of black hair tuned his guitar, intent on adjusting the instrument and the mic. I watched, fascinated at how well the imposter had assumed Travis' identity. It was like he loved playing this instrument, like playing in this band was the highlight of his life. My resolve wavered with indecision. What if Russell was wrong? Nothing in the ease and confidence of this guy sent up red flags or gave me any indication that he wasn't exactly who he was supposed to be.

"Are you sure?" I asked Russell, pointing at the lead singer.

The necromancer watched intently as Travis draped the guitar strap over his head, settling the instrument on his hip. "Yes. The ghost is very agitated and trying to take the guitar from him. He's becoming more distinct and I can definitely see the resemblance."

Time to trust a ghost and a necromancer over my own eyes and intuition.

I thanked Russell and watched him make his way through the crowd. I didn't blame him for wanting to leave before the band started. This was hardly his kind of music, and honestly he stood out. So did Tremelay and I, but one less out of place individual improved our chances of catching the skinwalkers before they got wind of us and vanished.

The band started playing to the screams of the crowd. A mosh pit formed and I backed away, keeping an eye on Travis as I also tried to look for Tremelay. I doubted the skinwalker was going anywhere until the end of the concert. I couldn't see him walking out on this unless he felt his life was in danger. And I had no intention of confronting him until I could get him alone, or after the concert when the crowd had left and there were less civilians to get caught in any crossfire. Just because he knew magic didn't mean the guy didn't have a gun in his pocket as I did. No sense in getting a bunch of kids shot just because I couldn't be patient.

I finally found Tremelay and nodded to him, jerking my head toward the stage and mouthing "Travis." He nodded back and edged to the other side, so we were flanking the band. I assumed the other skinwalker was here, too, but Russell hadn't seen any more than the one ghost. If the second skinwalker wasn't posing as Bradley or Gary, then we wouldn't recognize him. Which would make it all the more dangerous to confront Travis. His accomplice could be anyone in the band, or even in the crowd. I was even beginning to be paranoid about the pierced woman collecting money at the door.

I knew the exact moment when Travis spotted

the detective. He hit a wrong note, his eyes narrowing as he focused into the crowd, then he plastered a stiff smile on his face and continued to play. After a few sets, the band took a break and the canned music took over. Travis scanned the crowd and I tried to make myself look like I was with the group of teenagers behind me, turning my back on the stage and hoping I was unrecognizable from this angle.

When I turned around, I couldn't see Tremelay anywhere. Or Travis. I had a moment of panic trying to remember where I'd last seen the detective, and headed in that direction. The mosh pit had disbanded with the break in the live music, but the crowd was still thick and I wasn't tall enough to see over a good number of these kids. Tremelay was nowhere to be found at the far corner of the stage, but I did see a door half-hidden by the stack of amps. It looked to be to a rear storeroom, and was partially open. I edged forward cautiously and peered in to see duffle bags and spare equipment.

There were no exit doors, no windows, and no band members. I made my way into the room and looked at the duffle bags, open with articles of clothing spilling out, and at the coats draped over cheap metal chairs. This was where the band changed and got ready, but where were they? Smoke breaks? Most everyone in the crowd was vaping, catching their nicotine fix in a way that didn't violate Maryland's tobacco in public places prohibition. Not that the concert goers probably cared judging from the scent of cannabis and the open exchange of pills going on.

Rabid Rabbit was an industrial band, gritty and old school. No doubt they were smoking the real thing—joints included—out back behind the garage.

Now was the time to dig through Travis Dawson's stuff and see if there was anything here to indicate which skinwalker had assumed his identity. The first few bags held only clothing and an assortment of porn mags. I was ready to dismiss the last bag as clothing-only until I pulled out a handful of pictures. It was odd to find actual photos when most everyone stored images electronically. There was a worn and tattered picture of a man and woman smiling down at a small boy holding a puppy. Another of what seemed to be the same boy riding a tricycle while the woman cheered on. And another of the boy, the man behind him helping him hold a baseball bat. I went to put them back and saw one more, tucked against the side of the duffle bag. It was a boy and a girl— Brian Huang's children. Did this mean Lawton King was in Travis Dawson's skin? Or that he was posing as another member of the band?

I shoved the pictures back into the bag and turned to go, nearly having a heart attack as I saw someone standing just inside of the door. I hadn't heard him, and he'd managed to slip in without disrupting the flashing light from the garage bay.

He closed the door behind him with a firm click. Even in the dim light I recognized Travis Dawson.

CHAPTER 28

"WHAT ARE YOU doing in here?"

I recognized the tenor of those smooth words. He wasn't sure if I was a crazed groupie looking for souvenirs, or if I was a crazed groupie here to offer myself up as a notch on one of their bedposts. I was just surprised that even with the dim storeroom lighting he hadn't recognized me.

Which meant he was probably not the skinwalker who had been impersonating Huang, the one whose pictures I'd just been pawing through, the one who I'd suspected was Lawton King. *That* skinwalker would have known me on sight. The other one, Gary Jarvett, had only met me the once while he was impersonating Bradley Lewis.

I wasn't sure which option was better. Lawton seemed a scared boy who just wanted to go home. Gary...well, he'd been creepy as Bradley Lewis and judging from what the picker had said, he was the violent leader of the three. And he was the one blocking my exit. My hand snaked down toward the heavy pistol in my pocket. His eyes narrowed, dropping to follow the motion.

Shit. Think fast or draw and shoot. And I really didn't want to discharge a firearm in a crowded building where nothing but a thin plywood wall separated us from the main concert area.

"You're Travis Dawson," I said breathlessly, feeling like a total idiot. "I just wanted a souvenir. A T-shirt or something. I'm sorry. I'll leave now."

I jabbed a finger against the sewing needle I'd stashed in the cuff of my sleeve. With a quick word under my breath, I'd activated the rebound spell. All I needed now was for him to cast something to freeze or incapacitate me, and I'd have him.

Instead Travis advanced, still blocking my path to the door. "You look familiar. Older than the usual crowd here. Didn't I see you at the Midnight Visitor concert the other night?"

Double shit. I moved toward him, figuring I could dart around and toward the door if needed. I had the rebound spell in place, and was pretty sure I could take him if he got physical. Whatever he was originally, Travis Dawson wasn't muscular. A good elbow to the diaphragm or fist to the nose would do it.

But something weird happened when I got close to the skinwalker. I forgot about punching him or skipping around him and just stood there, staring at his shirt and wondering what I was supposed to be doing. Travis put his hands on my shoulders and eased them slowly down my arms. "I don't like you going through our stuff. Think it's best if you just stay here."

Part of my brain was perfectly okay with that suggestion but part wanted me to leave. I thought about which option I should take as his hands worked their way down my arms, coming to rest on the leather bracelets.

I felt his hands tighten, heard an intake of breath and the snap of the leather cuff. His index finger touched the tattoo and it flamed to life, clearing my brain and causing the skinwalker to yelp and yank his hands away from me.

What the heck was I doing? This guy had murdered, and I was just standing like a mannequin in front of him. He hadn't cast any spell to rebound back on him, so I tried the next suggestion of Garza's

"Gary Jarvett. I know who you are and I reveal your true name to everyone. Everyone in Baltimore." I was slurring my speech and wasn't sure how effective option two was going to be on the skinwalker. It'd better work, because option three involved bullets.

I didn't know if it hindered his magical abilities, but my words certainly had an impact.

"Fucking Templar." he snarled. His hand came at my face and I ducked, blocking it with my right and punching out with my left.

His head jerked to the side as my fist hit his jaw. Without his magic I felt pretty confident that I could best him, so I swung with the right, surprised at the sticky-slippery feel of blood on my palm. He took the blow, punching toward me with his right. I had on the flak jacket, so I braced for the blow and kept swinging, blood beginning to fly from the cut on my hand.

How the hell was I bleeding? My palm stung just as I realized that whatever Travis held in his right hand was stuck in the plates of my jacket. With a twist he pulled free, slashing me across the arm with something long and sharp. He had a knife. I hadn't seen one in his hand, but it was the only thing that made sense.

I punched and kicked and elbowed, trying both to stay free of the knife and disable him. No way I was escaping out the door and letting this guy get away. He was going down, whether it was by my fists or from a gunshot. Unfortunately I was too busy hitting him and trying to avoid getting stabbed to dig the gun out of the recesses of my cargo pants, where its weight slapped against my leg with each of my movements.

One of my punches went wide and I stumbled off balance, feeling the blade slice through the fabric covering my jacket. Before I could regain my balance, Travis punched me with far more force than a skinny teen should have. My head jerked to the side as I fell to my knee. I saw the foot coming toward my face and tried to launch myself upward and back, taking the kick in the chest instead.

Pain exploded across my ribs. I slid across the room from the impact, my back and head slamming into the concrete wall. Everything dimmed and I felt myself crumple in a heap on the floor. I struggled to catch my breath and with what was left of my foggy brain I dug in my pocket, feeling for my gun.

The door opened. "Hurry up, we're getting ready to..." the male voice tapered off in confusion. My hand closed around the hard steel, but I hesitated, uncertain if the new guy was a band member who'd just stumbled upon us or a roadie. I wasn't about to fire the gun and risk killing someone in the crossfire.

"It's that Templar woman," Travis told him. "Help me."

Shit. The other skinwalker was one of the guys in the band. I took a painful breath and looked out from partially closed eyes, slowly sliding the gun free of my pocket.

"Break her neck and get out of here before the others come looking for you," Travis said. "Stash her behind the benches and you can skin her later."

"No!" the other boy said, his voice panicked. "Just tie her up and we'll run for it."

"Fine. I'll kill her myself." Travis took a step toward me and the other boy grabbed his arm.

"She's a Templar, Gary. You can't kill her. It will cause a war. They'll exterminate every last one of us."

Gary/Travis pulled free. "I don't give a shit about the rest of them. They'll never catch us. We'll stay one step ahead of them."

The rest of them? I hesitated, my finger on the trigger. How many murderous skinwalkers *were* there? Everything had pointed to just these three teens, but from what Gary said, there were *more*? In Baltimore or spread all over the country?

I saw Gary walk toward me, saw the short dark-skinned boy with the bleach-blond hair behind him shut his eyes tight. *Not gonna happen.* I rolled to the side, yanking the gun from my pocket and firing at Gary. I know that Garza said to shoot them in the neck, but I couldn't bring myself to take a shot that might miss and hit the concert goers on the other side of the plywood.

Red bloomed on his chest and Travis looked down in shock. "The bitch shot me. Did you see that? She shot me."

Besides the brief stain of blood, my shot didn't seem to do anything so I proceeded to unload the magazine in his chest, scooting upright when the clip was empty and using the wall at my back to get to my feet.

Travis dove for me, and I clubbed him with the pistol, suddenly regretting how the wall at my back hindered my mobility.

"Help me," Travis shouted as I landed a hard blow against his jaw. In the background I heard people screaming and shouting. I kept hitting, every breath sending a stabbing pain through my ribs. The knife slashed along my arms and I kicked, trying to get room to maneuver out of its way.

"Help me you stupid fucker, before she knocks my brains out."

I smashed the butt of the pistol against Travis's nose, and he bent in half, head-butting me in the stomach. I looked up just in time to see a piece of lumber coming for my head and raised my arm a second too late to completely block it.

My arm went numb. I heard the pistol clatter to the floor. Everything spun as I went to one knee. Then I felt warm breath against my face. My eyelids grew heavy, my mind thick, then everything went black.

CHAPTER 29

M Y HEAD WAS pounding as if my brains were trying to exit my skull. Even the shallow breaths I was taking sent a rhythmic ache through my chest. I kept my eyes closed and took in my surroundings with my other senses, unwilling to give away to my captors that I'd regained consciousness.

Hurting as I was, regaining consciousness was a good thing. I'd expected them to kill me right there, but I guessed the gunshots and the stampede of people would not have left much time to murder someone and skin them in a back room. How they managed to drag an unconscious woman out of the concert garage and take off was beyond me. I hoped they'd been seen. I hoped that right now Tremelay was on their trail, bearing down on them like a detective with Templar blood would.

There was no light filtering through my eyelids, so either it was dim, or it was night, or I was somewhere with no windows. Dark. I shivered in the damp chill, feeling the uneven ground beneath my body, the sharp jab of either rocks or dirt clods against me. It smelled of chemical fertilizer, of mold, of turpentine and bleach. And very faintly of laundry detergent. I could hear nothing beyond the pounding in my head.

Taking a cautious breath I eased open my eyes.

I *was* in a basement—dirt floor with a cement pad in the corner serving as foundation for an ancient washer and dryer. Faint light filtered through a tiny window near the ceiling. A set of narrow wooden steps led up, presumably to the rest of the house. There was an old paint rag, stiff and rough in my mouth. My hands were bound together with silver duct tape, as were my ankles. I winced at the blood staining my shirt sleeves and pants, beginning to feel the sting of dozens of cuts and slices. Thank heaven for the vest or I would have suffered far worse from Gary's knife.

There was a metal support pole a few feet in front of me, paint peeling. What caught my eye was the jagged edge of metal where something had been cut from it. Perfect for sawing through duct tape— and probably adding to my wounds. I rocked up to my knees, practically throwing up at the motion. I had to get this duct tape off and find something that could act as a weapon. There was no way I was going to fit through that tiny window, which meant my only way out was up the stairs and past whatever skinwalkers were in the upper part of the house. I scooted on my knees across the uneven dirt floor, managing to make it to the pole without face-planting into the ground. There, I wiggled around backward and arched my back, trying to reach the jagged piece of metal.

It was up too high. The only way I was going to do this was if I managed to get to my feet, and I already felt like the room was a carousel on top speed. There was no other choice. These guys were going to kill me. It was a wonder they hadn't killed me already. So I braced my back against the metal pole and pushed myself upward, legs quivering with the effort. It put me at the perfect spot to rub the duct tape against the jagged piece.

I'd just gotten to work on my wrists when I heard the squawk of a door and the flick of a switch. A bright light blinded me and I panicked, dropping to the floor and closing my eyes. Idiot. As if they wouldn't notice that I'd somehow moved across the room from where they'd originally dumped me.

Realizing there was no way I could fake this, I kept my eyes open and got back to my knees, watching as two sets of legs came down the creaking stairs.

"Oh good, she's awake." Gary grinned. He was still in Travis Dawson's skin. I longed to punch that grin right off his face, but punching him before hadn't seemed to have any lasting effects. Neither had shooting him. Beyond the bloody holes in his clothing, he appeared unhurt.

"She's moved." The other boy, Lawton, was in the bass player's skin. He shifted nervously back and forth at the bottom of the stairs. "We'll duct tape her to the pole and get out of here. A new city, somewhere different. We can make a 911 call once we're clear of the state, so someone can come get her."

Gary rolled his eyes. "Or we just kill her and leave her here. Who cares if anyone comes and gets her? This place is a flop house. It will be weeks before anyone comes down here and discovers her body. Longer if we throw a bunch of lime on it and wrap it in plastic."

I liked the first guy's idea better.

"She's a Templar," Lawton protested. "You're crazy if you think they won't track us down. I know you don't care about the others, but we're gonna die if we kill her. That cop knows us. And Templars have magical stuff. They're like witches. No matter what skin we take, they'll find us."

For a brief second Gary looked concerned, then he shrugged. "Nah. They haven't done that sort of thing for hundreds of years. She's not chasing us on a sanctioned mission. She's doing this on her own. They won't spend any time or energy hunting us down."

He was right, except it was the Elders who wouldn't give a crap about my death. My family was another thing. I remembered the look on my mother's face when I'd told her of my demon mark. She'd find these boys and make sure they met their death at the end of her sword.

"If we let you go, you'll leave us alone, won't you?" Lawton pleaded, his eyes desperate.

I couldn't give him that reassurance. "You've killed people. You'll kill again. I can't let that stand"

I might be signing my death warrant, but I wasn't about to lie. They'd know it. And I'd rather go down fighting.

Gary barked out a short, harsh laugh. "Hey, at least she's honest. Kill her. Leave her body down here."

Lawton caught his breath. "Are we going to leave Baltimore? Go elsewhere?"

"No. I like it here. And I like this Travis kid. He's in a band. He gets the babes. Guys respect him. Did you see how we opened for Midnight Visitor? That fucking rocked. There's no way I'm leaving that behind."

"Where will we stay? We can't come back here." There was an odd look in Lawton's eyes as his gaze met mine, like he was trying to tell me something.

Gary shrugged. "We've got options. Maybe we'll just float for a while, or crash at this Travis kid's place, or at the band practice spot. Doesn't matter."

"Okay."

I felt sorry for Lawton, even though he was probably about to kill me. His face was pinched and white, his eyes wild and frightened. He licked his lips, hands shaking as he picked up an enormous wrench from beside the washing machine.

"Make sure she's pulverized," Gary instructed. "Take her skin and ditch it somewhere else. That way it will take longer for them to identify her."

Lawton nodded, shifting the wrench to his other hand and wiping the free one on his pants.

Gary put his arm around the other man's shoulder. "Your first kill. Sure you can? I had to kill Huang for you and this Strike kid you're wearing. I'm getting tired of doing all the heavy lifting in this partnership."

"I can do it." Lawton said, his voice shaking.

"Good." Gary patted him on the shoulder. "Because if I find out she's not dead, then you are. You're either all the way in or all the way out, and after that fiasco at the bus station and your brief stint in jail, I'm not sure I can trust you. I need to trust you. So it's her, or it's you. You heard her. You let her go and she'll come back after us. I'll check. And if I see her alive, then you won't be. Got it?"

Lawton nodded. "Got it."

Gary turned to walk up the stairs and Lawton swung. I dove to the side, rolling and the wrench slammed against the dirt. "Hold still," he ordered, his voice more firm than it had been all evening.

"Have fun." Gary laughed. I heard the squeak of

the stairs, the slam of the door, then the impact of the wrench on the dirt as I frantically rolled around the basement.

"Hold still." This time Lawton's voice was a concerned whisper. "I don't want to hit you."

I froze, more from shock than any inclination to comply with his command. He hit the ground beside me with the wrench, reaching out with his other hand to yank the rag from my mouth. I didn't have a drop of saliva left. The taste of dry fiber and old paint was the only thing on my tongue.

"Quiet." He hit the ground twice more, this time putting his back into it. There were dents forming in the hard, red, rocky clay from the wrench. I held still, and kept my mouth shut, wincing and blinking every time the wrench came down. Finally he stopped, cocking his head to listen to something.

"You need to get out of here fast. I wouldn't put it past him to come back to check on your dead body."

It was my turn to lick my lips. "He'll kill you if he doesn't see my dead, skinned body in this basement."

Lawton's eyes glistened with tears. "I'll lie and say I dumped your body elsewhere. I don't care. I'm not killing, and I'm especially not killing a Templar. Gary might not care about our family, but I do. I'm not signing their death sentence just because he's gone crazy."

The adrenaline faded with his words and I slumped, once again feeling the pain of my head, my ribs, and the myriad cuts all over my limbs. He was going to let me go. I was hurt but I'd live. I only wished I had the same confidence that *he'd* live.

"I didn't kill Brian Huang," Lawton said, his

eyes earnest as they met mine. "Gary did. Later that night he took my skin—Lawton King's skin—and hid it from me, forcing me to wear Brian Huang. I've been Lawton for ten years. It was...it hurt to be someone else. And now this kid."

"I believe you," I told him. I did. This poor kid was trapped and scared.

"Gary put Brian Huang's body in the closet to get back at me because I told him I needed to go home to Brian's wife and to work the next day. They were expecting me. There was a special exhibit and I had to be there."

Trapped, scared, and more than a little unhinged. Lawton was talking almost as though he'd *become* Brian Huang when he'd put the skin on. Was that what happened to skinwalkers? "It's okay. I'm going to find him and put him away where he can't hurt you or anyone else ever again."

"You'll never catch him." Lawton's voice was grim as he stalked over to a shelf of painting supplies and knocked it over, prying the lid off a gallon of red and dumping it on the floor. I watched as he smeared the red across the wrench, flinging drops of it onto the walls.

"I believe you, I really do, but you *had* to have killed someone in your past. A brother? A sister? Maybe you were really young and someone forced you to do it."

"I didn't kill anyone, not even Lawton King." His voice was wooden as he splattered the red paint across the room. "I didn't kill anyone. Sometimes when people die, and they're real fresh, we can use their skins."

Ew. But I believed him. There was something about this boy—when he was Brian Huang, as well as when he was this Strike guy—that made me believe him. He hadn't killed anyone. He was just a kid caught in a bad situation with no way out.

That meant what I'd read about skinwalkers was wrong. They didn't have to kill a family member to gain the ability. And I still had no idea how to stop them. Either the naming thing hadn't worked or Gary Jarvett wasn't really Gary Jarvett. I was at a loss on how to stop and apprehend these two—three if I counted the female running around north of the city as a vampire. But right now, the priority was getting out of this basement and to safety. And possibly getting some medical attention.

"There." Lawton threw the wrench into the corner and dug in his pocket pulling out a cell phone—my cell phone. He placed it by the stairs and began to make his way up. "Better hurry. And leave us alone. I'll try to convince Gary to leave the city. Just leave us alone."

I saw him disappear up the steps and heard the door close. He'd left the light on, and I took immediate advantage of my chance at freedom, scooting back over to the pole and shimmying upward to again saw at the duct tape on my hands. Once they were free, I tore at the strips around my feet, scooping up the cell phone and the wrench as I headed up the stairs.

The wooden treads creaked and I winced with every noise, unsure that I truly was alone in the house. But when I eased open the door I heard nothing.

This truly *was* a flop house. Plywood covered the windows on the outside. The front door had obviously been pried open. Fixtures and plumbing were ripped from splintered cabinetry. The ceiling hung in tatters, the linoleum floor was chipped and scuffed. Rags were piled in a corner. I doubted the skinwalkers used this for more than a dumping ground. Gary seemed far too fastidious to set up home in such a place.

I wasn't about to linger. I made my way to the rear of the house, climbing between the two-by-fours blocking the broken doorway and into an overgrown lawn with a dilapidated, rusty fence. Judging from the adjoining backyards, the whole block was vacant. I took advantage of that fact and climbed through the yards, breaking into a painful run once I'd hit the street.

After a few blocks the adrenaline had once again faded, leaving me ready to puke and pass out on the concrete. I sat against a brick wall covered with graffiti and pulled out my phone, eyeing the street signs and ignoring the curious stairs of the residents. There were messages—some from Tremelay and a few from Dario. I winced and glanced at the sky. It was close to dawn. I knew if I called Dario he wouldn't be able to get here before the sun came up, and judging from his texts he was hard at work tracking the skinwalker vampire.

So I called Tremelay. The detective shot off a panicked, incomprehensible stream of questions the moment he answered.

"I'm okay," I assured him. "Well, actually I have a concussion and some cuts, and probably bruised ribs, but I'm okay. Can you come pick me up?"

I gave him the cross streets, relieved that I wouldn't have to walk all the way back to Fells Point. Not that I knew exactly how to get to my apartment, or to my car. I hoped my sword was still in my trunk. Although anyone who tried to steal Trusty would have gotten a nasty magical shock.

"I'll be right there," Tremelay promised.

There was one more person I'd need to talk to. Again I looked at the gray tint to the east and dialed Dario.

CHAPTER 30

I'VE GOT A lead on your girl." Dario's voice was cheerful. I was about to change that.

"Let me know how you manage to subdue her because none of the stuff that crappy excuse for a supernatural expert Hakan Garza wrote about worked."

There was a moment of poignant silence. "You okay?"

"Concussion. Bruised ribs. Cut up like a spiral-sliced ham. Other than that I'm okay." Actually I felt better than I should have. Reaching up, I touched the lump on my head. It wasn't huge and the skin wasn't broken. I was beginning to think my unconscious state had been from whatever sleepy spell the skinwalkers used and not the board Lawton had smacked me with. But why hadn't the sleepy spell rebounded on them? And why was I not dead?

They could have killed me. They *should* have killed me. Lawton was the only reason I was still alive and him letting me go could cost him his life.

"You shot them?" Dario asked. His voice was now gruff and harsh, like he was chewing gravel and ready to rip the head off of someone.

"The one that was attacking me, yeah. I unloaded the clip. Now, in all fairness to Garza, I didn't shoot him in the neck. I was worried about missing and having the bullet kill someone on the other side of the wall. Still, it should have slowed him down. He didn't even flinch."

Dario swore. "How physically strong were they? If the humans are greater than human strength, then I'm wondering how powerful this vampire one is going to be."

Incredible Hulk with fangs? "This guy was a skinny, tall kid and he managed to take me down. I think I would have held my own if the other one hadn't hit me in the head with a board. Either way, you might want backup."

He grunted and I wasn't sure whether my suggestion offended his ego or he was considering how much backup to bring. "Sure you're okay?"

Awww. He was worried about me. "No. I need a box of cannoli and a good bottle of Chianti right now. When are you coming home?"

I practically heard his smile. "As soon as I catch this girl of yours. We've finally got the rogue situation under control. The only ones left alive are harmless and we definitely sent a message about hunting on the fringes of our territory."

I thought about the two boys, how Lawton seemed trapped in his circumstances, how Gary didn't care about anyone but himself. Which was this girl? And did I want to risk vampire lives to find out?

No, I didn't.

"If she's anything like these other two skinwalkers, then don't worry about bringing her in alive."

"Didn't know you wanted her alive." Dario's voice once again was amused. "But of course you wanted her alive. You're a Templar and she needs to face human justice."

If the past month had taught me anything, it was that human justice was flawed and sometimes it needed to come another way. "I just had my rear end handed to me by these two. Don't underestimate her, and if it looks like she might get away, I'd rather she be dead."

She'd killed two vampires and who knows how many people. I couldn't let her go free to continue killing.

"Okay. It's coming on dawn soon, but I'll get right on it tomorrow night. Hopefully I'll be back before sunup."

I hoped so. Hanging up with Dario, I saw Tremelay's sedan pull in. He jumped from the car and raced toward me, face full of concern.

"Ainsworth! You look like a crime scene photo. You sure you're okay?"

I repeated my list of injuries and waited while he checked my head and various cuts.

"What the hell happened?" The detective plopped down beside me, handing me a much needed bottle of water and a couple of aspirin.

I swallowed the pills and gulped half the contents of the bottle before replying. "I was rooting through the bags in the back room when Gary, the one impersonating Travis Dawson, cornered me. None of Garza's techniques worked. The guy attacked me with a knife, which may or may not have been coming out of his finger, and when the other one came in, I knew I was in trouble. So I pulled out your gun. Unloaded it in Gary's chest and it didn't do squat. Next thing I know I'm on the ground, unconscious, then waking up in the basement of an abandoned house."

"They didn't kill you?" Tremelay asked,

incredulous.

Obviously not. "Yeah. I know. Gary told Lawton to kill me, but the kid let me go. I'm afraid he's going to pay for that act of charity with his life."

The detective rubbed his face in his hands. "I lost sight of you when the band broke, and when the gunshots went off the crowd surged for the door. It was a damned mob. By the time I got free and went looking for you, all I found was the empty gun and shells. Oh, and blood splatter."

He must have thought the worst. Without thinking, I wrapped my arm around him and gave him a hug, resting my head on his shoulder.

"I had to preserve it all as a crime scene, report you as a possible victim. I'm so sorry, but I truly thought it was going to be your skinned body we found next." Tremelay's voice wavered and I hugged him tighter, even though the movement was killing my poor ribs.

"I'm fine. I've got no idea where these two skinwalkers are, but I'm fine."

He sighed and pulled away. "Do you need to go to the hospital? Stitches? X-rays? How hard did that kid hit you on the head?"

I felt the bump again, finding a second one from where I'd smacked the wall when Gary had thrown me. "Not that hard. I don't think I need stitches, and I'm pretty sure my ribs are just bruised. Honestly I just want a shower and a nap."

Tremelay grimaced. "It might be a few hours before that happens. I need you to come down to the police station."

I stared at him with huge eyes. He had to be joking. I'd had the crap beaten out of me, seriously thought I was a goner, and he needed me to go to the station? "Why?"

He squirmed. "Because the gun was registered to me. I told them I'd given it to you. You fired the entire clip and there was blood everywhere."

"At least half of that blood was mine," I retorted.

"I reported you as missing, possibly taken by the skinner."

Oh. Yeah. I was the victim. The only known survivor. Of course they wanted me to come in. "Can't my statement wait until I've cleaned up a bit and taken a nap?"

The detective squirmed again. "No. It's not just a statement. They're considering charging you with firing a weapon in a public place."

He had to be joking. He *must* be joking.

"If it had been me, I still would have needed to fill out a stack of reports to justify every bullet fired," he explained, his voice pleading with me to be cooperative. "I want them to see you injured, not all cleaned up and rested. I want the reporting officer to see you and know you were fearing for your life. That plus your very valuable information on the skinner case should make all of this go away."

I was never carrying a gun again. This was total bullshit. Supernatural baddies killing innocent people, and I was going to be hung out to dry for trying to stop them. With a gun. None of this would have happened if I had gotten my sword past the girl at the door. I still would have wound up duct-taped in the basement of an abandoned house, but at least I wouldn't be facing jail time.

"Okay. Let's get this over with."

Tremelay helped me to my feet. I made sure I shuffled to his car like a B-movie zombie, exaggerating every ache and pain. I knew it wasn't his fault, but someone needed to feel guilty about this whole thing.

This time it was my turn in the hot seat of the interview room. Five officers were squashed with me in the tiny space. I was pretty sure that was against regulations as well as the fire code, but there seemed to be a lot of interest in Tremelay's occult expert who'd gotten nabbed by the skinner and managed to walk away with her skin mostly intact.

The five officers looked carefully at me. My pants were shredded and stained with blood. My arms had diagonal cuts all over them. I took a few shallow breaths and tried to look miserable. It wasn't a stretch, even for someone with my poor acting ability. Once again I recited my story, carefully omitting the rebound spell and any magical details that would make me look like a crazy. Although I guess I could explain it all as confusion from my whack on the head.

"They were both cutting you with knives?" One of the officers asked. He was busy scribbling in a notebook. I assumed he was the one who was going to have to fill out the report on the shots-fired-at-the-rave call.

"Just the one. The other guy seemed reluctant to join in, but when I started bashing my attacker in the face with the pistol, he decided to help his buddy."

"Wait. You fired the gun, emptied it, but still didn't take down your attacker?"

Here's where I got to look like a complete idiot, someone who should never be allowed to even look at a gun, let alone fire one.

"Yeah. Maybe he was wearing a vest?" It was my only idea that might salvage my reputation as a sort-of badass Templar.

"At that range it would have knocked him back." The officer rubbed his chest, clearly remembering the feel of a slug hitting a vest. "It would have had some effect, even if it didn't kill him. But we didn't find any slugs in the walls either. Where the heck did you aim when shooting?"

Crap. Back to looking like an idiot. I rubbed the bumps on my head and blinked innocently. "He'd bounced me against the concrete back wall earlier. Maybe my vision was wonky? I'm trying to remember as best as I can."

It must have worked because my interrogator moved on. "Then the other guy hit you in the head and you don't remember anything until waking up, duct-taped in a basement?"

"Yeah. They came down before I could get free and started discussing how to kill me."

I saw the sympathy on their faces, especially the woman standing next to the guy scribbling in the notebook. "Did they rape you?" she asked softly.

"Thank God, no." I shook my head. "The one who'd attacked me at the concert told the other to kill me and dispose of my body."

The woman exchanged a glance with one of the other officers. "So it sounds like the one is more of a reluctant accomplice. Maybe the main killer has some kind of hold over him, a family member's safety perhaps?"

"He let me go, and left my cell phone so I could call for help." I'd already told them this, but it bore repeating. I really wanted Lawton to escape the death penalty if possible.

"And you recognized them?" The note-taking officer asked.

I nodded, thinking fast. Even though Gary had assumed Travis Dawson's identity, I really didn't want to sully the dead kid's reputation. "Bradley Lewis was the guy who attacked me. He seems to be the ring leader. I didn't recognize the other one. He was young, African-American, medium height and build. I think he was in the band? Or maybe not."

I hated to throw Bradley Lewis under the bus, but someone had to take the blame for this and Unknown Skinwalker Mage didn't seem a sane response. Hopefully I was vague enough on Lawton's description to allow him some legal wiggle room if he got caught.

"Bradley Lewis?" the woman exclaimed. "But I thought the body from the Lewis garage came back as his."

I shrugged, trying once more for the dazed-and-confused look. "It was either him or he's got a twin running around."

The officer finished scribbling in his notebook, then looked at the others. "Think I'm done here."

Thank heaven. They all filed out of the interview room, leaving me alone with my injuries on a hard chair with a Styrofoam cup of the worst coffee ever. It seemed like hours, but ten minutes later Tremelay came back in with a handful of papers.

"They wanted to charge you with discharge of a weapon in a public place, but given the circumstances they've decided to drop the charges if you agree to ten hours of community service."

Community service. Exactly what I'd been doing for the last month, and I'd sure as heck done more than ten hours of it. "Does time served count? Protecting the city from death mages, and skinwalkers? Can I include that or do I need to squeeze in some soup kitchen hours in between hunting supernatural killers?"

He winced. "I know, I know. Just go pick up trash in the park or something. Ten hours isn't much."

For him, maybe. For me ten hours of community service was like a slap in the face. This sucked. Really, really sucked. I was at the rave doing official police business, accompanied by a detective who'd *given* me the gun, and I was now being punished for helping out. Just peachy.

The rest of the process couldn't have gone quick enough for either me or Tremelay. He fast tracked me through the paperwork, I signed on the line, then followed him to his unmarked car to drive back to the rave site where my Toyota was still parked.

All I wanted to do when I got home was turn on some television and finish off that expensive chianti, then take a nap. Screw them all. Community service, my ass.

But I was a Templar and I couldn't let these skinwalkers run around my city killing people, even if the police had just given me the equivalent of a giant butt-hurt. There was no time for sulking. I had other things to do—like find out why my rebound spell hadn't worked against whatever the two skinwalkers had done to make me so sleepy. And how I was going to subdue these two. They were strong and fast and impervious to bullets. They could change appearance, but outside of the sleepy-time thing, they didn't seem to have any magical abilities. There had been plenty of opportunity to cast a spell, yet they hadn't. According to the Garza book, which I was beginning to think was a complete fabrication, skinwalkers were basically witch-mages. Outside of mauling people in their animal form, the majority of their violence was in the form of spells. These kids were teens. Surely they would have known some basic spells by now? If their mentor had taken the time to teach them the very advanced techniques of using skins to assume another's form, then he had to have taught them a few charms and hexes.

I drove home mulling over my complete lack of reliable knowledge on these creatures. Garza had let me down. There weren't many other texts I could turn to. In a wild moment I considered calling the National Museum of the American Indian in D.C. and asking them if I could speak to a specialist on Navajo spellwork. Maybe I'd been going about this the wrong way by checking my Templar books. I had no other ideas. Researching Native American myths and legends through the museum and internet sources might be my only option. Perhaps I'd get lucky and find a gem among the thousands of pages of muck.

Making my way through the wards and physical locks, I entered my shabby apartment and put my sword on the kitchen counter, wincing as my bruised rib muscles pulled with the motion. The painkillers Tremelay had given me were wearing off, and who knew how much aspirin I had left from last month's demon-attack injuries. I needed to start buying the stuff in bulk.

The little fox figurine stared at me from the coffee table, its eyes once again bright red. I picked it up and brought it with me to the dining room table strewn with books and my laptop.

"I'm glad you're feeling better," I told Raven. "Because I'm really going to need your help on this one." I told her of the night's, and morning's, activities then set her in front of the laptop.

Hopefully Raven could come up with something, because right now the only thing I was capable of was sleep.

CHAPTER 31

M Y EYELIDS WOULDN'T open. I couldn't move, but I could hear and feel everything. I recognized the dank smell of mildew and turpentine and my heart raced as I realized I was back in the basement. I'd just escaped...hadn't I?

"Don't mess up her skin," I heard Gary say. "It would be really cool to be a Templar. Imagine what I could do in that skin. I could take my Oath, gain entrance to the Temple, steal all that magical shit. Her family would never know. I'd visit them and slaughter them in their sleep. Everyone would think it was a Lizzie Borden murder."

I heard a girl's laugh. "I'll be careful. A Templar and a vampire. We'll rule the world. Forget about this stinking town. Forget about Lawton. He was always a weakling, always a cry baby. We don't need him."

It felt like a razorblade was slicing into my waist. I tried to scream but nothing came out. Inch by agonizing inch the pain moved upward and outward, my skin separating from the muscle. Why couldn't I wake up? I needed to wake up.

My own hoarse shriek woke me. I flailed against invisible foes before realizing I was alone in my bedroom, tangled in sweat-soaked sheets. My ribs ached with every deep breath, my head throbbed.

Desperately needing to check, I threw off the covers and pulled up my tank-top, running my fingers along my waist. There was nothing there beyond the rough circle of the demon mark.

It was bad enough losing sleep over my killing Dark Iron, now I was having nightmares about being skinned alive. This had to stop. I needed to come to terms with my choices, have faith in my abilities as a Templar, and face my fears head-on.

A Templar. Maybe that was my problem. I'd been chasing these skinwalkers like a mage with a research book in one hand and spells, or a gun, in the other. My faith had been shaken and I wasn't thinking of this as a Warrior of God. Research was good. Research helped you prepare for what you were about to face. But when you faced it, all a Templar needed was her sword and her faith.

I had my sword. Time to find my faith.

The shower felt good aside from the sting of dozens of slices on my arms and legs. Once I was clean I treated and bandaged my cuts, an entire box of Band-Aids now decorating my body. Refreshed, I headed toward the laptop with renewed purpose. Tremelay was, no doubt, checking all the addresses associated with Travis Dawson and this Strike kid. I'd spend the rest of the day in research and in prayer, and when the night came, I was going to hunt a skinwalker. Two actually, although I hoped I wouldn't have to kill the one.

The cursor blinked on my laptop. Raven had been hard at work while I'd slept. *Your> reversal spell was solid. The sleepiness must not be a spell. Chloroform? Some kind of nitrous gas maybe? When they cut you with the knife, did they dose you with something?*

Raven had come through, managing to type on the computer. I wanted to hug her, but hugging a three inch resin fox seemed kind of weird.

My spell was good. At least I knew I hadn't flubbed that one up, but then what *was* the sleepy-time thing the skinwalkers had used on me? "I would have smelled chloroform, although nitrous or some other knockout gas is a possibility." I said to Raven. "But if he had a canister of gas I think I would have noticed, and wouldn't he have been affected too?"

The keys tapped slowly, one agonizing letter at a time. *Maybe not skinwalker?*

I really didn't want to face that option but none of the methods Garza suggested had worked. And Lawton insisted he hadn't killed anyone—which was a key means in gaining the skill. And now the weird sleep thing. A skinwalker should use spells. These guys didn't use spells. And whatever they'd done to make me want to take a nap in the middle of a fight for my life it wasn't magic. It had to be a skill native to a non-human creature.

I'd been wrong. Which meant I was back to square one. Not skinwalker. Not shapeshifter. Not demon possession. What *were* these things?

In desperation I shoved the Peterson and Garza book aside and searched for "creature," "supernatural," "human skin" on the internet.

What came up was a mishmash of parasitic skin infections, video game references, and a whole host of very creative tattoo art. Out of desperation I added "South Carolina" to the mix, figuring the kids had been taken and held in the state for ten years. It was possible whatever creature took them was indigenous to the state.

Skinwalkers. Page after page of skinwalker lore,

a few articles about a taxidermist who gave ghost tours, and a legend from Gullah culture about something called a Boo Hag.

Hag was typically another name for witch, and I'd already determined that these two guys weren't casting spells, so I set that one aside and started reading the skinwalker articles, hoping outside of all the crazy misinformation on the internet, *somebody* would have insights into how to stop these guys. At this point I didn't care what I called them, I just needed to catch them.

I was on my third cup of coffee and on page two of my internet search when I heard a knock. It was Sean Merrill at my door.

CHAPTER 32

WHAT WAS JANICE'S boyfriend doing here? Without Janice. And how did he get my address? This was even more suspicious than him stopping by the coffee shop where I worked.

"Can I come in?"

There was no reason for me *not* to invite him in, other than the fact that he was my friend's boyfriend and he was carrying something that looked like a large hard-sided briefcase from the '80s.

I was curious, though. Even cut up and with a mild concussion, I was reasonably confident I could take down the tall, skinny developer if he tried anything. Especially with my sword at hand.

"Yeah. Come on in." I'd need to tell Janice about this visit. It was just too weird for her boyfriend to come calling on me solo.

Sean walked in, setting the odd briefcase on my kitchen counter and wandering over to the dining room table where my laptop sat open to a page on Shaman skinwalkers. He ran his finger down the monitor while I waited with growing impatience for him to speak.

"Skinwalkers mainly use animals to assist their journeys across the veil into the spirit world, as well as to assume the form and power of the animal, whether for benign reasons or not." He closed the laptop. "You're looking in the wrong place. You need to be researching Boo Hag."

Every muscle in my body tensed. A land developer, a patron of the arts, and now a man knowledgeable about North American paranormal creatures. Who was this Sean Merrill?

"Boo Hag." I let the words hang in the air, as a sort of prompt for him to go on.

"The killers," he explained patiently. "They're not serial killers or skinwalkers or demons. They're Boo Hag."

"They don't cast spells." I wasn't sure why I was telling him this. Perhaps it was because I was frustrated and desperate. Heck, if I was relying upon the internet to give me the answers, I shouldn't balk at listening to what this guy had to say.

"No. Boo Hag aren't the witches that the legends say. We're a race of creatures that live primarily in the Carolinas."

We. A chill went through me. Sean moved toward the kitchen, flipping the latches on his briefcase. I flinched with each snap, wrapping my fingers around the hilt of my sword.

"Sit down." A smile took the command out of the words. Out of the briefcase came two martini glasses, a bottle of Haymans 1850 Reserve gin, and a slew of accessories. "You a one or two olive woman?"

"It's barely after noon," I protested.

He opened the gin and poured a generous amount in the tumbler. "It's never too early for a martini."

This guy would have fit right in with my family. Martini lunch, indeed. I sat, not sure what to make of this. "Two olives. Dirty, please."

He wiggled his eyebrows, the first suggestive move he'd made since he'd come through the door. "I always figured that about Templars. It's the straight-laced ones with swords who like it dirty."

Sean poured the two martinis, placed one before me then sat down opposite me with the other. "Back to the topic at hand. Boo Hag generally live in clans. We survive by taking a small amount of life essence from the breath of sleeping humans. We seldom kill unless cornered and threatened. We're a secretive race, who only want to live in peace among the humans."

Yeah. Except there was something missing from his speech. "These three *have* killed. And what's with the human skins? That hardly seems peaceful."

He winced, taking a sip of his martini before answering me. "Our natural form is alarming to humans. There's no way we'd survive if we walked around looking like a skinned corpse. Each of us find a human to impersonate. We take their skin, and become that person, keeping that identity until the human skin ages to the point where we can no longer use it. Generally we need to assume a new identity every forty to sixty years, depending on the age of the skin when we take it."

I noticed he'd phrased this carefully to avoid the gruesome truth. "You kill a human being and assume their identity. You *do* kill."

His eyes met mind, steady and honest. "We make every effort to take the skins of those who are newly dead. Overdose victims, head trauma—as long as the skin hasn't suffered more than minimal damage we can repair it when we put it on. But sometimes...yes. Sometimes we have no choice but to kill a human and take a skin. If it's a matter of life or death, we will kill to preserve our anonymity, to protect ourselves and our family. Please understand, we'd be wiped out by the humans if they saw us and knew we were more than just an old folktale."

I sipped my martini, imagining a skinned corpse walking down the street, trying to get a meal in a diner, working at a call center, and I saw what he meant. "How many skins do *you* have? Does every Boo Hag have a collection of identities they can assume, like these teens are doing?"

He set his drink down. "I only have one skin, one identity. We don't collect. I've never heard of a Boo Hag doing what these kids are doing. That's why I didn't come forward at first. I honestly didn't believe they could *be* Boo Hag. I too thought this was a human serial killer, or some other kind of creature. We're peaceful. We don't want to kill, and we take every effort to avoid it. Yes, it's fraud, and technically identity theft, but we don't murder."

The three kids terrorizing Baltimore were committing murder, but right now I wanted to know about this man in front of me who'd presented himself as Sean Merrill. "Did all this happen two years ago? When you said you woke up and discovered you weren't the same person?"

There wasn't even a hint of malice in his expression, just honesty. And sadness. "I was a ninety-year-old man the day I met Sean Merrill. I'd been searching for almost five years for a suitable skin when I came across the accident. He'd been hit head on and died of internal injuries. It was on a back road, so it took a while for another car to come along and call 911. The doctors said it was a miracle I'd survived the accident, let alone walked away with such minor injuries. That was two years ago. I took Sean Merrill's skin, divorced his wife, and began a new life."

Immediately I thought of my friend who was already half in love with him and drained my martini glass "And Janice? What are you going to do about Janice?"

His gaze warmed, a smile turning up the corner of his mouth. "Just because I'm a creature in a borrowed skin doesn't mean I like living alone. For two hundred years I've lived by day as a human. I would like to have a companion—one who doesn't want children, one who trusts that I'm not cheating on her when I'm out late at night. Janice is a smart, kind woman. She's the sort of woman I could fall in love with."

"Will you tell her?" At this moment I was far more concerned about Janice than the killers running around Baltimore and any part this man might play in all of that.

The smile widened. "If things continue on between us, yes. I never thought I could tell someone, but Janice knows about vampires and mages, demons and angels. I hope she can accept the man I am under the skin."

It was one thing to know about the presence of supernatural creatures, another entirely to date one. But that was up to Janice. "You need to tell her. No waiting until she's in love and you break her heart. I want you to tell her this week, or I'll do it for you."

He nodded, taking another sip of his martini. "But that's not the reason I'm here. I would have been more than happy to keep my true nature a secret from you, but these three Boo Hag threaten us all with their murders and reckless actions. You need to know everything about them."

I did. Starting with how they managed to take me out. "So what's with the sleepy stuff? I encountered two last night and they had something that made me so tired that I could barely keep my eyes open. They actually knocked me out with it."

Sean grimaced. "We're only supposed to do that when we come upon someone who is already asleep. There's a narcotic in our breath that we use while we feed to keep the human in a deep sleep. I'm sure you can understand how alarming it would be for someone to wake up and find a monster inches from his face."

That would be more than alarming. "So you take their life essence through their breath? How much? What are the side effects to the human afterward?"

Sean held up his hands. "Let me step back and explain more about us. We're genderless, although after years of wearing human skins, we develop a preference. Obviously we cannot bear children with humans, but once every century or two, we do produce offspring asexually. Boo Hag live for approximately three hundred years. Each night we shed our skin and find a human to 'ride' stealing their life-force through their breath as they sleep. We do not kill our victims. They wake up feeling a bit tired and groggy, but recover within a few days."

It didn't sound too bad outside of the human skin thing. "Every night you walk around like a skinned corpse to feed? Sounds risky."

"It is, which is why the narcotic in our breath is so important. We also can move short distances by transforming into smoke. It allows us to gain entry to homes under doors or through cracks in the window sills."

And that was how Lawton as Brian Huang escaped the jail cell, although I was still amazed that he'd navigated the city in his Boo Hag form without anyone calling the police.

"We move fast," Sean added. "I'm sure humans have caught a glimpse of us over the years but at night with dim light and our speed, most probably think the monster they saw was just their eyes playing a trick on them."

All that was going to make it even harder to catch the murderers. "Do you know these three Boo Hag who are spree killing in Baltimore?"

He shook his head. "Not personally. They're just kids. They weren't even born last time I was home to visit. A few of us live outside of the main clan in South Carolina, but we all return there when we have offspring so that Grandmother may raise them properly. She ensures they have the skills and social training to interact and live among the humans, otherwise they could endanger us all. I can assure you, this sort of thing has *never* happened before."

"So this Grandmother lost a few of her young before they were adequately trained?" I went to sip my martini, and got a mouth full of olives instead. Time for a refill.

As if reading my mind, Sean took my empty glass and rose to make another. "Fully trained or not, young Boo Hag don't act like this. I didn't even suspect the killers were Boo Hag until a few days ago when Janice confided in me the gruesome nature of the crimes. Even then...Boo Hag aren't like this. We're peaceful. We just want to fit in and live without notice or persecution. Their taking of skins and wearing them seemed suspiciously like what we do, so I made a phone call home and discovered that, yes, three of our young had left the nest without permission."

I accepted the second martini gratefully. "Three

Boo Hag. They hitchhiked their way up with that picker, took a skin at the rest stop, took another at the museum. They took Brian Huang, Bradley Lewis, Travis Dawson, some kid named Strike—why do they need all these skins?"

Sean shook his head. "They don't *need* more than one skin. I think they're collecting. Maybe they aren't satisfied living as one human during the day, so they grab the skins of whoever is convenient, whoever appeals to them? Maybe they're trying out these lives like teenage girls in a department store dressing room, discarding the ones they no longer want? I don't know. None of this makes sense to me. If Grandmother hadn't confirmed these three were missing—these exact three—then I wouldn't have believed they were Boo Hag at all."

What had gone wrong with these three that hadn't happened ever before in Boo Hag history? Did they feed from the wrong person? Fall in with the wrong crowd? Whatever their past or motives, they were three teens, runaways who were drunk on freedom and power in a human world and killing whoever they wanted—vampire or human. Well, at least two were. Lawton had insisted he hadn't killed, and I believed him.

"They're not ready to be away from the nest, away from the supervision of Grandmother," Sean continued. "I know they're on a killing spree, but they're very young. They're just kids. Maybe they don't yet understand the nature of their actions."

Like amoral toddlers pulling the wings off butterflies? Regardless, they were killing people and they needed to be stopped. "So, what are you going to do about it?"

It was Sean's turn to drain his martini. "I don't know what I *can* do about it. They're not my children. Plus they are three and I am one. Only Grandmother has the power to rein them in. She is trying to get up here as fast as she can now that she knows where they landed but there are five other children who need her. She can't just drop everything and come."

"She needs to get a move on and stop them, or I'm going to have to kill them. I can't allow them to run around murdering humans while Grandmother takes her sweet time getting up here."

But could I? My stomach roiled at the thought. As deranged as Gary was, he was still a kid. It had been hard enough to kill Dark Iron. What would it do to my soul, to my sanity, to run my sword through teenagers? I envisioned plunging Trusty into the Boo Hag's chest, facing him head on as I hadn't done with Dark Iron. Gary would know I was both his judge and executioner. I'd see it in his eyes. I'd have to do this, and I'd have to do it with conviction—not delaying and wavering like I'd done with the mage.

It wasn't like Tremelay could prosecute them, and I was in no position to restrain them and transport them back to South Carolina.

Sean swallowed hard and nodded. "I understand. Rules are rules and I don't want these three to jeopardize the safety of all of us with their actions. But if you can find a way... They're kids."

Kids. There *had* to be another way. "Would it help for you to talk to them? Let them know Grandmother is on her way and she's not happy?" Sheesh, it sounded like a childhood threat. *Just wait until your father gets home.*

"They don't know me." He hesitated. "I can try. I'm not sure I can talk any sense into them, but I'll try. I just... I have a good life here. I don't want to have to leave. Can you promise to keep my secret? I don't want others to know what I am, that I'm not human."

"I can't guarantee that. My detective friend is going to have to know and probably the vampires. No one is going to want a public panic, and honestly, most aren't going to believe you all exist anyway. I think you can rest assured you'll continue to have some degree of anonymity outside of the paranormal community.

He nodded. "Thank you. I'll help you to stop and apprehend these three any way that I can."

Now that I knew what I was dealing with, I was about to pump Sean Merrill for information. "So your main clan is in South Carolina? How many Boo Hag are there? I've never heard of you before, and there's nothing in the Templar books about you."

He sighed. "We're not from Europe and we keep to ourselves. We're less than a footnote in most books on the supernatural. There are seven billion humans in this world, tens of thousands of vampires. There are fifty Boo Hag. Fifty. Worldwide. Most of us live in our nest in South Carolina. Fifty. We are no threat to humanity compared to all the other creatures in the world."

They were about to be forty-seven, maybe forty-eight, unless Sean could talk these kids off the ledge or Grandmother managed to put her scooter into high gear. "So how do I locate these young Boo Hag? How do I restrain them?" *And how do I kill them?*

Sean's jaw clenched and he stared into his empty glass. I knew he didn't want to tell me their vulnerabilities when I could turn around and use them on him or the rest of his family. "As far as weapons go, salt is horribly painful for us."

"Salt?" I used to wonder about vampires and garlic, but salt? That was in everything. How the heck did they avoid it without forsaking all restaurant dining and never leaving the home when the snow plows were treating the roads?

"The human skin lessens the effect. Like this." He held up the martini glass. "I can ingest it in moderation and touch it. On an open cut it would be agony. In my Boo Hag form, it would severely damage and possibly kill me."

Low sodium diet, but beyond that I wasn't sure how helpful the salt sensitivity would be. If I were lucky enough to catch one out of his human skin...but how likely would that be?

"Anything else?"

Sean nodded. "We're vulnerable to magic. A spell will work on us just as it would on a human." He eyed Trusty, his mouth twisting downward. "A Templar can permanently disable or kill us with their sword. Only a consecrated weapon will work. Guns or normal weapons have no lasting effect on us, but *that* will put us in the grave."

And he'd sat here, having martinis with me with a lethal weapon inches from him. It made me realize how much Sean wanted to help—both the humans in his town and his Boo Hag family. It made me realize that in spite of his fear of discovery he'd decided to trust me—his girlfriend's friend.

Now it was time for me to trust him.

"The three seem to have split up. The two boys are in the city, wearing the skins of musicians in a local band as of last night. The girl went up north a few days ago on her own. She's taken at least one vampire skin. Possibly two."

His eyes flicked toward mine. "A vampire skin?

We don't mess with vampires. In fact, we stay as far away from them as possible. I can't imagine what a Boo Hag would do with a vampire skin."

I pushed my half-empty glass away, needing a clear head for this. "I overheard the girl once, before I knew she was affiliated with the killers. She seems to have a thing for vampires, a kind of fetish. Is that normal?"

He shrugged. "Nothing about these three is normal. We educate all of our children. They have access to television, magazines, current culture—all this is so they can better assimilate when they move in the human world. I know there are humans who are fascinated with vampire culture. I guess a Boo Hag could be the same."

The movies, the books. Vampire folktales carried that forbidden erotic component that reality supported. How many times had humans been fixated on the legend, only to fall hard into a blood-slave life once they discovered there was truth to the tales? A human with an obsession with vampires would either cosplay, or take up with the real thing either as a blood slave or Renfield. I guess a Boo Hag that was equally obsessed would take a skin. Judging from what Dario said about the reported taste of their blood, the life of a slave would be off the table. And I doubted they could be turned. The only way a Boo Hag could get close to vampires was by becoming one the only way they knew how.

Yikes. "How bad is this going to be? How is a Boo Hag going to react to wearing a vampire skin?"

Sean slowly shook his head. "We're constrained by the knowledge and somewhat by the physical limitations of our skin's former owner, so I don't see how useful a vampire skin would be to one of us. At night we shed our skin to go ride. She couldn't wear a vampire skin during the day or it would disintegrate in the sun, leaving her exposed in her natural form. And if she wore it at night...she can drink all the blood she wants, but it's not going to sustain her for long. A Boo Hag needs to ride, or they'll starve to death."

"How long can she go without feeding?" I wondered how crazy this teen was, if her vampire fantasy would kill her before we managed to catch her.

"Six, seven days maybe. She's going to be really weak after a few days."

"So we've got vampire-wannabe Bonnie, and two rock musician wannabe Clydes," I mused. "Any ideas on how to find them?"

"You could try the victims' homes. We take on more than a human's form when we wear their skin. We have their memories, their skills, their knowledge, and a good bit of their personality. The longer we wear a certain skin, the more we become attached to that persona."

This had to be the weirdest thing I'd ever heard of, but it made Lawton's strange words in the basement suddenly clear. He'd loved being Lawton, and missed that person. And when he'd become Brian Huang, it had been hard to force himself away from the responsibilities the man had held dear.

"So you're a mix of the Boo Hag you've always been and Sean Merrill?" I asked.

He nodded. "I've never had a problem with snakes, but Sean was terrified of them. I jump three feet every time I see one now, and even though I know deep down there's nothing to fear, I can't help myself. I also now love baseball and find myself longing to vacation at a very specific campground in

Tennessee."

"These guys switched after being in Brian Huang and Bradley Lewis's skins for days. How easy is it to do that?"

"It's not. Switching skins daily probably wouldn't be too difficult. You wouldn't have time to get used to the human you're taking on. Keeping one on for a week and then switching would be very jarring, downright painful. A Boo Hag would need to have a good reason to switch, and afterwards they'd be very reluctant to switch again unless absolutely necessary."

"But these three came here as teenage kids— kids who had been reported as missing ten years ago. After ten years in those skins they switched?"

"It's like getting a static shock," Sean explained. "The first transition would be the hardest. I'd imagine they would slow down their identity changes either because of the discomfort or as a natural part of the maturation process. We *want* to live our human's life. We take on their mannerisms, likes and dislikes. If they find a human whose personality and lifestyle they truly enjoy, they won't want to give it up. From what you've told me, they'll probably want to stay as Dawson and Strike. Unless they feel their lives are in danger, they won't want to keep changing identities. They might keep killing, but as a Boo Hag, they'll eventually want to stay with one human form as long as they can."

But in the meantime they'd disappear into the crowd, never to be seen again. I doubted they'd ever be truly mature enough to exist in human society at this point. They'd always be murderous teenage runaways, endangering themselves and possibly the humans they encountered and rode.

"So right now I've got Travis Dawson and a kid named Strike, both late teens and both members of the band Rabid Rabbit. From what I overheard they like these two identities—at least Travis aka Gary does. So, would they head back to live in their parents' basement or something?"

"I don't think so. I'm thinking that these young wouldn't want to be subject to adult rules. It would remind them too much of Grandmother and the restrictions they ran away from. Maybe the band has a place? Or they're staying with friends of Travis and Sammy's?"

Possibly. I remembered them saying something about a rehearsal spot. "They can't be living on the street, can they? It's going to be hard to find them if they're holed up in a cardboard box beside a dumpster."

"Boo Hag want company, so I'm assuming they would be naturally drawn to the society their humans enjoyed. Check friends and places where Strike and Travis used to go. There might be a chance you'll catch them there."

That gave me good leads on the two boys, but what about the girl? "The one with the vampire skin, do you think she might actually try to seek out other vampires? The victim wasn't a member of the *Balaj*, but even rogues have a natural inclination to group together. Vampires don't like to be solo."

Sean shrugged. "I don't know much about vampires. Boo Hag don't like to be alone, and I'm guessing if she's wearing a vampire skin, she'll seek them out."

Which meant there was a good chance Dario would catch her. I sent off a quick text to him, asking him to try to not kill the vampire imposter if they caught her, and that I had more information for him.

"What happens to a skin that's not in use? Let's say they've got six or seven of them, do they stay preserved when they're not regularly worn?"

Sean shook his head. "The skins will last a normal human lifetime if worn continuously. Removing them at night doesn't seem to affect the preservation, but I'd assume a few days of non-use and the skin would begin to decompose."

This might be a self-limiting factor, eventually forcing the Boo Hag to narrow down to one or two skins at a time. I could only hope they were fond enough of Travis and Strike that they were still wearing them. Tremelay should be able to check out friends of those two and hopefully narrow down spots where they might be located.

"Thanks. This was a huge help," I told Sean as he packed up the martini supplies.

"Like I said, I was very reluctant to share this with you, but I like Janice and you're her friend. I felt you needed to know. I'm trusting that I'm not going to wake up one morning with a sword in my chest?"

My smile probably wasn't as reassuring as he was hoping for. "That's going to depend on you, Sean. You choose your path, but you better make sure it's a righteous one."

CHAPTER 33

AFTER SEAN LEFT I sat, stunned and a bit tipsy from my liquid lunch. I'd been at the end of the line thinking these guys were skinwalkers and in a matter of hours I knew what they were and how to stop them.

Boo Hag. And my friend was dating one of them. But I'd think about that another time. Right now I needed to prepare myself to be more of a Templar and less of mage.

I tried to meditate, tried to pray, but each time doubt disrupted my concentration, occupying my thoughts. How could I be true to the Templar purpose when I'd killed a man, stabbed him in the back as he'd turned to leave. How could anything justify that?

It had been so easy when I was a child riding through the fields with the sun's golden rays on the tall grass. I'd been so sure that God would guide me, would keep my aim true and my heart pure. I'd always felt the knowledge that had come with that fateful bite of apple in the Garden of Eden had been self-awareness, that the burden humanity bore in our eviction from paradise was free will. God's righteous path wasn't so easy to discern anymore. It was overgrown with briars and fallen trees blocking our way. Do we go around? Do we chop our way through? Are we even on the right path anymore?

I guess that's where faith came in—that elusive wisp that I'd left in a forgotten place. I was lost in the woods and I wasn't sure which path was the righteous one.

Yeah, I was dedicated to protecting Pilgrims on the Path and yet I couldn't even find my own way.

Giving up on the meditation I called Tremelay to fill him in on all I'd learned.

"Okay. Skinwalkers, Boo Hag...how do we catch these kids and how to I make sure they stay in jail this time? That's what I need to know." The detective sounded all business. His confidence was infectious.

"Salt can take them down and even kill them, but I'm not sure how that is going to help. Take their skin away and surround the jail cell with a thick layer of it? Coat the bars and windows with it?" Sword. Magic. Salt. None of them were practical for long-term incarceration.

"They could always make a deal with a prisoner or guard to scrape away the salt and poof they'd be gone. No one is going to understand the importance of surrounding one guy's cell with a mineral. And skinless? *That's* gonna cause a panic."

I grimaced. "Solitary confinement?"

Tremelay sighed. "Again, how are we going to convince both a judge and our correctional system the need to lock three teenagers up in solitary, in cells with salt cemented all over the place?"

"How are you keeping the Fiore Noir mages in place?" The prosecutor must have worked something into the sentencing guidelines, otherwise the mages would be charming and hexing their way into an early, and very illegal, release.

"We explained to the judge that allowing them magical items would cause a disruption and possibly make them targets for prisoners who would believe they were devil worshippers. The defense attorneys tried to pull the religious freedom card, but the prosecutor was able to prove this had nothing to do with religion. Heck, half of them went to church regularly and even took communion."

None of that would work. Boo Hag didn't need spell books or components. They'd just shed their skins and be gone. And I was beginning to rethink my original suggestion. "I don't think we can do the salt-lined cell anyway. They'd starve. They need to slip away each night and feed from sleeping humans. They can't do that if they're confined."

"We're just not set up to deliver justice to non-human offenders," Tremelay confessed.

We weren't, which was why the vampires took internal matters into their own hands. There would be the same problem with an incarcerated vampire. They'd either burn in the sunlight, starve to death, or bend the bars of their cells and strong-arm their way out come night time.

There was no way to make a justice system run by humans who didn't believe such creatures existed work in these cases. I was back to the torturous decision I'd made with Dark Iron. The one where killing the offender was the only justice available.

I looked at my sword on the kitchen counter. This was the sole solution. Kill Gary, Becca, and maybe even Lawton. Their only pardon would be if Grandmother could get here first. Even then, I wasn't sure I wanted to let her cart away murderers. What punishment would they meet at her hands? Sean was adamant this wasn't typical Boo Hag behavior. I'd like to believe him, but this

Grandmother had been negligent and allowed three of her charges to escape. Who's to say that wouldn't happen again? I'd need reassurance that it wouldn't, otherwise the Boo Hag and I were going to have a problem.

"Any leads on their whereabouts?" I asked, my eyes still on my sword.

"We've interviewed family and friends. We've got eyes on their band practice spot, and their hangouts. They think you're dead and that they're safe. I'm willing to bet these two will turn up in the next day or so once they're convinced the coast is clear."

I nodded, even though Tremelay couldn't see me. "If you get wind of them, even a rumor, call me. I'll take care of the situation. I'll deliver justice."

And I would, no matter how difficult that would be for me.

Tremelay was silent a moment and I know he was having a battle of his own. He was a cop. His whole life was dedicated to arresting offenders and seeing them judged by a jury of their peers, serving time through a human correctional system. He'd be green-lighting me as a vigilante, and even though these killers weren't human, that had to have been just as difficult for him as killing the Boo-Hag would be for me.

"I'll call you, Ainsworth." The detective's voice was soft. "This one's all yours."

CHAPTER 34

G OT HER." DARIO was downright smug.
It was close to midnight. He'd texted me
the thumbs-up emoticon in reply to my eight-
page message about Boo Hag attributes and how I
really needed this girl alive if at all possible. The
brief communication then radio silence had me on
edge. I knew he was on the trail of our vampire Boo
Hag.

"Where did you find her?" I asked.

"Getting beaten up by two girls behind a strip
joint."

That was unexpected.

"Cops showed up," Dario continued. "It was all
very entertaining. The dancers don't like other
women poaching their regulars. Drinks were
thrown, words were exchanged, but our vampire
wannabe persisted in trying to pick up the men at the
club. She went out back to meet a patron and instead
got pummeled by two of the dancers."

"Two women subdued a vampire?" It was
incredible. She might have been a Boo Hag in
vampire skin, but having recently been on the
receiving end of Boo Hag fists, I would have expected
a different outcome. Unless these two women
trained with Ronda Rousey, they should have been
easily overcome.

"There's something wrong with her," Dario told

me. "I think she's dying. Maybe they're not compatible with vampire skins."

Or maybe she was starving to death.

"What happened with the police?"

The vampire snorted. "We told them she was a friend of ours, that she was drunk and we were taking her home. She wasn't in any shape to protest. The dancers were clearly the aggressors, and were happy just to see her gone and not to wind up facing assault charges."

How badly had she been injured? Vampires healed fast. And from what I'd seen, Boo Hag did, too. "What did they do to her?"

"Not a lot. Scratches, kicking, punching. Like I said, I think she's dying. She was healing, but slowly. And she didn't protest or fight us when we took her."

That was kind of...sad. I couldn't feel sympathy for this woman, though. She'd killed at least one vampire. She was a murderer, not a starving runaway kid. A murderer.

"Is she still up north in Towson or Hampton? Where did you end up taking her?"

"No, we brought her back. There's nowhere adequate to hold a vampire up there, and she's got the same strength and speed as one of us. I put her in Leonora's holding cell for now, but I'm not sure how long even that's going to hold her."

Yikes. I wasn't sure which alarmed me more— the fact that the Boo Hag might escape a cell meant to hold a *vampire*, or that Dario had taken her to the Mistress's house. Leonora and I didn't have the most amicable relationship, and I'm sure she was less than thrilled to have a creature wearing the skin of a rogue vampire in her house.

"Should I meet you there?" Duh. He was hardly going to drag the Boo Hag through the city to my apartment. It's just that I was reluctant to go to Leonora's. I'd have my sword, and Dario would meet me, but I still hated that place with a passion.

"Yes. Armand is at the door. He'll escort you."

Which meant Armand would ensure no one snacked on me or harassed me. Those loyal to Dario always treated me with the utmost courtesy, but Leonora's followers tended to mirror her dislike if not expand it to a threatening extreme.

I hung up with Dario, grabbed my sword, but hesitated in the doorway. Should I call Sean? He was probably still in the city, although at midnight I wasn't sure whether he would be in his human skin or out "riding."

I wound up just texting him to let him know we'd found Becca and the vampires had brought her, alive but injured, back to the city. He'd promised to help. I was sure he'd get back to me as soon as he was able.

Driving to Leonora's, I tried to think of what tactic I should take in interrogating this Boo Hag. My main goal was to find out where Gary and Lawton were, but I could hardly lead with that question. I'd need to find out as much about her as I could.

Armand did meet me at the door, a favor for which I was quite grateful. The two vampires out front were Leonora's buddies and they made it very clear that without Armand, my drained body would have been found at dawn in a dark alley.

They were bluffing. That sort of thing would have meant war between Leonora and Dario—something the Mistress was eager to avoid. Even so, my palms sweated on Trusty's hilt, protection blessings ready on my lips as I followed Armand through the hallway and down a set of stairs. It was different stairs than I'd been down last time, making me think Leonora had her basement sectioned off.

She did. And evidently there were different levels. We continued down two more sets of increasingly creaky wooden stairs, the air turning dry and cool. It reminded me of a wine cellar—a wine cellar with a set of holding cells, one in each corner of the room. Dario stood next to the far left cell. It seemed far too large for the occupant, a woman huddled in a ball as far away from the bars as possible. White-blond hair shielded her face and arms from view, its length even covering most of her legs.

"Becca?" I asked softly. She looked so frail that I suddenly decided to take a kinder, gentler approach than I'd originally intended.

She didn't reply, or even look up.

Dario shrugged.

"Hon? What's your name?"

Armand strode forward, snatching a stick off the floor and banging on the bars. "Hey. Answer the Templar when she asks you a question."

So much for kinder and gentler. Or for keeping my identity a secret. This woman had never seen me. I'd hoped to keep the fact that I was a Templar from her as long as possible.

The woman looked up and snarled, baring her fangs. Yep, not likely to get any cooperation from her now—at least not without coercion.

In spite of the bravado she was drawn and paler than even a vampire should be. Bruises covered her face, and her bare arms still had the faint marks of scratches. Her eyes struggled to focus on me, her body slumped weakly against the back wall.

"She rallied a bit and tried to escape once we got her down here," Dario told me.

The cage did look like it had seen better days, but I couldn't tell what damage was from the Boo Hag and what had been caused by previous vampire occupants. Bars were twisted as if they'd been pulled apart then bent back into shape. Some had chunks taken out of the metal. Vampires were amazingly strong, but it would take one more than a few minutes to work their way out of this cage. An attentive guard would be able to subdue them before they managed to escape. Which made me wonder about *their* techniques of restraining prisoners.

"How do you guys keep vampires in the cage? The bars are just iron. Do you really have guards on them twenty-four seven to beat them back every time they try to break out?"

Dario got that blank, expressionless look that I was beginning to recognize so well – it was the expression he got every time he was about to tell me something I wouldn't like.

"Normally prisoners are only kept alive long enough to interrogate, so long term guards or confinement isn't an issue. We have ways of rendering them immobile for long periods of time so they don't attempt escape while we're holding them."

I read between the lines. Vampires healed quickly, but amputations or massive amounts of bone breaks with internal injuries would take time— a lot of time if the vampire hadn't fed recently. I could hardly complain, though. It's not like human jails could hold them. Paranormal criminals required a different method of confinement. I could hardly fault the vampires for their extreme methods given the nature of their offenders.

"Any idea what's wrong with her?" I asked. Dario wasn't a medic and neither of us knew anything about Boo Hag physiology, but he did know vampires. She was wearing the skin of one. Maybe whatever she had going on was a vampire thing.

"I think she's starving. The weird thing is she's been trying to feed like a vampire, but she keeps vomiting the blood back up."

"I am a vampire," the girl shouted. "I'm Marcielle and I pledge my loyalty and life to Mistress Leonora and her *Balaj.*"

I caught Dario doing something suspiciously close to an eye roll. "And she keeps yelling that," he told me.

"She's no vampire," Armand chimed in. "She's crazy, that's what she is. She smells funny, can't keep blood down, and her one finger keeps turning into some kind of claw thing. Looks like a knife."

Yeah, I'd had up close and personal experience with one of those. I'd no wish to repeat that.

"Has she tried to take her skin off yet?" I couldn't figure out why she hadn't resorted to that last ditch effort to escape. At night, or day, without the skin she'd be able to slip between the bars and be out of Leonora's house before the vampires could catch her. She had to have another skin stashed somewhere she could use once she got away.

Unless she was particularly fond of *this* skin. I remembered what Sean had told me. If the Boo Hag had grown attached to living Marcielle's life, she'd be very reluctant to leave it behind. That plus her vampire fixation and the difficulties in gaining a replacement skin could be keeping her here.

"Where are the other two Boo Hag?" I asked, deciding to cut with the small talk and go for the jugular.

She glared at me. "I don't know. I'm a vampire."

Was she trying to negate her real self, or did she really not know where the other two were? She could be telling the truth. When she'd left them behind to go vampire hunting up north, she could have broken off all contact with them.

"Why did the three of you leave your home, leave Grandmother?"

Loneliness flashed across her face before her expression hardened once again. "I'm a vampire."

"You're a renegade vampire," Dario responded. "You have no family. You have no territory. You've been cast out to roam the outskirts, and either starve or be killed."

Tears filled her eyes. "This is my *Balaj*. This is my family." Her voice shook with uncertainty and fear.

"It's not." Dario's voice was cold, impersonal. "We don't know you. We would have killed you on sight if this woman hadn't asked us not to. The only thing keeping you alive right now is this Templar. I suggest you answer her questions before we decide you're of no further use and rip your head off."

She burst into tears, curling into a little ball against the cell wall. "It wasn't my fault. Master said I was weak, that Richard never should have turned me. I'm so hungry, so lonely, so scared. I don't want to die. I want my family. I want my Grandmother."

Finally. The emotions of the Boo Hag and the vampire seemed to be in alignment.

"You're hungry because you can't live on blood,"

I told her. "I know you want to be a vampire, but you're not. In time you'll be able to fit into the human world, but you'll never be able to fit into a vampire one. They'll always know you're not one of them. They'll never accept you."

"I'm a vampire," she sobbed. "I'm a vampire."

I was beginning to agree with Armand that crazy is what she was. But I wasn't sure if her mental state was due to the disconnect of wearing a vampire skin, the fear that Marcielle would normally have being captured and caged by a strange *Balaj*, or the sudden realization that she was a young Boo Hag, alone and woefully unprepared for the world around her.

"Do you want to go home?" I asked her in as kind of a voice as I could manage. "Do you want to go back to Grandmother?"

She shuddered, drawing herself up and taking a deep breath. "I'm a vampire. My name is Marcielle and I want my family."

"And we're back to that," Armand commented dryly.

I pulled Dario aside. "Is there somewhere we can talk privately? I'm assuming she has the hearing of a vampire, too."

He nodded and motioned for me to follow him up the stairs and into the main-floor room where Leonora tended to hold court. Neither of us sat on the gigantic, ornate chair that served as a throne.

"I know someone who might be able to help," I told the vampire. "But I need to make sure he can come and go safely. He's another Boo Hag who has been living here in the area as a human for the last two years. He might be able to get through to her."

He nodded. "One of her own kind. That might work. How human-like is he? She looks and smells like a vampire, but there's something strange about her scent. I'm assuming we'll notice the same difference in this Boo Hag?"

"I don't know," I confessed. "Honestly he seems completely human to me, but I don't have your heightened senses. I had some hesitation about him at first, but I figured that was just me being paranoid because he's dating Janice and I don't want her to get hurt."

Dario blinked in surprise. "The developer? Sean Merrill? Suzette met him. She would have said if he'd seemed off, or smelled odd. Unlike our friend downstairs, he must be more skilled at impersonating a human."

"She met him in the last two years? Because that's when Sean Merrill became the Boo Hag Sean Merrill."

The vampire nodded. "Suzette works with a lot of the city government, just to keep track of what's happening with various buildings and long range planning. She met him last week at an evening community planning function.

"I'd like to bring him here, if that's okay with Leonora. This Grandmother that raises the young is supposedly on her way, but I don't know when she'll arrive."

Dario got my unspoken question. "We can continue to hold her until her Grandmother arrives, but she doesn't look well. I'm not sure she'll last more than a day or two, especially since she's refusing all food but blood and can't seem to keep that down."

***

"SHE'S BEING HELD in a vampire cage?" Sean asked. "All she has to do is shed her skin and she's gone."

He'd called me back and left a message, but our game of telephone tag ended with my most recent call. Reluctant to show up at the Mistress's house without an escort, I'd agreed to drive out and meet him down the block at a gas station.

"I know. She's really sick, Sean. Dario thinks she's dying. She keeps insisting that she's this vampire Marsielle. I don't think she'll leave that skin without a fight."

Sean ran a hand through his blond hair. "I've got no idea what being in a vampire skin will do to a Boo Hag. We've never assumed anything but a human identity, only worn human skins. I'll do my best to talk to her, but for all I know wearing that skin might have caused her permanent damage—physical as well as emotional."

Great. We might not be able to get anything useful out of this girl. And she might die, wasting away in a vampire cage. "Is your Grandmother on her way?" I had hopes that their elder nanny-figure could bring these three into line.

"She's on her way. Grandmother is a calming and stabilizing influence. She couldn't just leave the other young or there's a chance what is happening here will also be happening in South Carolina. She's had to bring in other Boo Hag to ensure the other children's safety before she could leave. I'm confident she'll be here by early morning."

I hoped that would be soon enough. "The vampires have said they'd keep Becca contained until Grandmother arrives, but I really need to know where the other two are so we can secure them before they kill again or flee the city."

Sean wrinkled his nose. "The vampire cage probably won't work with them. You're going to need something more durable, like a spell of holding and a circle of salt."

Neither of which I knew how to do. I wondered if Raven was strong enough to help me. Probably not, given that just typing a few sentences on the computer seemed to wear her out.

"I'll do my best." I hated to tell Sean that I'd reconciled myself to the fact that I'd probably need to kill the two boys. I hated the thought. Even though they'd murdered more humans than Dark Iron had, they were children and somewhat amoral in their actions. At least I thought so. As squeamish as I was at the idea of killing them, I'd have to do it. I couldn't let more humans die.

We drove in silence out to Leonora's, Sean twisting his hands together as we pulled in the circular drive.

"I've met vampires before. I don't think they recognized me as anything but human, but I've always been cautious. I'm really concerned about revealing who I am to them."

"Dario has promised me you'll be safe," I assured him. "They have human allies, business interests in Baltimore. They're mainly concerned with continuing to hold their territory against other vampire groups and keeping their presence hidden from the majority of the humans. They won't see any reason to run off or harass one Boo Hag in a city this size. As long as you don't cross each other, you should be safe."

"That's not exactly reassuring as a developer," he commented, eyeing the vampires standing guard on Leonora's porch. "We might sometimes have business interests that oppose each other."

"Then negotiate." I parked the car smack in

front of the house, pulling my sword from the back seat. "I've found them very agreeable to work with. If a Templar can forge alliance with vampires, then so can you."

Sean seem loose and casual as we walked past the porch vampires and into the house, but I could tell he was nervous. The vampires looked at him with curiosity, but kept their distance. Armand met us inside, staring at Sean in surprise.

"This is him? Wow, if I had met him out on the street I totally would have tried to pick him up. Seems totally human to me."

"Thank you." Sean smiled stiffly. "I try."

When Marsielle saw Sean, she blinked in surprise, but didn't otherwise acknowledge him. As he approached the cage, she shrank farther against the wall. "I'm a vampire," she told him defiantly.

"I see that." His voice was sympathetic and kind. "But you'll starve if you don't come out of that skin and feed."

"I just need blood. If they bring me a human to drink from, I'll be fine. They're starving me."

She was like a petulant child, lying to gain sympathy. Luckily I'd already told Sean about the blood.

"They did do that, but you can't drink blood. Boo Hag don't drink blood. Take the skin off, Becca. I'll protect you. I won't let them hurt you. Take the skin off and we'll get you someone to ride."

"I'm not Becca. I'm Marsielle and I'm a vampire. This is *my* skin. It's me and I'm not taking it off."

She wasn't completely delusional. She knew she was wearing a skin, even though she was insistent on keeping this particular identity.

Sean put his hands on the iron bars, leaning in. "Why did you leave Grandmother, Marsielle? You're too young to be out on your own. Even vampires need family."

"They're not my family." Her jaw set in a firm line and she tilted her chin upward. "I'm not Boo Hag. I'm a vampire."

"But you once were Boo Hag," Sean countered softly. "Why did you leave?"

Her lips quivered. "They made fun of me. The others made fun of me. Gary said if I helped him and Lawton escape, he'd get me a vampire skin to wear. But then Gary started to make fun of me too, so I left. I'm not a Boo Hag. I've never been a Boo Hag. I just needed to find a vampire skin and nobody wanted to help me."

"Where are Gary and Lawton?" Sean asked.

The girl began to rock. "Lawton never made fun of me. Lawton was nice. He was always nice. I'm so hungry. Why are they starving me? I need blood. I need my family. Where is my family?"

"Where's Lawton? Do you know where they are, Marsielle?" Sean insisted.

She looked up, her eyes shining with tears. "I left them. Gary wouldn't help me like he promised, so I left them."

"But where were they staying?" Sean continued to press the girl. "Was there a place where they liked to hang out? A place where if you all got separated, you could meet up again?"

"The nice house." She furrowed her brows in thought. "I was only there once, but Gary called it the safe house."

That could be anywhere.

"Do you know where it is?" Sean asked.

"I can get there, but I don't know the street names," she confessed. "It's east. It's a pretty place with flowers and neighbors who water their lawns and have dinner with their families every night." She wrinkled her nose. "There's white carpet everywhere. I had to take my shoes off at the door when I went there because the woman would go crazy if I tracked mud in on the white carpet."

White carpet. Amanda Lewis. And now that she'd been killed, there was no one living there. It would be all the more easy to sneak in and out without a nagging sister to yell at you about taking your shoes off.

I left Sean to continue trying to get Marsielle out of the vampire skin and went upstairs, dialing Tremelay in spite of the obscenely early hour. Becca might be starving herself, but Lawton and Gary weren't. There was a good chance they were out "riding," and if so, we could possibly catch them with their pants down. Or with their skins off.

CHAPTER 35

I'M GONNA GET fired for this," Tremelay grumbled.

I'd just be happy if we didn't wind up dead. Sean had remained with Marsielle, promising to text me the moment Grandmother arrived. We were too close to daylight for any of the vampires to assist. Which left Tremelay and me sneaking around an upper-middle class neighborhood at the crack of dawn. The whole thing with Marsielle had taken too long and I feared we'd lost the window of opportunity to catch the Boo Hag out riding. So instead of taking their skins and setting a trap for when they returned, we were planning for a fight.

We didn't even have the cover of darkness to hide us as we slipped from behind the car to the row of forsythia by the garage. The plan we'd come up with was for Tremelay to enter through the front and distract them with his shotgun and official police arrest-the-bad-guys mode. I was to sneak in through the back cellar door and flank the two from the rear, dispatching them with my sword. That plan only worked if they were in one of the open floorplan rooms, like the kitchen/dining/greatroom area or hallway. If the two were up in a bedroom somewhere, or separated, we were going to have to wing it.

Which meant we were going to have to wing it. I

knew our chances were slim that we'd catch the two unawares, in the same room that happened to have multiple entrances. It was pretty much going to be the Boo Hag trying to beat on Tremelay and me until I could manage to kill them.

The thought made my stomach revolt. I was going to kill again. I was going to kill two children. Yes, murderous non-human children, but still children. I'd come to like Sean, and I knew he was trying to bring the one woman who might end this bloodshed. But if she didn't get here in the next five to ten minutes, it was up to me.

And this time I would not hesitate.

Tremelay waved me on and I darted around the corner of the garage. Around back was a basement door. Unfortunately the basement door was in clear view of the back deck and anyone who happened to be looking out a window at the time. My bigger fear was that a neighbor would see us sneaking around the house like amateur ninjas and call the police. Then Tremelay's career would *really* be over and I'd have to explain to the cops why I'd broken into the crime scene of a murder victim with a large sword in hand.

Edging along the side of the house I slipped down the cement steps and gently tried the handle. Locked. I'd expected as much and touched one of the charms on my bracelet, whispering the incantation as quietly as possible. The bolt slid free and I heard the "snick" of the handle lock retreating. Slowly easing the door open, I led with my sword and breathed easy to see the huge basement room was empty of living occupants.

Amanda Lewis's house was huge. The thing had to be four thousand square feet—plenty of room for a single woman and her deadbeat brother. The upstairs was carefully decorated, but the basement was unfinished. Color-coordinated storage tubs were stacked against one wall, labeled with their contents. A few shelving units held paint cans, furnace filters, and an assortment of home repair items. I got the feeling that no one ever came down here, even though the place was free of the usual cobwebs.

I darted past the furnace and made my way up the stairs, holding my breath as I opened the door to the main floor of the house. Warm air hit my face along with the smell of cooking bacon and the lingering odor of blood.

It seems we *were* lucky after all. Making my way down the hall I peered into the open space adjoining the kitchen and saw them. Ducking back I pulled the mirror from my pocket and angled it to better see what was going on in the room.

Mirrors. Good for fighting Medusa. Good for spying on Boo Hag.

The kitchen was a mess of dirty pans and burned bacon draining on paper towels. Beyond that, I saw three figures. Gary was once again Gary. A skin that I assumed was Travis Dawson's was carefully folded on a chair like it was a beloved shirt. There was a guy with a mess of dyed-green hair slumped in the chair next to him, the now-familiar duct tape around his arms and legs.

Angling the mirror I finally saw Lawton and stifled a gasp at his appearance. The other boy had no skin on at all and was sitting on the floor, knees drawn up to his chest, his head bowed onto his crossed arms. I could only see a portion of him as he was hidden by the dining area furniture.

"I really liked being the band guy." Gary looked

with regret at the folded skin. "I hate wearing this skin. I want to go back to being Travis. Or even Bradley. Anything is better than this loser."

"The cops are looking for Bradley," the other boy told him. "And the one who was at the concert knows you're Travis. Just stay Gary."

"I don't want to be Gary." The Boo Hag kicked at the chair, his expression petulant. "Gary is a loser. That cop doesn't know shit. And if you'd killed the Templar girl like I'd told you to, I could stay Travis."

"I *did* kill her." Lawton's voice held a faint tremor.

Gary laughed. "Right. That's why you won't tell me where you dumped her body or her skin. Weak piece of shit. I'm sorry I brought you along. You're deadweight. You're of no use to me at all. Because of you I can't be Travis again."

I tensed, hand on the hilt of my sword. Was he going to kill Lawton? Why was the boy without a skin? And could I intervene without risking the man duct taped to the chair?

"I dumped her by the MLK, under an overpass. Homeless people sometimes stay there. It's risky to go back to check on the body. People might see us. We've already gone through most of the skins we have. You get ID'd as Gary and the only one you'll have left is that rest-stop guy."

"And the Strike kid you were wearing."

Gary moved closer to Lawton. I waited, biding my time until I felt I could get between him the potential hostage.

"And this guy's," Gary added, moving back to the dining table and yanking the guy's head up by his green hair. I saw the wide terrified eyes of their soon-to-be victim and clenched my jaw. He was awake.

He'd be a witness to me killing the Boo Hag. In addition to my moral dilemma, I now had a practical one. I'd save my Baltimore pilgrims, but I'd face a whole lot more than ten hours of community service for this one.

"I'm gonna have to cycle between Strike and this guy and ditch Gary's skin. The cops might not know me like this but if Grandmother gets wind that we're up here, she'll spot Gary a mile away."

"If Grandmother comes looking for us, it won't matter whose skin you're wearing." Lawton looked up, his eyes weirdly bulging without lids. "You don't need to kill anyone else, Gary. Just take the rest-stop guy and Strike's skin and get out of town."

Which would leave Lawton with nothing. He had seemed to appease Gary with his explanation of my body disposal, but the kid clearly knew he wasn't getting out of this house alive.

"I don't like Strike." He kicked the duct-taped man's leg. "I'm not sure I like this guy either. Maybe I'll run out this afternoon and see if I can find someone else. Someone who's cool. Someone who's not a loser like this guy."

I saw a movement at the opposite doorway and panicked. Oh no. Not now. Not when Gary was so close to the hostage.

"Police." Tremelay appeared in the doorway, shotgun poised. From his angle he couldn't see either Lawton or the green-haired kid. I could only hope he'd heard them talking and figured out their locations from their voices.

It might not be ideal, but it was time for action. I ran, trying to get between Gary and the human, but was not match for his speed. Gary grabbed the human, yanking him off the chair and pointing his knife-like finger at the kid's throat. I hesitated, knowing that I couldn't manage to kill Gary before he killed his hostage.

Gary pivoted, dragging the kid in front of him as he angled himself in a defensive position. Tremelay moved to the side, trying to flank him, but the Boo Hag jabbed his finger into the human's chin. Red trickled down. The hostage's scream was muffled by the duct-tape across his mouth.

"Stay right there, both of you. Sword on the ground."

Of course he was more nervous about my consecrated weapon than he was Tremelay's shotgun. I'd seen the negligible effect bullets had on a Boo Hag. I doubted bird shot or slugs would be any different. I'd worried that when it came time I wouldn't be able to kill the Boo Hag teen, but now that he had his knife against another's throat, I was finally onboard with the plan. But I knew Gary wouldn't think twice about killing this man, so I gently eased my sword to the floor and slid it away with my foot.

I might not have my sword, but I still had a few spells up my sleeve, and hopefully if Tremelay could get in a distracting shot, I'd be able to use one and get Gary away from his hostage.

"Too many have died, Gary," Tremelay said, his gun still trained on the human shield. "We've caught Bella. We know what you are. Grandmother is on her way. Let the kid go and you'll live to go home with her."

"If you know what I am then you know that gun of yours isn't going to do shit to me but mess up my clothes." Gary's voice was cocky. He edged backward toward Lawton dragging the bound human along with each step.

"There's no way out," Tremelay warned him. "Wait for Grandmother and you'll live. Kill that man or escape today, and you'll die. She'll find you, Templars always do, and when she finds you next time, she'll kill you."

Gary laughed, his eyes still on me and my sword as he continued to back up. "Idiot. You think Grandmother is going to spank me and send me to bed without cake? We're all dead, whether by that Templar's sword or at Grandmother's hands. We've put the whole community at risk. There is no punishment for that except for death."

My immediate reaction was to glance at Lawton with sympathy. He'd done all he could to help. A death sentence seemed rather harsh in his instance, but it's not like I could offer any alternative.

"Then pick your death, because this is over right here, right now."

I admired Tremelay's confidence, but couldn't see how anybody but Gary had the upper hand right now. He had the hostage, and I just couldn't let him kill this guy right in front of me.

The Boo Hag laughed. "Wrong. You're both going to stay here while I leave. Do whatever you want with Lawton. I don't give a shit about him. Let me go and you can have him."

Mirroring Gary's move I came around the dining room table and realized what was going on with the other Boo Hag. Lawton wasn't just naked, he was huddled in a huge, thick ring of salt. Gary had stripped him, trapped him, and now was ready to sacrifice him to us. Jerk. But Lawton wasn't the only one I had sympathy for at the moment. The poor kid with the green hair was shaking like crazy, whimpering noises coming from behind the duct tape. I was sure he'd read the papers and knew what his fate was going to be.

"Let that human go," I told Gary.

He laughed. "Maybe. Maybe not."

Tremelay took a step forward and I edged to the side, no longer trying to flank the Boo Hag. At this point I had a different idea. "He'll slow you down," I commented. "And you'll need to really hustle once you get out of here. We'll be right after you."

He shrugged, still backing toward the door, but at a different angle. Just a few more feet.

"Let the human go, Gary." Tremelay took another step forward. "Let him go unharmed and neither of us will follow you wherever you go. I'll give you my vow and so will she."

No I would not. I shot a quick glare at Tremelay, not sure where he was going with this. I most certainly was going to hunt this kid down, whether he let his hostage go or not.

"You can go somewhere on your own—you and Lawton and Becca," the detective continued. "You can either make a life somewhere else, or go home to South Carolina."

"Fuck that," he yelled. "I'm not going back. I'm never going back. And I don't give two shits about Lawton or that vampire-loving freak. Kill them both for all I care."

I caught Lawton's eye and hoped he got my unspoken message. Gary's attention zeroed in on me as I moved a few steps toward him. His finger-knife dug deeper into the hostage's skin. "Stay there or I'll kill him," he ordered.

I held out my hands and stayed where I was, but

it was clearly too close for Gary's comfort. He moved backward, right into the salt surrounding Lawton. The other Boo Hag jumped forward, grabbing his friend around the neck and slamming him face-down into the salt. The human crashed against the floor with a muffled cry, and then I heard Gary scream. A horrible smell hit my nose, of burning flesh.

But it wasn't Gary who was burned, it was Lawton, hurt far worse than the other Boo Hag as his naked flesh hit the salt. Instinctively I reached out to grab him, wincing at the feel of wet slippery muscle and sinew in my hands. I kicked out, slamming my foot into Gary's face and throwing Lawton to the side.

Hands grabbed me and now I was the one with a finger-knife against my throat. The back of my head barely reached his shoulder, his long arm pinning me to his chest. "Bitch. I should have killed you after the concert."

"Yes you should have," Tremelay told him. The shotgun roared and I ducked my head, feeling the knife nick the skin of my throat. My heart stuttered as the shot hit both me and the Boo Hag.

It stung like a thousand scorpions. The arm around me dropped as the Boo Hag clawed at his face. I doubled over, rolling away as I hit the floor. The shotgun roared again and again and again, the sound closer with each shot. Gary screamed like he was being eaten alive and I opened my eyes to see Tremelay standing over him, loading more shells into the shotgun. The Boo Hag flailed and convulsed on the floor, crimson blood pouring from tiny wounds all over his face and body.

I jumped up and ran to grab my sword. Tremelay's weapon seemed to have had more effect than the pistol had, but I knew it wouldn't kill the Boo Hag. Only I could do that.

I picked up the sword, hearing the shotgun roar again. I turned, ready to save my friend from an angry Boo Hag and abruptly halted. The room was silent aside from the faint sound of weeping from the green-haired boy and the low moans of Lawton. Gary lay still on the floor, smoke curling from the hundreds of tiny wounds that dotted his body. One eye stared sightless at the ceiling, the other was a mess of oozing red flesh.

How...how had that happened? Was the shotgun Tremelay's consecrated weapon? Had his family not gone underground as I'd expected?

I looked over to see the detective on the phone, calmly calling 911 as he held the shotgun at the ready, still pointed at Gary's body.

Everything hurt—my neck where the Boo Hag had cut me, little places all over my torso where I felt like I'd been bitten and some particularly mean person had rubbed salt in my wounds. I didn't feel cold or fuzzy-headed. There was no light at the end of a long tunnel. I'd been shot, but I wasn't dying. I hurt too much to be dying, so I looked down and saw crystalline chunks of white scattered around the floor.

Salt. Tremelay had loaded his shells with rock salt. That clever, clever man. And what merely hurt me had done Gary in. The Boo Hag was still in his human skin, but the salt had eaten through beneath the flesh. Tremelay had acted, and this time it had been him who had saved the day.

I stared at him as he continued to speak to dispatch, nothing betraying what the detective must have felt. I'd killed a man. I knew Tremelay. I knew this wasn't how he wanted the situation to end. But he was a cop and safeguarding many meant he had to take actions that would no doubt cause him many sleepless nights.

I might have the sword, but he was more the Templar than me. He did this every day, protecting his own Pilgrims on the Path, with a badge and a gun. If he was strong enough to do his duty, then who was I to be angsting over a smudge on my soul. I was God's Warrior. It was my job to sacrifice myself, and even my afterlife, for the safety of my Pilgrims. Tremelay had faith in his institutions and system. I needed to have faith that God would guide my hand, and that at the end of the day, when my judgement came, I'd be found to have done far more good than evil.

CHAPTER 36

TREMELAY TOOK CARE of the hostage, carefully peeling the duct tape from him. I went to Lawton, unsure what I could do to help the Boo Hag. His feet were mangled bits of black and he was missing two fingers on his left hand where he had touched the salt while knocking Gary to the floor. I cleared away as much salt as I could, then brought him the folded skin of Travis Dawson.

"Will it help if you put this on?"

He looked up at me, his red-face twisted in agony. "It hurts so much. Please kill me."

Not if I could help it. "Put on the skin and let me know what to do. Should we wash your feet and hand? Soak them in water?"

He shook his head, taking the skin from me with trembling hands. The Boo Hag slipped it on as if it were a jumpsuit. It molded and shaped around his body like a living thing. Now instead of a skinned corpse, a naked young man huddled before me. His hand was still missing two fingers, and his feet were still mangled, but somehow he managed to look better.

"They'll never heal," he told me, his voice weak. "It hurts so bad."

Well, he was going to have to buck up and deal because if he wanted any chance at a future, we needed to get out of here. We. Tremelay might have taken the killing shot, but I didn't need my name in another police report.

"Here." I threw Lawton an armful clothing that I found in a duffle bag against the wall. There was a backpack next to it which I didn't look in, sure it contained the skin of rest-stop guy and Strike, possibly also Bradley Lewis.

"I found that guy holding a knife to you." Tremelay pointed to Gary's body as he spoke to the trembling hostage. "He was going to kill and skin you, but I shot him and killed him. No one else was here."

The boy might have green hair, but he was quick on the uptake. His dark-brown eyes glanced at me, then briefly at Lawton before he shuddered and turned away, nodding. "No one was here except for me and the killer."

"Can you walk?" I asked Lawton. The Boo Hag was busy wrapping his feet in extra shirts, tying them in place with socks.

"I'll need help."

I got him to his feet then put my arm around him, catching my breath as I half-carried the boy over the fat ring of salt. Sirens sounded in the distance. I was still hurting from last night, but there was no time to baby my injuries. We needed to get out of here fast, or we'd both be facing questions neither one of us wanted to answer.

Lights were on in the neighbors' houses but thankfully no one was outside to see us leaving or hobbling down the street. I'd parked two blocks away and I'm sure that was the most agonizing walk Lawton had ever made in his life. Mine too, since I was supporting much of his weight and still feeling the effects of my bruised ribs.

We collapsed in my Toyota. I dialed Sean and watched Lawton with concern. The boy's face was ashen, his eyes glassy as he stared blankly out the window.

"Gary's dead," I told the elder Boo Hag the moment he picked up. "I've got Lawton, but he's hurt. He was without a skin and being held in a salt circle and got it on his feet and hand."

I heard Sean's sharp inhale. "There's not much you can do to help him. He'll either heal or he won't, and in the meantime he's going to be in pain. Where are you?"

Silent police cruisers, lights flashing, roared by us. "Canton. Tremelay is dealing with the police reports. Gary had a hostage, who is thankfully alive and unhurt. But what should I do with Lawton?"

"Grandmother is here with me and Becca. We can meet you at your house."

"Okay." I disconnected and stared at my phone. I wasn't thrilled about taking Lawton to my house, or playing host to the matriarch Boo Hag. And I wasn't sure I wanted to turn him over to her. I shot the kid a questioning glance and he nodded weakly.

"I want to go home."

"But she'll kill you," I reminded him softly. "I know you're hurt, but I can drop you somewhere and if you can make your way out of the city, you'll be fine. I'll tell them you're in a different skin to delay them."

"No," Lawton replied, a bit of firmness creeping into his voice. It was the first time I'd ever heard him so lacking in fear. He'd helped take down Gary, had saved that green-haired kid's life with his actions. Maybe the boy was growing up.

"I just want to go home," he continued. "I don't want to be on the run all by myself. I'm hurt. I can't make it out here in the human world. I just don't have it in me. I'd rather go home and die in peace."

It was his decision, and one I couldn't really fault him for given all he'd been through.

"Okay." I started the car and headed toward Fells Point and my apartment.

***

GRANDMOTHER WAS A tiny woman with wiry salt-and-pepper hair and the face of a dried apple. Beady black eyes stared intently at me as Sean made the introductions. I wasn't sure of the proper etiquette for greeting a Boo Hag elder, so I shook her hand.

She nodded at me, her hand cool and dry in mine. Then she turned to Lawton with a tsk sound. "Boy, you three have caused me quite a lot of grief. Why did you run off like that?"

Lawton was standing respectfully, his head bent low. Blood had seeped through the makeshift bandages on his feet. My carpet had seen worse. I was more concerned about the poor kid's fate than any cleanup I might need to do later.

"Gary said you'd decided to kill us, that you'd made a mistake letting us live past infancy. He said we could live free if we just got away. Becca could become a vampire. He'd help me with skins and adapting to human life. And we'd all live."

Grandmother tilted her head and looked intently at the boy. "So Becca stole the keys and you slipped me a little something in my late-night tea. I'm ashamed of you Lawton. To so easily come under the influence of someone like Gary... I'm so ashamed."

He reddened. "I'm sorry Grandmother. You

were right. We shouldn't have lived. I'm ready to accept my fate. I just want to die at home. I miss home."

The woman sighed and turned to me. "Have you ever taken a life, Knight Ainsworth. One of your own kind, not in the heat of battle or while defending yourself. Have you coldly judged another a threat to your people and a danger to all and played God with their life?"

It was as if every one of her words punched me in the gut. I didn't reply, but I knew she read the answer in my eyes.

She nodded in a quick sharp motion. "It's even harder to make that decision about a child. For hundreds of years I have culled those Boo Hag children who, in my judgement, might be a danger to us, whose personality might put us all at risk of extermination. Might. It's never a clear decision and each time I took a child's life that action took a piece of my soul."

"Isn't there some way...some kind of rehabilitation or institution you could keep them in? A way of separating them from the human world?" My conscience was guilty enough, I couldn't imagine how *she* must feel. I thought of my nephews, of Jet, and knew I could never make that call. Never. I'd reconciled myself to killing teenagers, but babies? No.

Grandmother shook her head. "We're only fifty, give or take. We have no way of securing the wayward and dangerous ones, as you've just witnessed. Centuries of taking the lives of babies... I'd decided to try something different. Instead of killing these three, I spared them. I'd hoped I could change them, that in time they'd come around. And now many have died and we are exposed. I fear the day may have come where we will be hunted and put down like monsters."

"We have no desire to hunt you down as long as you can live peaceably with the humans." I told her. Sean had said they avoided killing unless there was no other alternative, or in cases of self-defense. We did the same. There was no reason to annihilate the entire Boo Hag race just because of identity theft and the actions of two disturbed teens.

I wasn't exactly good at judging who were and weren't the monsters, but at least I could give her this reassurance that neither Tremelay nor I would target the Boo Hag. Gary had paid for his crimes with his life. Marsielle was insane and likely to die either by starvation or at Grandmother's hands. Lawton...well, I saw a glimmer of salvation in Lawton. And it was Lawton's life I wanted to leverage in this situation.

"I have a request though." I pointed at Lawton, the boy staring at us wide-eyed. "Give him a chance. He saved my life, risking his own to defy Gary's order to kill me. He saved a human hostage and help us take down Gary just now. He's injured. He's scared. But I think he might be okay."

Grandmother narrowed fierce dark eyes at the young Boo Hag. Lawton trembled, but I hid a smile, seeing the glimmer of relief in their depths. She didn't want to kill Lawton either. She hadn't wanted to kill him as a baby, and she didn't want to kill him now. "You hear that boy? I'm gonna grant her request, but that means that your life is hers. Shape up, because you know I do not give second chances like this, ever."

He nodded vigorously and the elder woman turned to me. "He escapes again and kills anyone, that's on you. I don't want any backlash for us, but you do what you gotta if he starts running wild. I'll take him home with me, but he's your boy from now on."

Great. I had a Boo Hag teenage boy. I wondered if I could fit him on the shelf with the figurine collection Gran had been sending me. What should I expect from the kid? Cards at major holidays? Did I need to send him birthday gifts?

"It will be okay, Lawton," I told him instead. "It's going to be okay."

"I know." He smiled. "I'm going home. Whatever happens now doesn't matter because I'm going home."

CHAPTER 37

THE SETTING SUN was warm on my back as I leaned forward to put the paper boat at the edge of the Patapsco River. It bobbed in a muck of sludge and oil, a rusted soda can and a plastic grocery store bag by its side. I lit the note I'd written, placing it in the boat and sending the whole fiery mess farther into the water.

The Boo Hag who'd wanted to be a vampire had died, starved to death according to Sean. I wasn't sure whether to address her as Marsielle or Becca, so I wrote both names on the prayer I sent to heaven on the wings of smoke. Sean didn't have any news for me on Lawton. I wondered whether the Boo Hag grandmother had kept her word to let him live, or had delivered a merciful death as soon as they'd returned to South Carolina. Would I ever know? Hopefully I would receive a Christmas card that told me he was okay and safe at the Boo Hag sanctuary. Sill I launched another boat, this one with a prayer for Lawton's future, whether it be in this world or the next.

The whole thing had been blamed on Gary Jarvett who had died at the scene and had evidently killed his partner, Bradley Lewis. All the others were being labeled victims. Lawton King and Becca Campbell were merely other hitchhikers, briefly traveling with Gary, Becca lucky to have escaped him alive. She was still missing, listed as a runaway teen even though she'd been reported missing ten years ago by her parents.

And how sick those parents must feel, to know their child had surfaced after ten years only to vanish in the wind again. They'd never realize Becca had truly died ten years ago, and the teen sighted thumbing a ride up to Baltimore wasn't her at all.

I watched the boats burn to the waterline, feeling a chill as the bulk of the sun dipped below the city skyline behind me. Prayers were all I could give Lawton and Becca right now. I had to prepare for a Halloween ritual to remove this demon mark, for my visit with Chuck at the prison next week, and for my nightly dinner with Dario.

I stood and stretched, turning to see the golden sky fade to salmon and violet, the skyline black in silhouette against the sunset. My city. My Pilgrims. And I was walking the path right along beside them.

Book 4 in the Templar Series, Famine's Feast, will be released at the end of 2016. Make sure you're signed up to receive New Release Alerts at http://debradunbar.com/subscribe-to-release-announcements/

ABOUT THE AUTHOR

After majoring in English with a concentration in Medieval Literature and Folklore studies, Debra promptly sold out to the corporate world. By day, she designs compensation programs, after dark she feverishly writes her novels.

Debra lives in a little house in the woods of Maryland with her sons and a slobbery bloodhound. On a good day, she jogs and horseback rides, hopefully managing to keep the horse between herself and the ground. Her only known super power is 'Identify Roadkill'.

Connect with Debra Dunbar on Facebook , on Twitter @Debra_Dunbar, or at her website, http://debradunbar.com.

Sign up for New Release Alerts at http://debradunbar.com/subscribe-to-release-announcements/.

Feeling impish? Join Debra's Demons (http://debradunbar.com/debras-demons/), get cool swag, inside info, and special excerpts. I promise not to get you killed fighting a war against the elves.

Thank you for your purchase of this book. If you enjoyed it, please leave a review on Goodreads, or at the e-retailer site from which you purchased it. Readers and authors both rely on fair and honest reviews.

Other Books By Debra Dunbar

The Imp Series
A DEMON BOUND (Book 1)
SATAN'S SWORD (Book 2)
ELVEN BLOOD (Book 3)
DEVIL'S PAW (Book 4)
IMP FORSAKEN (Book 5)
ANGEL OF CHAOS (Book 6)
IMP (Imp Series, prequel novella)
KINGDOM OF LIES (Book 7)
EXILE (Book 8) Summer 2016 Release

Books in the Imp World
NO MAN'S LAND
STOLEN SOULS
THREE WISHES

Half-Breed Series.
DEMONS OF DESIRE (Book 1)
SINS OF THE FLESH (Book 2)
UNHOLY PLEASURES (Book 3) Spring 2017
Release

Templar Series
DEAD RISING
LAST BREATH

BARE BONES
FAMILE'S FEAST, Winter, 2016 Release

71855197R00184

Made in the USA
Columbia, SC
05 June 2017